Little Bird

LaRita Dixon

Editors: Earl Tillinghast and Regina Cornell

Cover Design: 3SIXTY Marketing Studio - 3sixtyprinting.com

Interior Design: 3SIXTY Marketing Studio - 3sixtyprinting.com

Indigo River Publishing
3 West Garden Street, Ste. 352
Pensacola, FL 32502
www.indigoriverpublishing.com

Ordering Information:

Quantity sales: Special discounts are available on quantity purchases by corporations, associations, and others. For details, contact the publisher at the address above.

Orders by US trade bookstores and wholesalers: Please contact the publisher at the address above.

Printed in the United States of America

Library of Congress Control Number: 2018961517

ISBN: ISBN: 978-1-948080-51-4

First Edition

With Indigo River Publishing, you can always expect great books, strong voices, and meaningful messages.

Most importantly, you'll always find . . . words worth reading.

Prologue

Her home and love is Syria. Amal was born and raised in the paradise that is her country. The narrow alleyways, with their twists and turns, are the passages to her heart, and the sound of the flat drum is the beat. Although she could leave, it is a country that would always beckon her back—for Syria is always with her.

Amal was born to a simple man and woman. Her childhood was built under her baba's beard, and its soundtrack was his throaty laugh. And her mama's loving kindness was what molded her. They weren't rich people, but they were happy. She had her parents' love and a country that gave her meaning and belonging. Without them, she was nothing.

She had no words to describe the feeling she had the day they were taken from her in the cruelest of ways, leaving her an orphan. Now she was without family or country. But as long as she was standing, Syria lived within her. And as long as she lived, she would never forget that day.

The day that everything changed.

Chapter

ONE

A Glimpse into the Past
Homs, Syria

Thunder roared around Amal as she gripped the rough, wet rope. It tore at her skin as she braced herself against the tumultuous waves that crashed into the small life raft. Although the storm raged loudly, she could still hear the terrified screams of her fellow passengers. Waves rocked the tiny inflatable boat violently, making her sick to her stomach. Amal was surrounded by darkness, except for the brief flashes of lightning that stabbed through the sky and illuminated the terrified faces of those around her for brief moments. Their faces, all sharing the same look of distress and sorrow, would always be etched into her memory.

Another clap of thunder sounded as the raft made a giant leap over the angry waves before crashing down hard, sending the craft toppling around like a toy boat.

"Ya Allah, where are you? Help us!" Amal said to herself as she clutched the boat for her life.

The wind howled angrily as it blew furiously around her. She just wanted it all to stop. After another stab of lightning illuminated the violet sky, she glimpsed the familiar figure of her friend toppling overboard. Without thinking, Amal jumped to action, pushing past a few people to the side of the life raft where Hala had been sitting. She reached out to her, screaming for her to take her hand, as the woman struggled to stay above the surface.

The giant life vest she wore proved useless against the fury of the night's storm. Salt water stung Amal's eyes as it splashed in her face, blinding her momentarily, but she refused to lose sight of Hala.

"She's the only thing I have left! Ya Allah, please!" she cried. She watched helplessly as the woman was enveloped by another large wave and succumbed to the darkness below.

Amal searched the water frantically, but Hala never came up. She sat back, feeling empty and hopeless, with numbness overtaking her limbs from the coldness of the water that soaked her body, though she couldn't tell if the chill was from her broken heart or the coldness of the water coating her skin. Amal took in her surroundings almost emotionlessly. These were her neighbors: some she knew and some she didn't, but what they shared at that moment made them all the same. They were all unwanted, left to fend for themselves and to be eaten by the big black monster that was the ocean below.

Another wave crashed against the boat, and Amal wasn't holding on. There wasn't enough time to grab hold of the boat, and instantly she was thrown into the icy black water. The battering waves pushed her down as she struggled to swim. Amal couldn't keep up; her tired body grew weak, and she closed her eyes and gave herself to the waves. People nearest to her reached frantic hands out to try to save her, but it was no use. As salt water filled her lungs and the coldness overwhelmed her, she just let it be.

There's nothing to live for anyway, she thought as she let herself slip into oblivion.

Amal
Saint Joseph's Hospital
Present Day

Amal was bathed in darkness so deep and thick it weighed her body down like there were mountains of sand covering her. She listened carefully for anything that would let her know that she was alive. The screaming and the sounds of the ocean that once deafened her were gone. Her surroundings were still, and the more she concentrated, the more her hearing improved.

She could hear a steady beeping noise. Not like the sound of a car—this was the sound she had heard on television on hospital shows. Even though the rhythmic beeping kept her company, there was a stillness about the environment. The silence made her want to cry. Her chest ached with sadness as she fought the tears and tried to be strong. If these were her last moments, she didn't want them to be spent sobbing.

Suddenly she became aware of her arms and her legs, wiggling a toe just to be sure. Not knowing what death would feel like, she had seen enough dead bodies to know they didn't move. She then moved her mouth around, like she was rolling a piece of hard candy around her teeth, and felt the heaviness of her eyelids; the thought of opening them made her tired. If she could move her body, then surely she could open her eyes. Uncertain where she was or what was there, she listened and waited. There was still a faint beeping in the background, now mixed with the hum of mysterious, low voices.

Amal was about to panic, but she heard Baba's voice in her memory, saying, *"One step at a time, Little Bird,"* as if he were talking to her right then. The pain she hadn't felt in a while hit hard in her chest. She missed her baba and mama, but what would they want her to do? Knowing they wouldn't want her to succumb to fear, she strained with everything in her to open her eyes.

As soon as they opened only a crack a blinding white light flooded in, making her shut them quickly. Her head pounded, like her brain was trying to kick its way through her skull. She didn't know if it was because of the light, but was determined not to let that stop her. So Amal tried one more time, just slower this time, until she could faintly see her surroundings.

She was in a white room with the sun pouring through a window to her right. Blinking her long black lashes, Amal tried to adjust her eyes to the light. *How did I get in a hospital?* she thought while looking around.

And as if on cue, a bouncy woman in pink scrubs, with blonde hair and two ponytails that bounced as she walked, came in whistling some lighthearted tune. Her shoes made a rubbery squishing sound as she stepped. The nurse saw her before she could pretend to be asleep again.

"Morning, sleepyhead!" the nurse announced her presence brightly. "I'm so happy to see you're finally up! So tell me how you're feeling." The nurse moved her hands over Amal's body, checking her pulse and blood pressure with ease. "Look at me." She took a small flashlight from her pocket and shined it in Amal's eyes, which made her head swim.

Her accent was so thick that Amal could hardly understand what she was saying. Amal just tucked her hands in her lap and looked down.

"There's no need to be scared, sweetie. You're safe now," said the nurse. "We're here to take care of you. Poor little thing like you being found washed up on the beach. I know you must be terrified." The nurse gently smoothed the hair out of Amal's eyes after she put her flashlight away.

So that's what happened, Amal mused. *Found washed up on the beach.* She wasn't satisfied with that thought—wondering where she was and why she wasn't dead.

"I'm sorry, I didn't even introduce myself," said the nurse. "I'm Jaclyn, but everyone calls me Jackie. If you need anything, just call me." Amal watched as she pointed to the remote on the side of her bed. Amal nodded her head to show she understood.

Jackie left the room the same way she came in. She walked like she was bouncing on springs, with her ponytails swishing left to right.

Amal guessed it was near noon when Jackie came back with her lunch. The tray held pizza, a cup of fruit, apple juice, and a little white cup with ice. Amal hadn't realized how hungry she was until she saw the food sitting in front of her. Food, where she was from, was scarce. She was lucky if she got bread and water. So she hungrily and shamelessly ate as Jackie watched her.

"You don't talk much, do you?" asked Jackie. Amal just ignored her and kept eating. "Well, you're going to have to talk sooner or later. We need to know what happened."

That was enough to make Amal slow her eating. Amal looked up at the nurse with her big honey-brown eyes, not sure what to say.

"I'm not here to hurt you. You can talk to me," Jackie said with a soothing voice.

Amal put her tiny plastic spoon down and just peered down at her plate. She didn't want to be rude, but she didn't want to talk either.

"I don't want to right now," Amal said. Hearing her voice startled her, as the words came out in a croak. She couldn't remember the last time she had heard her own voice. After sitting in perpetual silence for more than a week, she had forgotten what her voice was like. Soon she was aware of her throat and how much it hurt. The pain brought back memories of the salt water that had rushed into her lungs, filling them up like water balloons.

Jackie smiled. "Now we're getting somewhere. You don't have to tell me anything now, but the doctor and the people from social services will want to know. How about you ask me a few questions? You have to be curious about where you are."

Amal was curious as to how she had gone from being in the ocean to a hospital bed. She swore she had died that night, but she knew the nurse had no answers for that. No one could answer that, as only God knew, and she wasn't sure if he would let her in on the secret or not.

"Ummmm . . . ," Amal mumbled and quickly shut her mouth. Nurse Jackie looked at her curiously until she realized Amal wasn't going to say another word.

"Okay. Let's start with this. What's your name?" Jackie asked. Amal just sat with her head down, not daring to look the woman in the eyes. "Come on! It's not fair that you know my name and I don't know yours."

Fair enough, Amal thought. This nice lady had brought her food. She could at least tell her what her name was. "My name is Amal Al-Ansari," she croaked before covering her mouth with her hand. A plastic bracelet dangled from her arm, and when she raised her hand it slide down her thin arm.

"Okay, okay! Now we're getting somewhere! It's nice to meet you, Amal." Jackie held out a hand, and Amal placed her small hand in hers and shook it awkwardly.

"Do you have any questions for me? Don't be shy! Ask me whatever you want," the nurse exclaimed.

"I'd just really like to know where the bathroom is."

Jackie burst out laughing, showing her dazzling smile. "You know, I think you're just the cutest thing. Come on. Let me help you."

Normally, going to the bathroom would have been no big deal. At home, Amal was always zooming about in the safety of those walls, but now the once-simple task became tedious and painful due to the events that had put her in the hospital. She wasn't prepared for how badly her body and lungs ached; moreover, nothing could prepare her for what was to come. She could still taste salt water in her mouth, mixed with the taste of bile. It burned her teeth and throat.

When she rolled over to sit on the side of the bed, the room seemed to spin around, making her dizzy. Jackie must've noticed, because she put a hand on Amal's shoulder and said, "Take your time, sweetie."

And that she did. She sat at the edge of the bed until the room stopped spinning, and then attempted to slide off to the floor. As soon as her feet touched the floor, her legs felt like jelly and almost gave out. She was happy the nurse was there to help her, or else she would've surely fallen.

"Easy now. It's not a race. We'll get there when we get there," Jackie said reassuringly while holding on tight to her arm. Once Amal gathered enough strength she took a few weak steps. "See? You're doing good! Only a few more."

Amal took her time, walking shakily, until they were finally at the bathroom door. The nurse helped her onto the toilet, then gave her some much-needed privacy. All the while, she chatted on about her favorite foods, books, and everything in between. Jackie was definitely a talker. Amal could tell that she loved her job. She distracted her with her lighthearted conversation that made her feel normal for once.

"How old are you, love?"

"I'm twelve." Amal's voice echoed slightly in the stark white bathroom.

"Oh, I remember when I was your age. I was a troublemaker, though. I stayed on punishment. My mom never spanked me, but boy, could she talk. My brothers and I would get in trouble, and she would lecture us for hours. One night she talked to us until the sun came up. Of course we still had to go to school." Nurse Jackie laughed, remembering her childhood. "You okay in there?"

"Yes, I'm almost done." Amal had a bit of a hard time relieving herself as she was sore all over, but after sitting there for a few moments she finally did. She couldn't find any water to wash with, so she did the best she could.

Looking back at the situation, she wasn't sure what had happened to trigger the waking nightmare. But as soon as she heard the sound of flushing water, she wasn't in the hospital anymore. She was back on the boat, and the same feeling of being unsafe and panic washed over her. The sky was dark, and she could feel the rope cutting into her hands again. She looked at them and they were bleeding. The smell of blood and salt water was so overpowering that she had to make a conscious effort not to throw up. The floor rose and fell under her feet, swaying wildly with the wave that was underneath her. She gripped the sink to keep herself steady. *What's happening to me?* Lightning cut through the bathroom with a deafening rumble and landed right beside her.

"Stop it! Stop it!" she screamed, placing her hands over her ears. She shut her eyes tightly, trying her hardest to rid herself of the horrifying hallucination.

She lost her balance and hit the cold floor with a smack. Her hospital gown splayed out around her, but was she on the floor or in the icy ocean water that once claimed her small body? Jackie ran in, grabbing hold of her on the floor, and pulled Amal to herself.

"It's okay! You're fine!"

Jackie shook her a bit as she tried to snap her out of it, and when this didn't work she yelled for another nurse and said some other things Amal didn't understand. She clawed at Jackie's arms trying to get away, writhing like a wild animal until she felt a pinch on her left shoulder. And like that, it was over. She blinked rapidly as she tried to clear her vision. The storm was gone in an instant; the shot brought her back to reality as Jackie tucked her into her arms and took her back to the bed. Her eyelids became too heavy to hold open, and she realized she was falling asleep. She tried to fight it until she just couldn't help but close her eyes.

A few hours later, under warm white sheets, Amal's eyes popped open. She was back in the hospital bed. Although her head was foggy, she could make out strange voices outside the room. Amal wasn't sure what they were talking about, but she had a feeling that they were talking about her.

"So we're thinking PTSD and what else?" asked a gruff, masculine voice.

"Oh, okay. Just keep an eye on her," said a subdued voice.

Amal wanted to get out of bed; she wanted to know who was talking and if they were talking about her. As she attempted to pull the covers back to get up, she felt a sharp pain in her arms. She couldn't lift them. Both her arms were bandaged and shackled to the bed. She panicked when she saw the underside of her nails held dried blood: these were recent injuries. The last thing she remembered was going to the bathroom. The last voice she had heard was that of the nurse.

Amal sat for a while trying to remember, looking at her arms. They stung with pain every time she moved them. In a way, she liked the pain; it helped clear her head. She didn't know how long she had been awake, but when she tried to hear more of the voices outside the room, they had stopped.

The door creaked open, and a black man in a white coat quietly walked in. When he saw Amal sitting in her bed and looking straight at him, his demeanor changed. He was short and, by his features, looked like he was in his early thirties. Though he was brown, his face was full of freckles, which made him look childlike. He put on a friendly face and introduced himself, but Amal wasn't listening. She'd had enough of men to last her the rest of her life. She didn't trust them and wanted nothing to do with anything male. They were vile creatures as far as she was concerned. All of them except her baba.

The doctor held out his hand, but Amal didn't take it. She didn't want to shake his hand, so she just stared at her arms while he asked her questions.

"What's your name? What happened the night you were found? Where are your parents?"

The last question struck a nerve, and she locked eyes with the doctor for a moment before saying, "I don't remember anything, and my parents are dead."

She then turned her head away from him, refusing to say anything else. She didn't know if he was still standing there, and she didn't care. After a few moments, she heard the door close, before drifting back to sleep.

Chapter

Two

A Glimpse into the Past

Homs, Syria

Before that tragic day, Amal had had a normal life. She had a family, went to school, and loved to play with the kids in her neighborhood, who were more like family to her, not just friends. Amal and the neighborhood kids were a group of about thirty. They would walk the streets talking and laughing or would sit in the park a few blocks from where Amal lived and play games. Soccer was their favorite thing to do, and they had made their own teams. The Reds and the Blues are what they called themselves, and they took their teams very seriously. Amal was a Red, and she was known for being an excellent goalie. Nothing got past her, even on a bad day. Their parents and the rest of the people in the neighborhood even got in on the action, and every Saturday they would bring drinks, cook food, and enjoy the game. After the game was said and done, the winners were rewarded with ribbons made by Amal's mom. After, they would eat and enjoy each other's company until the wee hours of the night. Her life was simple, but she was happy, and that's all that mattered.

It was a usual Sunday afternoon when Amal's sister, Jannah, was preparing for her upcoming wedding. Amal sat on Jannah's bed, surrounded by the bridal wardrobe their mother had been making for Jannah since she was little. Amal had one as well; however, she doubted she'd ever need it. She thought marriage was weird. She had told her mother it was just an excuse to dress up and have a big party, just to become someone's maid.

Her mother simply laughed and said, "You think all I do is clean up?"

She saw what her mother did on a day-to-day basis: wash dishes, do laundry, dust, and cook dinner. So she said yes.

"Well, you may be right about some things. I do clean and cook, but I enjoy it. I love my family, so I do those things. If I didn't, I wouldn't be a good mother."

Amal thought about that. She thought about how hard her life would be if she didn't have her mother's help and the help of her sister. She hated the idea of her sister leaving and living elsewhere. She was so used to having Jannah there with her. For Amal, her sister was like a substitute mom.

Jannah's room was a pale yellow. The scent of the incense burning around the house snuck its way between the cracks of the door, like a ghost, slipping sneakily inside the room and leaving a rich scent in its wake. The aroma was thick and clung to all their linens. Her sister had always been a neat freak—everything had a place. Her craft supplies and books were neatly stacked against the wall. Her closet was even color-coded, down to her shoes, which were set by height as well as color. Each drawer in her dresser held specific things, and that's the way she liked it. Everything had its place, so it was strange to see her room in such disarray, even if it was just a few dresses on the bed.

Jannah turned to Amal, holding up a heavily beaded dress in magenta, plum purple, and red. "What do you think? Should I wear this first?"

"Well, I think—"

"Or this?" Jannah cut Amal off midsentence and grabbed another equally heavily beaded dress. It was bright blue with pink and gold detailing.

"I think–"

"But I just don't know!" groaned Jannah. "I feel like I should wear Mama's dress as well. What do you think?"

Amal threw up her hands in frustration. "Well, if you'd let me talk! I think you should wear whatever you'd like. It's your wedding. Plus, you look great in everything, anyway."

Amal had always loved her sister. Where other siblings often fought, they never had that problem. And if one made the other mad, they knew just how to make each other laugh, so arguments never lasted long. Jannah had always been beautiful, even when she was just a little girl. And she would probably age with grace like their mother. Although Amal had only seen a few pictures of her mother when she was younger, Jannah's resemblance to her was undeniable. Amal could tell that her mother's features, from what she had seen, had softened over the years rather than changed. Amal was sure that Jannah was going to remain beautiful forever–just like Mama.

Jannah's hair was bone straight and hung down her back like a silky jet-black curtain. Her eyes were honey colored, and her thick eyelashes framed them. Her eyelashes curled up with such length, she couldn't wear sunglasses, because when she blinked they scraped against the lenses. Jannah wasn't fair skinned or dark. She had the complexion of the heavily creamed tea their mother loved so much–sweet, hot, and fragrant. Even in the black abaya and hijab she loved to wear, she stood out in the crowd. She had a certain graceful way that she walked that made the boys stare. Jannah was as graceful as a ballerina, with her cape of black fabric flowing behind her. So it wasn't surprising when one of the neighbor's sons came to ask for her hand in marriage. Although he was tall and handsome, everyone knew he was the lucky one. Amal didn't know much about love; however, the way Jannah's fiancé looked at her made Amal feel a light tingling in the pit of her stomach, making her want to giggle every time.

"Of course you think I look good in everything. You're such a suck-up!" Jannah said, dropping the dress and racing across the room playfully to tackle her sister.

They rolled on the bed and on top of the beautifully tailored dresses, without a care in the world, laughing like nothing else mattered. It was just then, in that moment of happiness, the Adhan (call to worship) cut through their playing, and they stopped.

"Girls, come! Time for prayer!" their mom called from the living room. Jannah and Amal both jumped up, quickly straightening out the things on the bed.

"Come on, Amal!" Jannah said with a flourish in her voice. "After prayer we can go down to the store to see Baba, and I'll get you some candy." She flashed the bright smile that told Amal she was up to something, but Amal could never say no to candy.

"Race you to the living room?" Amal asked, excited.

"You're on! Count down?" Jannah braced herself.

"Three, two—"And suddenly Jannah ran off, laughing in that high-pitched tone that made her laugh so contagious. Amal was right behind her and yelled, "Cheater!"

After prayer, Amal and her sister changed their clothes and were off to their baba's store. They walked through the neighborhood and side streets, speaking to neighbors they had known and grown up around. The wind swept briskly through the alleyway, lifting her sister's abaya to expose her ankles and hot-pink sandals she'd worn for years. No matter what color of outfit she wore, which was normally black, she always wore those sandals. Her feet were always lightly dusted with earth when she came inside.

Their father's store was several blocks away, but they enjoyed the walk. Amal looked up at the sky, which hung over the top of the narrow alleyway like a bright blue carpet. The clouds were chunky and white, gliding through the sky smoothly and effortlessly. After they took a right turn and got near Noor's house, they could smell the fresh bread baking. It made Amal's mouth water. Noor made the best flatbread, which she served with honey and tea. Uncle Uthman was beating a drum on the porch, singing an old song to himself, while tapping his foot to the rhythm. He promised to play at Jannah's wedding reception, and Amal couldn't wait to dance. The clacking of her sister's sandals on the cobblestone walkway kept time with the beat. Amal bobbed her head left and right, hopping on one foot and then the other, while humming with the tune.

They wove in and out of the walkways; the way was etched in their brains. They rounded another corner and were at Baba's shop. He sold clothes and jewelry, and sometimes he got beautiful pieces from Dubai, and sometimes even from Africa. Amal told her baba she wanted to travel to those places when she got older. He would just smile and call her an adventurer. She was a free spirit, like her mama.

When they walked in the store, their father was talking to some man they'd never seen before. Their father laughed his hardy laugh and ran his hand through his thick, curly beard. Everyone said Amal got her looks from her baba, which always made her happy to hear. The older ladies in the neighborhood often pinched her cheeks and fawned over her, telling her stories of how her baba had been when he was her age. His cheeks would turn red at their recounter of his childhood.

Her sister went into the back where his office was, and Amal stayed out, looking around at the abayas that hung against the wall. He never got any in her size, but she still liked to look. She looked around until Jannah came out.

"Assalaamualaikum, Jannah!" her father's deep voice boomed as he embraced her with a hug. "This is the bride here, inshallah."

"Look at her blushing. Leave the girl alone, Abdul!" his friend said, laughing. Jannah was red cheeked and smiling.

"Baba, I'm taking Amal to get candy." Amal, upon hearing her name, came around the corner and nearly knocked over a display of scarves. Baba smiled at her.

"You got money? If not, get what you need." He waved his hand at the cash register.

"Thank you, Baba!" Amal exclaimed and hugged his legs. He lifted her up into his arms and embraced her with the warm bear hug she loved so much, before putting her back down on the floor. After saying their goodbyes, they were out on the street again, walking past street carts selling food and hungry working people looking for a cheap lunch. Other vendors were selling vegetables, spices, and even cattle. Colorful jewelry behind thick panes of glass sparkled in the daylight. The market was packed with people happily shopping, selling, and walking around. The second adhan rang out over the city from the tower atop the masjid, serenading the busy city below. Vendors started closing up to head to prayer, but the market was still bustling with life.

Thinking back on it now, Amal thought she should've known something was going to go wrong. Things were just going so well that neither she nor her sister saw it coming. In a flash, the happy buzz of people was turned into a mass of flesh, smoke, and shrapnel when the bomb fell right in the middle of the market, sending a shock wave through Amal so strong it blew her back. The hellish inferno turned the hum of conversation and laughter into screams and sirens. Amal's ears rang furiously as she stood in shock trying to process what had just transpired. A lady dressed in black ran in front of her, screaming so loudly and shrilly her whole body shook; her clothes were covered in blood and dust.

Amal was paralyzed on the spot, in the middle of the chaos, while crowds of people moved around her, until a man she didn't recognize grabbed her arm and told her to run. It was as if that word fueled every muscle in her body, and she took off. Years before, she had heard the expression "run for your life." In this instance, the phrase didn't seem fitting. There was much urgency in her stride. It was as if her feet weren't touching the ground as she passed people who were in shock and despair. Some just stood in place, screaming as loud as their voices would let them, but Amal ran past them, making their faces turn into nothing but blurs in the corner of her vision. Her lungs burned and her muscles ached, but years of playing soccer paid off. She could run forever, and she planned to until she found safety.

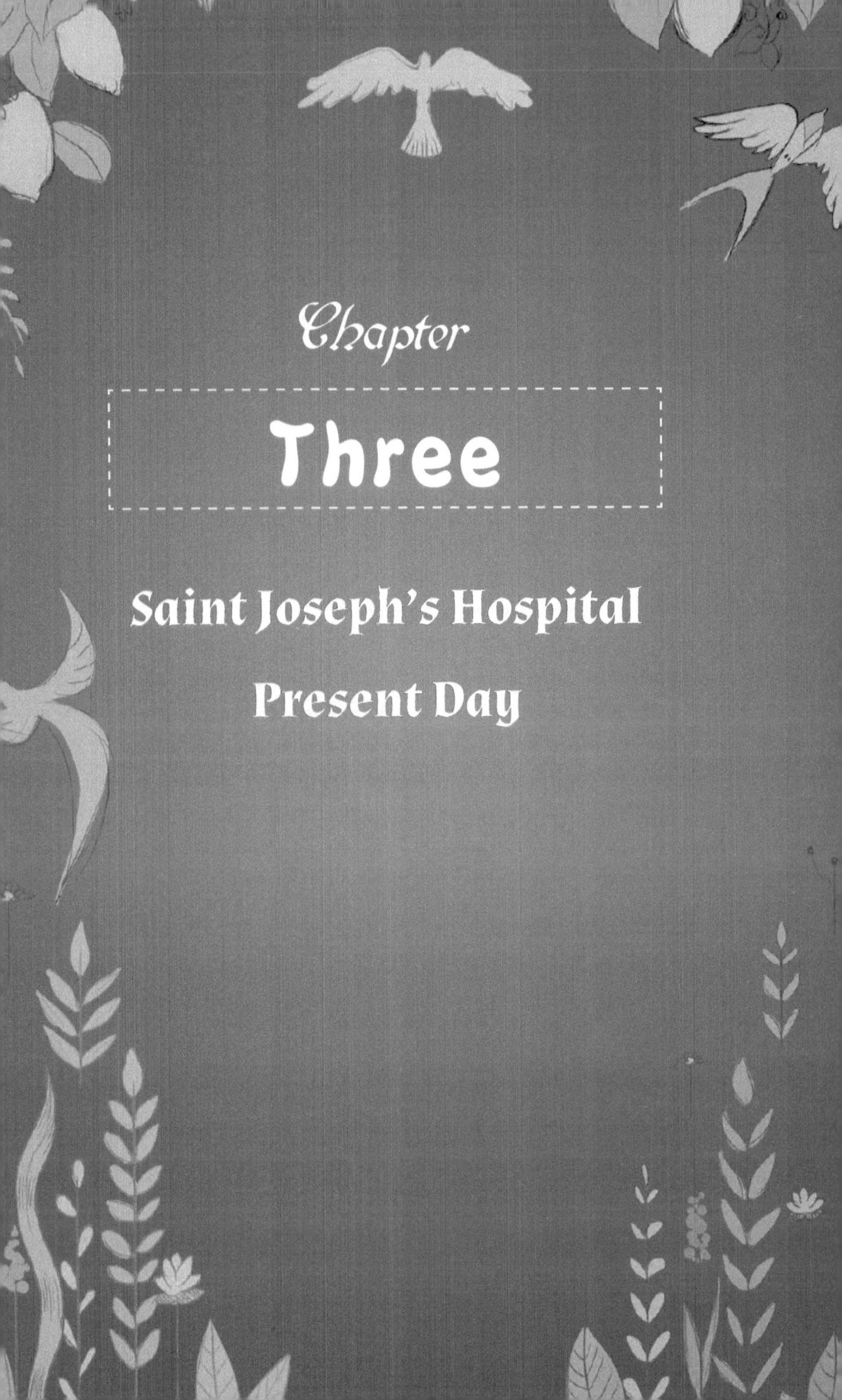

Chapter

Three

Saint Joseph's Hospital

Present Day

Amal was tucked in a tiny office in the hospital, studying the woman in front of her. She was thin, with dark hair and green eyes, and wore a black pencil skirt and a plum-colored top that ruffled around her neck. Her lips were red, like fire, and when she smiled her teeth shone as white as snow. When they first met, the woman had told her to call her Amelia. It was funny to Amal at the time because she didn't think the well-dressed woman looked like an "Amelia," but she called her by that name.

Amal felt small as she sat in the huge leather chair that squeaked noisily every time she moved. Her hospital gown and pea-green socks were two sizes too big. They made her feel odd and out of place in Amelia's immaculate office, which was painted a neutral shade of light brown. Large paintings hung on the opposite sides of the room, with no real pictures on them, just globs of color with no form or shape. Her desk was large and menacing, and Amal wondered why she would pick out such a harsh-looking piece of furniture. It didn't look like Amelia at all, but despite the surroundings, she felt comfortable here. It was the one place that was quiet, as the hospital had its moments when it could be too noisy.

Amal lay back against the back of the chair, breathing in the essential oils that Amelia had burning in a little lamp on a small table in a corner behind her desk. She loved the smell of the wood and oils, mixed.

"How are you?" Amelia asked as she sat behind the desk with her hands folded in front of her. Her nails were pointed and painted a shiny burgundy. They reminded her of claws freshly dipped in the blood of some unfortunate creature.

"I'm fine," Amal said, fidgeting in her chair a little.

"Are you sure? I heard you had an episode last week. Can you tell me about that?"

"'Episode'?" Amal hadn't heard this word before.

"Yes. Do you remember what happened?"

It took her a minute to figure out what Amelia was talking about. Then Amal remembered the event like it had happened moments before. She wouldn't call it an episode; it seemed more like a nightmare. No matter how much she wanted to forget about it, she couldn't. Amal had been trying to steer clear of the bathroom and running water ever since by holding her bladder for as long as she could, which she knew wasn't good. Nurse Jackie had to stand outside the bathroom whenever she went in.

"Are you going to tell me?" Amelia asked calmly.

"There's nothing to tell. I just blacked out." Amal shrugged. The chair smelled of fresh leather and let out a squeak as she leaned back.

"I haven't known you for very long, but in my line of work you learn how to read people, and I know there's more to it than what you're telling me. I think you remember but you're afraid to talk about it, which is fine, but don't lie and say you don't remember. It's okay to say you don't want to talk about it."

Amelia stood and smoothed out her skirt, then walked around her desk and sat on the edge of it. Amal looked down at the woman's shoes, which were unbelievably high-heeled, and black with red bottoms.

"I'm just trying to help you, but I can't unless you let me."

"Why do you want to help me? You don't even know me," Amal asked.

"Because it's my job and because I know you need me. I don't have to know you to care about you, Amal. You do understand that, right?"

She thinks I need her? I need my family, not her. No matter how nice she is, she can't make the fact that I'm an orphan any less painful, she thought. The word *orphan* stung as it formed itself in her thoughts. Only months ago she had a family, a home, and a country. She was happy and loved, but was now alone in someplace that was foreign to her, with doctors all around saying they were there to help. She didn't know who to believe, and for the most part didn't care. She just wanted to be left alone, as she was tired of the questions and nurses waking her up every hour. It would be so nice to just go home, but she knew there was nothing to go back to and she would have to make do.

They sat in silence until Amelia gave an exhausted sigh and walked back to her chair.

"Social Services will be here tomorrow to place you with a family. I was hoping to make some kind of progress before then, but it's fine. It'll all come in time," Amelia said as she opened a yellow envelope and sorted through a few papers.

"Social services? A family?" Amal asked a little louder than she had meant to.

"You didn't think you would stay here forever, did you?" Amelia looked up from her papers to look at Amal. Tears filled her eyes at the thought of leaving here to live with people she didn't know. Though Amal didn't like the hospital, she had become used to her surroundings and now would be leaving all that she had come to know in the past few weeks. She didn't know if she was or would ever be ready to brave the world outside those walls.

"But I don't want to go." Tears ran down her cheeks.

"Hey, it'll be fine. You'll see. I'll continue to be your doctor and will be here whenever you need me." Amelia walked around her desk and reached a manicured hand out and held Amal's hand in hers. "It'll get better and everything will be okay. I promise."

Amal blinked fresh tears away as she held Amelia's soothingly warm hand. Her gaze was filled with love and something else Amal couldn't understand. Maybe she would be okay. She didn't know for sure, but she would give it a try. *It couldn't be worse than what I've already been through,* she thought.

After her appointment, she slowly walked the halls while counting the marbled tiles on the floor. Her socks flopped around at the toe, making her feet look smaller than they really were. Amal walked past a maintenance closet and two sets of elevators, and thought about escaping for a moment, but where would she go? A feeling deep inside told her that it wouldn't be a good idea; she could end up in even worse trouble. Who knows what would happen if she fled the safety of the hospital into a world she didn't know? So Amal just kept walking, slowly feeling a sense of freedom as she weaved through the halls and smiled politely as she passed other patients in hospital gowns tightly gripping the railing on the walls. Once back to her room, she settled into bed and peered out the window, half expecting to see darkness, but it was still daylight. She thought of watching a little TV, but was exhausted from her walk and found herself falling asleep.

She wrapped herself in the blankets, like a caterpillar in a cocoon, with nothing but her head exposed. Maybe when she woke up, instead of a normal girl, she would be a beautiful butterfly and fly back home. As her eyelids closed she thought of her parents. Amal closed her eyes and imagined laying her head in her mama's lap and basking in the sweet smell of her perfume. She could feel her mama's hand on her back, patting her softly, with the Quran playing low in the background. She fell asleep feeling like she was back in the comfort of her home.

The day finally came when the person from social services arrived. He was a tall man, probably around six feet or so. When she saw him she was immediately uncomfortable and had to crane her neck to see his face when he walked into her room. Jackie must have sensed her discomfort and said she would be waiting outside the door if she needed her, leaving her alone with him. Mr. Wright was a man of few words and seemed to have to think before he said anything. His voice was light for a man, but Amal didn't care one bit. This is the man that would be taking her away to live with someone else, and she needed to know where she was going.

Days before his arrival she had thought about their meeting so much she dreamed about it. There were nights when she would wake up in a cold sweat after dreaming about the terrible person who would grab her and throw her in a bag and take her away, kicking and screaming. Amal assumed she'd be meeting a woman, but it wouldn't have made their meeting any less uncomfortable. Despite his asking many questions, their meeting was quick. He asked her personal questions about her life, and she nervously answered as many as she could without giving away too much. Did she have a birth certificate? Where was she from? How did she get here?—all the questions people had been asking since she arrived, but this time she felt like she had to answer, but didn't know what to say.

Words seemed to stick in her throat, like the time she choked on gummy candy. Before she left her country, her baba had told her not to say where she was from or they would kick her out, so she said she was American. Then came the flood of other questions: Did she know her social security number? What state was she born in? How old was she? What was her last name? What race was she? The questions seemed endless. He asked so many questions that she became overwhelmed and began crying. Amal was never much of a crier, but tears seemed to come to her quickly these days. It turned out in her favor because as soon as she heard her crying Jackie rushed in and quickly shooed the man out. He wore a confused look on his face when he left.

"That's enough for today," Amal heard Jackie say.

"Well, I think I have enough information from what was given by the hospital and from the questions that she did answer. I'll be in contact when I've found a match," the man said. Amal heard the sound of his fancy shoes clicking on the floor, and the sound got softer as he walked to the elevator.

***

"It's your turn," Jackie said.

Amal looked down at the checkerboard and contemplated her next move. When she wasn't busy Jackie liked playing games with Amal. Amal didn't want to admit it, but she had come to love Jackie, and she hoped she felt the same. She found herself wondering what she would do when she had to leave the hospital. Jackie's kindness and bubbly attitude reminded her of her mother. Amal missed her mama, but being around Jackie made her grief less painful.

"Sometimes I wonder what's going on in that pretty head of yours." Amal looked up to find Jackie smiling at her.

"I just . . . I was just thinking that I'll miss you when I leave," Amal said, wringing her hands together.

"I'll miss you too, sweetie." The nurse's eyes got misty for a moment, but she blinked it away. "You won't forget about me, will you?"

"Never!" Amal said. "I promise."

Jackie held up a finger to Amal and caught her off guard. "You pinky swear you won't forget me?" Amal had never heard of a pinky swear and didn't know what to do until Jackie grabbed her hand and locked her pinky around hers. "It's a promise that you can't break, and if you do, I'll have to cut your pinky off."

"Cut my pinky off!" Amal exclaimed. She didn't know much about hands, but she was sure she would need her pinky for something.

"Just kidding, kid!" Jackie smiled her bright, wide smile at Amal and ran a hand through Amal's hair. "Hurry up and move. My lunch break is only thirty minutes! I don't have all day!" Jackie said, giggling, teasing Amal.

"Okay, Okay! Let me think!"

Amal wished she could stay in this moment forever, where it was just she and Jackie playing checkers together. No worries or fear, just happiness and contentment. She finally made her move, not caring about the outcome. She watched the nurse as she looked at the board thoughtfully, wishing she didn't have to leave but knowing her time there was coming to an end soon. She said a silent prayer, asking God to bless Jackie for being so kind to her for the past weeks and helping her through the darkest times. And as Jackie finally moved a piece, she asked for Jackie to be blessed with what she'd wanted for so long: a baby. Amal closed her eyes and prayed a small prayer for her family as well. Wherever they were now, she hoped they were happy and waiting on her.

Little Bird

Chapter

Four

Saint Joseph's Hospital
Present Day

Rain beat heavily on the building as she lay in her bed looking at the wall. Something about the day just felt off to her. When Amal woke early that morning to the sounds of thunder, she knew today would be her last day there. She had no way of knowing, but it was just a feeling deep in her gut. Her stomach flipped and fluttered, so naturally she had no appetite; so when the nurse brought her breakfast of raisin toast, Cream of Wheat, and apple sauce, she just picked at it.

As long as she got to say goodbye to Jackie, she'd be okay, but she hadn't seen her all morning. She was so nervous; her stomach kept turning, making her even antsier. Amal could hardly keep her legs still when Amelia came in. She was wearing a black dress today, with a red jacket and heels so thin and high they made her look professional and put together. She looked like the women on TV and movies she had seen with her sister.

Amelia sat on the edge of the bed with a bag.

"Good morning!" Amelia beamed. Amal learned early on that Amelia was a morning person. While others looked worn down and tired, she always looked fresh faced and happy, greeting people as she walked through the halls to her office.

"Good morning," Amal said, her feet twitching under the blankets.

"I don't know if anyone told you, but we found the perfect placement for you."

"When will I be leaving?" Amal asked nervously.

"You'll be leaving in a few hours. Sorry for the short notice, but we just got in contact with the family last night."

Amal sat looking down at her hands. *A few hours? Will I get to say goodbye to my friend?*

"I brought you a few things to wear. I didn't know what your favorite color is, so I hope you like them," Amelia said, sounding hopeful.

She pulled a dress and a pair of shoes and socks from the bag. The dress was knee length, pale green and brown, with little cap sleeves, and the shoes were white strappy sandals. The dress wasn't her favorite, but she wouldn't complain. Amelia had even bought her bows for her hair. She looked at the clothes expressionlessly. Amelia must've seen the look on her face and took it as she didn't like the gifts.

"I should've asked what color you like. I'm sorry. I can get you something else."

"No! It's nice! I love it!" Amal said, putting on the biggest fake smile she could muster.

With a relieved sigh Amelia smiled. "Oh, I'm glad! At first I thought you hated them. I haven't been blessed with children yet, so I really had no clue what to get."

Amal heard what she was saying, but couldn't have cared less; she needed to see her friend. "Have you seen Jackie? I would like to say goodbye."

"I don't think she's working today, but I can tell her for you."

Amal's heart sank. Not only would she be leaving but she wouldn't be able to say goodbye to her friend.

Amelia checked her watch. "They're expecting you within the next few hours, so go ahead and get a shower and change. I already have your discharge papers. Everything's ready to go. I'm just waiting on you, my dear."

She pulled the covers back, revealing her bare feet and thin legs, before slowly getting out of the bed and gathering her clothes. This was it. She was leaving. She held her head up and willed herself not to cry in front of Amelia, but when she closed the bathroom door she lost it and silently sobbed while sliding to the floor, holding her new clothes.

"You okay in there?" Amelia called from outside.

Amal quickly wiped her face and replied with a weak yes.

She turned on the shower and stepped into the ice- cold water while giving herself a pep talk. *Everything is fine. I'm just in the shower. I'm safe,* repeating it to herself while washing. Amal turned off the water and towel dried as slowly as she could, savoring her last moments there. When she was dressed she walked out, her heart beating violently in her chest. It was actually happening. Amelia was smiling at her when she walked out of the bathroom. Clearly proud of her fashion choice, she patted the bed next to her. Amal sat down without a word, as if she were on autopilot. Amelia brought out a comb and gently began detangling her hair. After a few minutes of combing and after the bows were placed lovingly in her hair, Amelia turned Amal's head toward her to admire her work.

"You look so cute! Do you want to see?" Amelia led her to the bathroom and turned on the light. Suddenly Amal was met with the vision of herself in the mirror. If it had been a regular day back home, she might have agreed, but now she just felt hollow. Not wanting to offend Amelia, she smiled as big as possible and thanked her.

Since Amal didn't have any personal belongings, leaving was a breeze. Amal and Amelia walked hand in hand past the nurses' desk. Two nurses she knew were behind the desk doing paperwork as she passed. They looked up, gave sad smiles, and waved goodbye.

Once they made it downstairs Amal saw Mr. Wright standing at the entrance, looking awkward. His nervousness made it seem like he had never been there before. Then it hit her that Amelia wouldn't be taking her. When they were a couple feet away from the man, Amelia bent down, laying a warm kiss on Amal's cheek. She thought about her red lipstick staining her skin, and she didn't care. She would keep that kiss there forever if she could.

"Everything will be fine. You're going to go with Mr. Wright, but I'll be seeing you even if I have to come myself." Amelia gave her shoulders a squeeze. The kiss left a lump in Amal's throat as she tried not to cry. "You have my number. You can call me anytime, day or night."

Amal abruptly wrapped her arms around Amelia, startling her for a few seconds; then she embraced Amal back. They stood there hugging each other for so long that Mr. Wright cleared his throat, their public display of affection clearly making him uncomfortable. They pulled away, and Amal dropped her head.

"Time for us to go," Mr. Wright said, and he proceeded through the hospital doors.

He opened an umbrella for her, and they began walking toward his car, avoiding puddles of murky water on the sidewalk. It was so hard for her not to turn around and run back. She wanted to beg them to let her stay. She even contemplated throwing herself in front of a moving car so she would have to go back, but in the end she did none of those things. Amal just kept walking as the rain beat down on the umbrella. She looked around to see the city was a wash of gray and the street lights poorly illuminated the surrounding area. Rain began to come down harder as Mr. Wright opened the car door for her and helped her in.

As they rode through the streets, the car kicking up gray waves of water, Amal looked out the window intently. She wanted nothing to do with the situation. Mr. Wright had tried and failed to hold conversation, so they just sat in silence and the sound of rain. She was much too deep in thought to hold a conversation. *Where am I going? Who will I be living with?* She hated that her life was at the mercy of people who didn't know her, but she would have to get used to it. The buildings were stacks of metal, tall and important looking. Amal wondered what went on in those buildings, but she would probably never find out.

The car rode smoothly under Mr. Wright's command, and she watched the landscape change from huge buildings and paved streets packed with cars to trees and wide-open spaces lush with trees or crops. She saw a few cows grazing happily, not phased at all by the rain. They rode past a fence that held beautiful horses which ran along with the car until they were cut off by the fence. She wondered if they cared about being caged in and if they ever thought about being free, because she did. The hospital, this car, and wherever she was going next were like her cage. *Will I ever get free?* She hoped so.

The ride was long, and they rode until Mr. Wright slowed the car and turned down a small dirt road. The tree line was dense here, and she watched as the rain and wind made the branches move like the trees were waving at her. For a moment, she pretended they were, and that thought made her smile a bit. When they reached the end of the road, there was a small brown house sitting in the middle of a cleared space between the trees. The yard was surrounded by a rusted fence, and a broken-down car sat, missing tires and half rusted away, in the driveway. Children's toys left abandoned outside were shiny and dripping wet with moisture. If the yard looked like this, she didn't want to know what the inside looked like.

Mr. Wright turned off the engine and reached back for his umbrella.

"I'll come around and open the door for you. I don't want you getting sick."

When she put her feet on the ground, her legs were shaking like jelly, and she had a hard time holding herself up, but somehow managed. It took extra effort for her to make it to the porch. Once they were there, Mr. Wright knocked on the faded wooden door. The paint had chipped in places and came off on Mr. Wright's knuckles when he knocked. He dusted his hand off, as though he had been contaminated. Amal got a chance to look at the house more closely and found that plants lined the windows and porch. The bushes at the fence and walkway were overgrown and looked like they hadn't been trimmed in years.

Amal heard a commotion behind the door, which snapped her back to attention. The door opened to reveal a round woman in a pink robe standing in dim lighting, studying them with suspicious eyes. The sounds of a TV could be heard from where Amal was standing.

"It's about time you showed up. I almost thought y'all wasn't coming." She had a cigarette between her lips. The whole time she was studying Amal. "Well, come in!" she said more forcefully than courteously.

The first thing Amal was hit with was the smell of smoke. The smell was so strong, Amal's eyes began to water and burn. The woman ushered them to her small kitchen, where they sat. The woman glared at Amal like she was trying to read her mind. In the light, she was ugly, to say the least. Probably the ugliest person she'd ever seen. Her skin had a slight yellow tinge, like her teeth. She had sweat stains under her arms, and her nails were chewed to the bone. She took another drag on the cigarette while Mr. Wright fished out paperwork.

"Thank you for taking her in on such short notice. I have a few things for you to sign."

"You didn't tell me she was a foreigner."

Mr. Wright looked taken aback and cleared his throat. "She's not a foreigner. She's from here."

"She don't look white, and she don't look like a nigger. What's your name, girl?" Her eyes seemed to pierce through Amal's skin as she looked her up and down, blowing a cloud of smoke from her nostrils.

Amal dropped her head and answered, "Amal."

The woman scoffed, making her fat jiggle in places. "See. You can't tell me she ain't foreign. What kind of name is that? She's probably from one of those God-forsaken countries with the stupid names you can hardly say."

"Now, now, Miss James, please. Her nationality has nothing to do with it. I'm sure after a few days you'll see that she is a wonderful young lady. Now, if you would sign the papers . . . I have a busy day ahead of me."

"Well, get me the papers, then!"

Mr. Wright passed her the papers and watched in silence as she signed them. "She's to be enrolled in school soon, and she has to go to therapy session every two weeks."

"So she's foreign and retarded?" Ms. James huffed like it was a personal assault on her.

"No, she's not," Mr. Wright said, rising to his feet, clearly as disturbed as Amal was.

He brushed some cigarette ash from his coat and looked at Amal. "Well . . . If you need me, this is my number." He stood, handed Amal a business card, and stared at her for a moment before leaving abruptly.

The house was old and smelled of wetness and decay. After Mr. Wright's abrupt departure, Amal was left alone under the icy glare of Ms. James.

"You can call me Ms. James. I'm not your momma and I'm not your friend, so don't get comfortable around here. If the money wasn't good, I'da left your little ass outside where you belong. Damn immigrants, always thinking someone owes you something. You won't be eating for free around here!" she said, with an exaggerated neck roll. "Now get up and let me show you what you'll be doing. And pay attention because I'm only going to say this once!" she said, getting up from her chair.

She gathered her bathrobe around herself, and Amal got to see how big Ms. James really was. Her bottom looked like a ripe peach under the fuzzy fabric. It left a bad taste in her mouth, but she managed not to make any faces at the woman's appearance. She followed her down the home's only hallway. Ms. James flipped on the dim light so they could see. The carpet was mustard yellow and gave off an odd smell, like old fruit and smoke.

"This is my Ann's room. You don't go in there while she's in there. Don't talk or make any eye contact with her. I don't need her getting comfortable talking to A-rabs. You hear me?"

Amal nodded. She wasn't sure what an A-rab was, but she didn't ask. This was her first day there, and she was already being insulted and bossed around.

"Speak up!" Ms. James demanded.

"Yes, I understand," Amal said quickly.

"Yes, what?"

"Yes, ma'am," she said, looking down at the floor.

A smile spread across Ms. James's face that was so evil, Amal felt it in her bones and the hairs stood up on her arms. Her teeth weren't yellow, as she'd first thought. It could have been the lighting, but now she could see that the woman's teeth were black in spots and clearly hadn't been brushed in a while. A smear of lipstick on her teeth spread a sickly red color across them. She looked like she had eaten something small and defenseless. Amal just hoped she wouldn't be her next meal. When she pulled the cigarette out of her mouth it had the same red ring around the end. They went from that door to the next one, which Ms. James pushed open with one hand. A fancy washer and dryer were up against one wall, with washing powder in a hanging rack on the other wall. It was full of other cleaning supplies as well.

"I hope you know how to use a washer and dryer. I don't suppose they had them in whatever cave you lived in?" Insults flew from this woman's mouth just as easy as air came in and out of her lungs.

"Yes, ma'am, I know how to use them."

"Good. Laundry gets done every day. I made a list of what needs to be washed and what day. You stick to the schedule I will give you. All cleaning products will be found in this room."

As Ms. James walked down the hall, the back of her robe shook so much Amal wondered how the fabric didn't rip.

"This is your room." She pushed open the door to reveal a tiny room that was just big enough for a twin-sized bed and a dresser. It smelled just as stale and stuffy as the rest of the house, and the light was so dim she had to squint to see everything. The round woman faced her, holding a piece of paper in her hand.

"I'll let you have the rest of the day off, but I expect you up at 5:00 a.m. tomorrow morning. Do everything the way I say, and everything will be fine." She moved in so close Amal could smell her breath and see her missing teeth. "But if you cross me, you will regret it," she said, and she shoved the paper into Amal's hand.

Amal shook her head and walked into the room, looking at her new space. Only when she heard the door shut behind her did she feel safe, but she felt so alone; not even God was with her in that room. She wanted to call Amelia and tell her to come get her now. She wanted Jackie to find her and take her away from this place. They could go somewhere quiet, somewhere they could play checkers together, forever, so she would never have to come back to this place.

Chapter

Five

A Glimpse into the Past

Homs, Syria

She just kept running, but she couldn't help but think, *Is my mind playing tricks on me? Is this real?* Suddenly she remembered her sister, and she had to go back. Her sister had been walking ahead of her the whole time. Amal turned around and ran back. All the while she kept thinking, *Please don't let her be dead! PLEASE!* Tears streamed freely down her dirty face as she ran back, searching the ground for what felt like hours. Moving past death and destruction, with emergency sirens blaring, she ran and ran until she saw it. It was as if her whole world crumbled around her.

The noise around her stopped when she saw a hot-pink sandal covered in blood. She dropped to her knees, and shards of glass dug deeply into her skin, but she didn't feel it. Even if she had felt it, she wouldn't have cared. Amal picked up the shoe, as though it were made of glass, and brought it to her chest, cradling it like the shoe itself would fill the emptiness in her chest and stop all this havoc.

Something told her to look ahead, and there was the body no more than fifty feet in front of her. *Jannah* . . . She won't remember if she said it or just thought it, but her sister was there, lying in a pile of rubble that used to be a restaurant. Amal crawled to her and scooped Jannah up into her arms and rocked her as her head lolled against Amal's left arm. Her body was so limp and heavy, but Amal kept rocking her and prayed the prayer her mother had taught her. It would calm them down after a nightmare, but there was no calm to be had. She still tried even though she knew better. Amal didn't know if she was praying for herself, her sister, or everyone around her, but she closed her eyes, still rocking her sister, and she prayed with everything in her: "Allah!

There is no God but He—the Living, the Self-subsisting, Eternal. No slumber can seize Him nor sleep. His are all things in the heavens and on earth. Who is there can intercede in His presence except as He permitteth? He knoweth what appeareth to His creatures, as before or after or behind them. Nor shall they compass aught of His knowledge except as He willeth. His throne doth extend over the heavens and on earth, and He feeleth no fatigue in guarding and preserving them, for He is the Most High, the Supreme (in glory)."

Amal didn't know how her baba found her, but when she saw him she just looked at him, not sure what to say. Relief flooded his face when he saw her, but his face immediately changed when he saw whom she had in her arms. He picked her sister up and threw her over his left shoulder, with Amal in his right arm, and he ran. He ran so fast it was as if he were flying.

"We have to get home! We have to find your mother." His voice cracked, as he was crying and breathing hard. His oldest daughter was dead, and for no reason at all. Amal was still crying too. "It's okay. She's fine. We'll take her to the doctor. He'll fix her." He was not talking to Amal but to himself. He just needed a way to cope, but Amal knew she was gone. As they flew through the alleyways, he kept repeating himself that everything would be okay and he was going to fix her and fix everything.

They were almost to their house when another bomb fell, and this one Amal heard and felt harder than she had felt the first one. It sent shock waves through the ground. Its vibrations resonated deep within her small body. As hard as this one was when it dropped, her baba didn't drop them. He turned his back, shielding his children from the blast.

After what seemed like an eternity, he looked back. "No, no, no!" he shouted as he ran toward a huge pile of rocks.

Her baba stood there crying. *Why have we stopped?* Amal thought, until she realized the pile of rocks used to be her home. Her mama had been in there. Numbness overtook her body, spreading the same way a body part would fall asleep. Amal wanted to cry but couldn't. She pictured large pieces of the house falling from the sky, killing her mother on impact. She wanted to feel the pain of loss, but nothing came. How had her whole life turned this bad so quickly?

Thousands of screams echoed around them, like the gates of hell had been opened. Fires blazed and the air was thick with dust from collapsed buildings. She looked around in awe. It was so surreal. She had to be dreaming. This couldn't be real. Then Amal remembered reading a book on PTSD on one of their many trips to the library. At the time, it had seemed strange for a ten-year-old to want to read something like that, and she wasn't sure what had made her pick up the book, but she'd learned a lot from it. It's strange what traumatic events do to people. Some people become paralyzed in the moment, so shocked that they don't move a muscle. Others panic; they run, scream, cry, and yell with a wild look in their eyes. Most internalize it and fight their battles on the inside, but there are a few that take their fear out on others in what the book called mob mentality.

As she stood with what was left of her family, she saw it all; the fear, rage, confusion, sadness, and loss. Her ears and eyes were filled with tragedy. She tried to find some good in the situation and thought maybe she could fool herself into thinking everything was okay, but it was like trying to swim in turbulent waters: as hard as you try to come up to the top, you still get pushed down into it again and again.

She kept asking herself, *Is this real? Why is this happening?* A few large military vehicles hummed down the street, and before they could get to them, her baba grabbed her and ran like hell toward a nearby pillar from a building that had somehow survived the second blast, and hid them behind it. He was still carrying her sister's bloody body, and as they hid, he held her like he used to when they were little.

In the midst of the chaos, a vivid memory flashed before her: Baba coming home after work with a new movie and Amal, Jannah, Mama, and Baba cuddling under a huge quilt Mama had made. The patches were each unique but seemed to suit each other so perfectly. Hiding among the rubble, she imagined the feel of the soft fabric on her skin and the warmth and love of her family. It was strange how things changed so quickly. In that moment, she felt small and helpless.

She looked over at Baba cradling Jannah with his eyes closed. He was so still Amal almost thought he was asleep until a tear dropped from his eye and he sniffled. He turned to Amal and looked her over. She was covered in dust, dirt, and bruises, with shards of glass sticking out in awkward positions from her legs and knees. He stared at her for a long time before bursting into tears. She crawled to her baba, wiping his tears away with a dirty hand. It didn't matter how many fell, she would be there to wipe them up. She would wipe every last one of them until there were no more. Just like her mama would do if she were here.

Her mama was the most kind and loving person she knew. She would do anything for anyone, and she never asked for anything in return. Her heart was as big as the ocean, and when you were around her, you couldn't help but feel happy. Her skin was as toasty brown and warm as desert sand, and she always smelled of the finest perfumes. Her black abaya made her look regal as she walked arm in arm with Baba. Her clothes trailed behind her in billowing black waves and left the beautiful scent of her perfume in the air. No matter how hot it was, she seemed to never break a sweat. Love was her language of choice, and she was proficient in it. Her mama always had a smile for anyone who looked her way, and she never met a stranger. She would often strike up conversations with people she didn't know, making friends everywhere she went. She was what Amal wanted to be when she grew up. While other mothers complained about their children, she loved the chaos Amal and her sister brought to her on a daily basis.

No matter what time of day, Mama was always bubbly and happy. Songs spilled from her lips and echoed through the house in the mornings, setting a tone of lightheartedness that Amal and Jannah soaked up. She sang about Baba and the love she had for him, and when they were sick, she'd sing their illness away with her sultry voice. Her parents also sang sickly sweet love duets together. Mama loved to stay busy and could do just about anything, but crocheting and sewing were her favorite hobbies. She could make anything and everything, but loved making dresses for Amal and her sister. They never wanted to admit it out loud, but they loved those dresses and the time and care she took to make them. Kids in school would ask where they got their outfits, but they would simply smile and keep quiet. They'd made a pact that they would keep their source for clothes a secret.

As she looked down at her torn and dirty outfit, she felt tears sting her eyes. *Mama wouldn't be happy with the way my clothes look now,* she thought.

Chapter

Six

Amal
Monroeville, Alabama
Present Day

Amal awoke to the sound of an alarm blaring in her left ear and peered at the clock with one eye open. It was 4:30 a.m. and Amal needed to start getting ready for her long day, so she rose slowly from the hard bed and had a good stretch and yawn. Her hair was a mess and hung like a curtain over her eyes and face. She looked around, not knowing what time prayer came in, but she decided to pray, regardless of the time.

Looking out her small window, she shrugged and got up from her bed and tiptoed barefoot down the hall to the bathroom, the dirty carpet giving under her feet. When she got inside and flipped the switch on the wall next to the door, the light came on abruptly, blinding her for a few seconds. The floor was freezing and somehow unusually sticky under the bottom of her feet. It was unpleasant, but it helped wake her up. Pulling her plain cotton underwear down, she sat on the cold toilet seat. Was everything in this house terrible? While sitting on the toilet, she examined her to-do list, which read:

1. Make Ann's lunch

2. Serve breakfast 5:30 a.m.

3. Wash dishes

4. Dust furniture

5. Vacuum

6. Wipe down countertops

7. Clean bathroom

8. Wash clothes

9. Make dinner

10. Wash dishes

11. Wipe down table

12. Bed 9:30 p.m.

She got up from the toilet, flushed, and walked over to the mirror. There was a new toothbrush with a note on it by the sink: "Keep yours separate." She didn't know why she had to keep her toothbrush separate from everyone else's, but she did as she was told and brushed, then wrapped her toothbrush in tissue, placing it in her hand with the to-do list, and closed the bathroom door behind her. Had she been looking up, she would've see a little blonde girl with the same features as Ms. James walking toward her, but she didn't and she ended up bumping into her, making the clothes the girl was holding fall to the floor and Amal's toothbrush go flying. She was glad that she had covered it before leaving the bathroom.

"I'm so sorry!" Amal said, helping the girl gather her things.

"It's no big deal! My name's Ann. You must be the new girl."

The girl seemed happy to see Amal despite the circumstances of their meeting. A memory of yesterday's interaction with Ms. James made her nervous, and she didn't want to get caught talking to her daughter, so she just nodded with her head down. The girl was about the same age as Amal and seemed nice enough.

"Don't worry. I won't tell Mom about this. I know you didn't mean any harm," Ann said, handing Amal her toothbrush.

"Thank you," Amal said, and she walked back to her room, keeping her eyes away from Ann. As she closed the door, she heard Ann enter the bathroom and close the door. With all the commotion she had forgotten to wash up for prayer. *Oh well, the bathroom is taken now.* She was still determined to pray, so she took the daisy-print pillowcase off the bed and placed it on the floor and answered the call to prayer.

Finishing at 5:00 a.m. on the dot, she dressed quickly, then left her room to check off the first thing on her list. Walking into the kitchen, she decided to look around first to get familiar with the layout as she needed to know where everything was kept if she was going to be doing the cooking. The kitchen was small with black and pink tiles on the floor and half the wall. The stove was tucked away in a small niche in the wall. She quietly opened cabinets and doors, finally finding Ann's lunch box. Satisfied with her search, she turned to the fridge and grabbed some bread and jelly. The peanut butter was tucked away in the pantry. Her mind raced as she made the sandwich. Her brain wanted her to think she was dreaming and soon she would wake up in her bed in Syria and she wasn't at a horrible woman's home in the middle of a strange country. Shutting her eyes and envisioning herself in her family's tiny kitchen, she couldn't help but see her mama's smiling face as she made them food.

"Good, you're up. I'm going to need you to wash my sheets and flip my mattress when you're done with breakfast," Ms. James said, startling Amal with her sudden appearance. She was dressed similarly to the way she had been when they first met, except this robe was blue and had a brown ring around the collar.

She sat down at the table and began looking through a magazine with a smiling white woman on the cover. Amal hadn't even heard her come in.

"You do know how to make *American* food, right? Not bugs or whatever you're used to eating," she said with a wave of her hand.

"I can. Yes, ma'am." Amal had never eaten a bug in her life, but she had watched a lot of The Food Channel back home.

"You better not waste my food either. Damn devil worshipper. You burn it, you eat it!"

Amal cut the sandwich she was making in half with shaky hands and added a small bag of carrots and celery. Then she made breakfast for everyone while Ms. James sat on her round bottom, complaining about magazine articles and how some famous person wore her hair. She made pancakes, eggs, and fruit salad from canned fruit.

Hours later, she lay on the moldy-smelling couch, staring up at the ceiling. Her muscles burned, and her arms and legs were tired from all the things Ms. James had wanted her to do that weren't on the original list but were things she had added. The house was quiet, and she preferred it that way. She was sick of hearing the fat woman's racist rants. Ms. James had even made fun of the way Amal spoke.

It was that day that she learned that Ms. James liked to keep a lock on the fridge. Amal would have to eat quickly when she got up the next day before she did anything else.

When the weight of the world seemed to be on her shoulders, Amal closed her eyes and thought of her home in Syria and how much she missed it. Her parents' faces came into view. She could see her mother's warm smile and eyes and her father's perfect white teeth and well-groomed beard; she pictured them arm in arm, like they used to be. She shooed the thought away before it got too deep, but it still left its wounds on her heart.

Her body was so sore, and her muscles had become as hard as rocks, and her stomach protested loudly. If she hadn't been in so much pain, she would've cried. She couldn't imagine doing all those chores again the next day.

Ms. James had gone out to get her hair and nails done, and Amal was just waiting for Ann to come in from school so she could cook. She thought about Ann and how nice she had been to her that morning and wondered if she would still get in trouble for talking to her. Ms. James scared her, and she didn't want to see the menacing lump of the woman's temper.

Around 3:00 p.m. she was still lying on the couch when she heard the door. She jumped up and pretended she was fluffing the cushions. She was relieved to see it was just Ann. She came in looking exhausted, wearing hot-pink jeans and a pink-white-and-purple top with Hello Kitty all over it. Her shoes, bag, and keychain were decorated with Hello Kitty as well. When she finally got inside, she dropped her bag on the floor and finally noticed Amal standing there.

"Hey!" she said with a smile.

Amal didn't understand how this girl could belong to Ms. James. She was beautiful. Her blonde hair was tied into a tight ponytail that hung down her back. She had light blue eyes and a beauty mark next to her right eye. When she smiled her teeth sparkled, but Amal noticed she was missing one on the side. She was still a very pretty girl, and her attitude made her look even better.

"I was told I can't talk to you," Amal said cautiously.

"Yeah. My mom is mean and I'm sorry about that. She isn't here though, so it's okay. I won't tell her," Ann said as she dragged her backpack to the table.

She went to the cabinet to grab a cup, and Amal almost ran over to her.

"I'm supposed to do that," Amal said, nervously wringing her hands.

"Dude. Chill! I can get my own water. Like I said, she isn't here. It's fine. When she isn't here don't worry about me. Just relax," Anna said, pouring herself some water from a pitcher. "I know you've been working all day. Come sit with me."

Amal slowly walked toward the table and sat across from Ann, keeping her distance. She didn't know if she could really trust her or if it was just a setup. Amal knew nothing about this girl other than their brief meeting that morning in the hallway. For all she knew, she could be just like her mother.

"Would you like some water or juice?" Ann asked, looking like she was about to get up.

"No, No! I'm okay," Amal said, raising a hand to stop her.

"Just making sure. So you any good at math?" Ann asked as she dug through her backpack.

"Umm . . . I'm okay with math, I guess."

"What do you normally score in it?" Ann asked.

"I got As last year," Amal said, half talking and half concentrating on the front door; she was ready to bolt at the slightest jiggle of the doorknob.

Ann sucked her teeth at Amal, "And you're just okay at math? No, you're a freaking genius. I hate this stuff. Can you help me?"

"Me?" Amal asked, still uneasy.

"Yes you! Come on!"

Ann reached over after pushing the chair that sat directly beside her out of the way, and slid Amal's chair next to hers. They spent an hour or so together as Amal showed her how to work out a few problems. Ann was a quick learner and before long got the hang of it. This was the best Amal had felt in a while. She loved helping people, and Ann was very appreciative. It only took moments before she began to get comfortable with her new friend, and they began goofing around, passing a paper back and forth with a little comic strip on it. Each would take turns drawing a scene.

They did this until about six o'clock, when the sounds of keys jingling outside the door could be heard. Amal didn't know what to do, so she just jumped up and stood at the sink. She didn't know why, as there were no dishes to wash, but Amal felt it was best to look busy. Ms. James came in wearing a skintight leopard-print jumpsuit and hot-pink heels that were extremely high. Her hair was done up in curls that were pinned on top of her head, and she wore a smear of bubble-gum-pink lipstick on her lips. She looked like someone had dressed up a pig.

Ms. James took one look at Ann and knew something was amiss.

"Doing homework?" It was a simple question that came out like a threat.

"Yes, Mama. I was just finishing it," Ann said, slowly sliding the comic under her book.

She wasn't fast enough, though. Ms. James saw her hand moving as she walked as fast as Amal thought she could in those heels and grabbed the paper. She looked at it with disgust.

She turned to Amal. "Didn't I tell you not to talk to my child?" she asked.

"I'm sorry." Amal apologized. She looked at Ann and saw tears in her eyes.

"It wasn't her fault, Mama. She was just helping me with my work. I was stuck," Ann said, trying to take up for Amal, but it was no use.

She didn't see the hand coming, but she felt it. Her right cheek went cold; then it felt like it was on fire. That was the first time Ms. James struck Amal, but it wouldn't be the last.

"Mama, no!" Ann cried out as if she were the one who had been hit. Amal stood still, holding her cheek, shocked, as she had never been hit like that before.

"I told you and I'll tell you again: no talking to my daughter! You are in my house and will do as I say! Understand?" Ms. James was livid, standing over Amal, menacingly breathing as though she had run a mile. When Amal didn't answer she lifted her hand again, ready to strike her a second time. If it weren't for Ann rushing over and grabbing her hand, she surely would've.

"You understand, don't you, Amal?" Ann asked in a calm voice, bringing Amal out of her state of shock.

"Y-yes, ma'am!" Amal stuttered. Her teeth even hurt from the hit. Ms. James forcefully pulled her hand from Ann's grasp.

"For disobeying, after Ms. Friendly makes dinner, she can clean the floors with a toothbrush since you seem to need more to do and all." Taking one last look at Amal and Ann, she turned and walked away, clearly happy with what she had done.

***

Amal didn't know how long she had been cleaning, but when she was finally done it was dark outside and the house was quiet. She lay on the couch for a while, trying to calm her angry muscles. She popped her knuckles that were beyond sore from holding the old toothbrush for hours.

She rose from her place on the couch and turned off the lights as she went to her room. That tiny space made her feel sick whenever she was in there. There was no life, no happiness of any kind in that room; just a musty smell and hopelessness. Amal's life was exactly that. She lived with someone who hated her, and she felt like a slave.

Wrapping herself in a towel, she prayed, but in the middle of her prostration she wondered where God was. If he was so strong and powerful, why hadn't he helped her yet? The longer she prayed, the angrier she became, until she was livid. She threw the towel across the room, and it hit the wall and slid down in one fluid motion. If God wouldn't answer her, why should she pray? In her heart, she knew he was there, but her anger won out, and she ended up cutting her prayer short. She couldn't pray in that mindset, so she slid into bed without a shower. *I'll just take one in the morning,* she thought.

The house was quiet around her, filling her room with the sounds of the night. The crickets and frogs sang their "Midnight Sonata" as she drifted off to sleep. She wished she could be anywhere but there. Being outside with the animals would be better than this. Amal closed her eyes and imagined running away and living in the forest. She'd befriend the animals and spend her nights sleeping in the trees, using leaves as her blanket. At least they wouldn't hurt her or make her feel like trash. Before long, the warm hand of sleep gently pulled down her eyelids. She dreamed of being curled up in a huge nest in the top of a giant tree, surrounded by a thick forest of other trees, with a number of animals lying next to her, keeping her warm and safe.

The alarm on her small bedside table went off at 5:00 a.m. She should've gotten up, but the chores from the previous day had made her tired. She would only sleep for a few more seconds. *It won't hurt anything,* she thought before drifting off to sleep.

She dreamed of sand, blood, and people screaming. The sound of their voices rang in her ears, making her dizzy, so she pressed her fingers in her ears and willed herself to wake up. Another bomb dropped right in front of her, stinging her legs and face. Screaming, she tried to shield herself, but the pain kept going in her legs, stomach, and face. The wounds stung and throbbed, as if someone were hitting her with something.

"Wake up, you lazy-ass little bitch!" Amal awoke to Ms. James, with a belt in her hand, beating Amal's skin raw. She tried to shield her face with her hands while screaming and crying.

Her daughter, Ann, beat on the door, screaming, "Momma, stop! Please don't hurt her!" But she kept going, hitting her as hard as she could with the leather belt. Ann's presence seemed to fuel her fury.

It wasn't long before she replaced the belt with her thick fists, bringing them down on Amal with no mercy. "I told you to get your ass up as 5:00 a.m.! You thought I was playing? I told you not to cross me, girl!" Ms. James said as she punched Amal's body with no remorse.

It felt like years had passed when she finally stopped beating her, and Amal was left alone in her bed, injured and weak. She slipped in and out of consciousness, but it didn't matter. Suddenly she felt a warm hand on her face. She couldn't see through her swollen eyes, so she braced for another beating.

"It's me." Amal recognized Ann's voice.

She placed a cold towel over Amal's face and gently wiped away the blood that was caked between her eyelids. Amal tried to push her hand away, but she was too weak.

"Don't worry. She's gone," Ann said, sounding far away.

Amal's head throbbed, and she just wanted to sleep. She heard a faucet turn on from down the hallway, then moments later felt hands coaxing her to stand. Amal didn't want any help and just wanted Ann to go away, but she couldn't fight her off. Amal was led down the hall at a slow pace until she felt the tiled bathroom floor under her feet. Ann gently began removing Amal's clothes.

"This will sting at first, but it'll help with the soreness," and she lowered Amal into the hot water in the tub. She was right: it stung like hell. And she would've jumped right out if she were able to see, but Ann kept her hands on her shoulders, pushing her into the healing water. "I put in some Epsom salts and a few other things to help you relax."

Amal sat as still as possible, letting the warm water soothe her body.

"Feel good?" Ann asked.

She wished it could flow over her heart and heal its bruises. She felt a towel rub her back softly, startling her a bit. Ann worked with delicate hands, working the small washcloth in circles over her skin. Neither talked; they were just there, in the moment, together. Amal wondered how she knew how to do all this, but she understood that she probably wasn't the first person Ms. James had taken her anger out on. It made her feel sad that this girl, who was being so nice and gentle with her, had to deal with someone like that.

Ann washed and rubbed Amal until the water lost its warm temperature, and covered her in a towel before helping her out of the tub and taking Amal to her room. Amal was still afraid of the kindness that Ann was showing her. If Ms. James came back, she would beat her again for talking to her daughter, but Ann assured her that she wouldn't be coming back anytime soon. Apparently Ms. James had a boyfriend and often spent a lot of time at his home. That is, when he wasn't there. She could tell by Ann's tone that she didn't like him much. He couldn't be a nice person if he had someone like Ms. James for a girlfriend.

"I'm going to find you something to wear," Ann said. Amal tried saying no, but all she could do was shake her head. "Don't worry. I have things that she won't know I gave to you."

Ann disappeared before coming back in the room. She dried Amal's wet body one last time and helped her into a button-up long-sleeved shirt and pants.

"Here, take these," and she placed some small, round pills and a glass of something in her hand. "They'll make you sleepy, so I'll do your chores today."

Amal stood holding the pills and water. She wanted to say thank you, but her body hurt so much, she couldn't muster the strength.

"Don't be stubborn. Take them." Ann put a hand underneath Amal's and pushed it toward her face. Amal winced as she opened her mouth to put the pills in. Her hand brushed her lips, and she felt just how swollen they were. She swallowed the pills, and Ann took the glass from her and led her to the bed, tucking her in tightly.

"You just sleep now. I'll do the cleaning," Ann said.

Amal heard the door close and suddenly felt alone. She was thankful for Ann's kindness and spent a few minutes thinking of how she could make it up to her, when she felt the pills start to kick in and felt her body go limp with sleep.

Little Bird

Seven

Monroeville, Alabama
Present Day

Buckets of water were positioned around the house. It was another rainy day, which Amal didn't mind, as it gave them a break from the heat. She was sitting at the small dining table counting the drops and heard Ms. James's car pulling up in the driveway. Immediately jumping up, she pretended to be doing the dishes as they walked in, talking loudly and laughing. Amal knew she heard a man's voice and was curious as to whom it was, but she was too afraid to try to peek.

"This damn house is a mess. I swear, that girl is so stupid. She can't even follow simple instruction," Ms. James exclaimed as she walked through the kitchen with her friend.

"I'm sorry, ma'am. I'll get everything done before dinner." She smiled politely trying to hide her fear.

The man that was standing next to her was sort of tall and very hairy. His arms looked like the tacky carpet that covered the floor. His hair was brown and wet with the rain and clung to his forehead.

"This the girl you been talking about?" he asked.

"Yeah! This is the little bitch." They both laughed.

"She doesn't look that bad."

Amal hated the man's voice and the way he looked at her. His voice alone was enough to make her feel like she needed to shower. He gave her a sly smirk and a wink. Amal spun back around, pretending to do the dishes again, and hoped that when she turned around he wouldn't be there. She let out a sigh of relief when she heard the door to Ms. James's bedroom closing. Without hesitation she went about doing what was on her list for the day and was making much progress when she heard the steady sounds of thumping coming from down the hall. She froze in place, holding the broom she was using to her chest. A high-pitched giggle came from the closed door. She didn't know what was going on, but she knew it couldn't be anything good. It made her feel gross all over, and she couldn't wait to take a shower and hide in her room.

After her first two weeks Amal had gotten used to the verbal abuse, but the one thing she couldn't get used to was Percy, Ms. James's boyfriend. He was a disgusting man. The way he walked around with nothing on but his underwear made her uncomfortable, not to mention the way he looked at her when they were alone. Amal felt his gaze on her constantly, as she did her daily chores, and she didn't trust him. She could tell Ann didn't either. He would often come behind Amal and play with her hair. All she could do was stand there and try to ignore it.

He would whisper things in her ear like, "You know you like me," or "You're so pretty, I wish you were my girlfriend." He would only do this when Ms. James wasn't around. When she was he would just settle for subtle winks and smiles or he would ignore her altogether.

One night, Amal was lying in her bed waiting for sleep when she heard footsteps coming toward her door. Her heart beat wildly in her chest as she sat up waiting for whomever it was to reveal himself. Ms. James's boyfriend had started spending the night quite often, so she braced herself. She had nothing to fight him with, but she would fight him if she had to. The door swung open to reveal Ann standing there in her doorway. Amal relaxed for a few seconds, but couldn't stop thinking about Ms. James.

"Don't worry. She's busy with Percy. She doesn't notice me when he's around." Ann closed the door silently and lay across the end of Amal's small bed.

"I can tell you don't like him either. I never feel safe when he's around. Momma likes him, but he isn't a good person."

"I can tell. He makes me uncomfortable," Amal said.

"Yeah, me too. When he's here be sure to lock your door. He'll come in if it's not locked."

"Why would he do that?" Amal asked.

Ann sat up and was quiet for a moment and then shook her head as if she were trying to wipe her memory clean.

"He'll hurt you, and Momma won't believe you," Ann said as she sat up and pushed off Amal's bed. She walked to the door with her head down.

"Did he hurt you?" Amal asked.

Ann didn't say anything at first; she just kept her head down. "Just remember to keep your door locked."

And with that she was gone. Amal rose from her place for rest and locked the door. She climbed back in bed and looked up at the ceiling. The thought of that nasty man hurting Ann was all she could think of. She tried to beat down the anger that was trying to push its way up into her chest. It was nestled warmly in her tummy. She would leave it there, but she wouldn't feed it. She would let it die, like an untended fire, the way it was supposed to.

Chapter

Eight

Saint Joseph's Hospital

Present Day

It was about 10:00 a.m. when Amal and her foster mom arrived for her appointment with Amelia. Amal had been nervous all day yesterday, as this would be the first time she'd seen her since she left the hospital. Amal sat nervously in the waiting room, waiting for her name to be called. Ms. James had beaten her this morning for accidentally burning the bacon, so Amal was wearing a long-sleeved shirt to hide the bruises as best she could. The evil woman had already coached her on what she could and couldn't say. Amal knew she needed to tell someone, but she couldn't be sure that she would get saved from her foster mom before she tried to kill her. Ms. James had assured her that she would do so that morning, so Amal would have to be extra careful when talking to Amelia.

When the nurse finally called her back, Amal looked at Ms. James as she walked past her. She was giving her the evil look she gave her before she hit her. Amal felt her bladder go weak, and she had to hold in the urge to wet herself from fear. As she walked down the long hall, she rehearsed what she would say, until they got to Amelia's office. It was a metal door painted creamy beige, with her full name on it. As the nurse opened the door and ushered Amal in, she could smell the familiar smell of her office: expensive coffee and perfume. She almost broke down right there in the doorway, but she pushed through. Amelia was sitting at her desk, typing away at her laptop, when she looked around to see Amal. A huge smile spread across her face, and she was around the desk in no time, wrapping Amal in a tight hug. Amal smiled and hugged her back, trying not to scream from the pain. Amelia backed up and looked at Amal as if she was checking her over to make sure she was alright.

"You've lost weight," she said with a frown. "Is everything okay?"

Everything was not okay, but she smiled and faked it. "I just haven't been hungry, is all. I'm good!" She spread on the lie as thick as she could without being too obvious.

"How's everything going with your foster parent?"

"She's nice." That lie almost burned her throat as the words worked their way up to her mouth.

"Yeah? Good! See, I told you it would all work out. I'm so glad to see you're doing well."

And the rest of the appointment went on just like that. Amal lied for Ms. James, and Amelia believed every bit of it. At the end of her session she didn't want to leave. She left her office feeling so empty inside. Here she was, in a place where they could've helped her, and she wasn't brave enough to say anything. No one questioned why she was wearing long sleeves in the summer heat, but what did Amal expect? These people really didn't know her. To them she was just another poor, unfortunate case, and that was it. She felt less than human in that moment.

Once she came back to the waiting room, Ms. James was waiting on her. She looked nervous until she caught sight of Amal coming back.

"Everything went okay?" The "okay" sounded more like a threat.

"Yes, it was fine."

Ms. James nodded, clearly happy with the outcome, and began walking out. Amal followed her like a lost puppy until they got to the car. She wasn't allowed to ride in the front, so she got in the back and sat uncomfortably all the way back to the house.

Amal had been living with Ms. James for three months and hadn't seen the inside of a school. She was supposed to have been enrolled when she moved in, but Ms. James was against it. Amal wouldn't be able to do her job if she was in school. So she claimed she was homeschooling Amal. She had her do little assignments in old workbooks she had found at a yard sale. The idea of going to school in a foreign place made her nervous, but she knew she wouldn't feel as lonely if she were going.

She spent her days thinking about her old school, teachers, and friends. Her life had once been so full of happiness, but now felt like she was just surviving. Amal thanked God between each beating because Ms. James hadn't killed her yet. Each day was a struggle, and to be honest, she didn't know how much more of this she could take. Everything was supposed to be alright when she got here. This was supposed to be her fresh start, but it was anything but that.

Amal had just moved the mattresses back in from dusting and cleaning them when the rain started. *It rains so much here*, she thought. Her arms and back screamed from lifting the heavy mattresses and pushing them around, so she decided to rest a while. Ms. James was out getting her hair done, and Ann was about to come in from school, so she lay on the couch with her leg propped up over the back and thought of what to cook for Ann. Amal basked in her time with Ann, even if they couldn't speak around Ms. James, and loved doing things for her, even though she didn't like it. She was the one person there who appreciated Amal.

She was in mid thought when the doorbell rang; then came a strong pounding, so hard it sounded like the person was trying to break the door down. She dragged a chair across the carpet to look out the peephole and saw Percy leaning against the door, his hair soaked with rain.

"What do you want?" she yelled.

"Just let me in! It's raining like hell out here!"

"No. Ms. James said I wasn't to open the door for anyone while she isn't home," Amal said, standing on her toes, on top of the chair.

"She told me to come over and get her wallet. Just let me in!"

Amal thought about it for a second. He could be lying, but what if it was the truth? Ms. James would beat her within an inch of her life if she disobeyed, so she moved the chair out of the way and opened the door only a few inches, enough for her to see him swaying back and forth, with the same sly half smile on his face. She apprehensively opened the door wide enough for him to slide in.

"Thank you! Damn! You act like you don't know me or something."

He smoothed a wet hand over his hair. Amal could smell alcohol and a strong, musty smell on him. Something about it made her regret letting him in. He took off his coat and let it fall to the floor while he swayed to the kitchen. The way he moved, she imagined seaweed moving with the current underwater.

"Want to come help me find her wallet? She said it was probably in one of her other purses."

Amal didn't want anything to do with the situation and shook her head no.

"Come on! Please?" he asked, putting on the same sly grin as he stumbled toward her.

She was afraid she would get tangled up with him by the way his body moved. He was so close she could smell him strongly now. Frozen with fear she dropped her head and backed away. He reached out a rough hand to grab her arm, but he was too slow.

"You know, you're just so damn beautiful. Why don't you and me go in your room and talk for a little while?"

He stumbled closer. Amal tried to back away again, but he grabbed her arm. He was strong, and it terrified her. He was squeezing her arm so hard she thought it might break between his fingers.

"I have chores to finish," she said, tears coming to her eyes, fear making her voice squeaky.

"You're always doing chores. Come have fun with me."

He put his hand on her lower back, pulling her into him. She tried to pull away, knocking him off balance, while she ran for her room, but he was right on her heels and grabbed her by her hair and threw her onto her bed, where she landed face down. He slammed the door shut behind them, locking it in one quick motion. He was drunk, but he was quick and stood over her while he undid his belt and unbuttoned his pants.

"You and Ann are always teasing me! You knew what you were doing!" He spat as he talked and dropped to his knees, rolling her over on her back. She kicked wildly and screamed, but he was too strong. In a minute he was on her, moving forcefully inside her, but she still screamed and fought. He punched her in the ribs, knocking the wind right out of her, then placed a strong hand around her throat.

"Both of you are little whores. You knew what you were doing! Don't act like you don't like it!"

He squeezed her throat tightly in one hand. She thought he was going to tear through her, the way he was moving inside of her. Her surroundings started to get hazy, and she knew she couldn't fight him too much longer, but she would keep fighting; she couldn't give up. She promised herself that if she were to meet God that day, he would know that she hadn't lain still and let this man kill her, that she had fought with all her strength. She wouldn't let another man hurt her again without a fight. He crushed her beneath his weight, but she bit down on the side of his neck, taking out a chunk and spitting it in his face. He screamed as blood shot across the room and sprayed the wall. His face contorted into a hellish form, and he began beating her. Punches landed on her ribs, her face, but she fought him still, until he placed his hand over her throat again and squeezed until she finally lost consciousness.

A Glimpse into the Past

Homs, Syria

There were no speeches to be made, nor kind faces or hands to hold. It was just she and Baba when they buried her sister. He worked half the day digging the hole with a flat piece of rubble. Sweat clung to the ridge of his eyebrows as he panted from the heat and exhaustion. There had been nothing to wash Jannah's body with, but Amal still tried to wipe her face clean with her shirt. It was beyond dirty. Amal tried to lick the end of her shirt to wipe the blood from Jannah's face, but it was dry and hard; nothing could remove it. Realizing this made her give up on her attempts to make her sister look somewhat decent, and she plopped down on her bottom, inches away. Amal stared at her emotionlessly when realization hit her. This would be the last time they would see her face. Here in all the chaos, she would be buried, where all she would have as company would be the sounds and smells of death. Would she be lonely? Hungry? Would she be afraid of being down there in the dark? As her baba prepared to pick Jannah up and place her in the ground, Amal felt her heart shatter one last time. She just wanted to wake up and have this all be a bad dream.

After laying her sister in the ground her father and Amal prayed over Jannah, asking God to make a beautiful place for her in heaven where she could be at peace. Amal also asked God to give her the wedding she wouldn't be able to have and lots of babies to play with. She was always good with children, and Amal knew she had wanted them. After the prayer, her baba halfheartedly began to bury her. He moved as if the action of burying his own sweet girl were killing him slowly. His back was hunched over, and with every handful of dirt there were tears.

"Jannah," Amal said without thinking. Her baba paused and looked at her curiously through his tears. "I don't know if you can hear me or not, but I hope that wherever you are or are going to be is better than here. You deserve it, and I'm sorry. I'm sorry for being mean and annoying sometimes. The reason why I'm saying this is because I love you." Tears streamed down her cheeks. "I love you so much, and I know your time with me is over, but know that, no matter what, you'll always be in my heart, even though there isn't much of it left."

Standing in her tattered clothes, she sobbed into her hands. Her baba dropped what he was doing and gathered her up into his big arms, and they cried together until they couldn't cry anymore.

They finished burying her before nightfall. They were exhausted physically, mentally, and emotionally, but they couldn't stop moving, as they had to find a safe place to sleep for the night. Walking in the darkness that covered the land, they searched for any place that would be ideal for the night, but passed nothing but dilapidated buildings and houses. Amal normally felt safe walking these pathways and streets, but the night gave off an eerie feel that was amplified by the sounds of suffering. She walked up and grabbed her baba's hand and looked up at him, trying to make out the hard features of his face.

"Shouldn't we try to find Mama?" Amal asked. When she heard her baba take in a sharp breath, she wished she hadn't. They walked for a while before he spoke.

"I think your mama is with Jannah" was all he said.

Amal immediately understood. Their house was destroyed, and her mama had been in that house. The realization was like a punch to the stomach. She couldn't be alive, so they walked the rest of the way in silence.

The first week was spent walking during the day and sleeping in random places, as most of the town was completely destroyed. She could hardly tell where they were now. They slept in abandoned houses and buildings; any place that was safe enough was where they called home, but they never stayed at the same location twice. After waking up one morning her baba told her of news that the government had been sent to help them, and there was a camp for them a few miles away. It was on the outskirts of town, but there was a place for them to sleep. It was the first glimmer of hope they had felt since the bombing. Amal sat up and finger-combed her messy hair. She found that something was living in there and didn't take too kindly to being uprooted from its new home. There was no shower, no clothes to put on or breakfast to be made and eaten, so she dusted herself off and took her baba's hand, and they were off.

They walked for what seemed like days. Amal's shoes were torn beyond repair, but they kept going. Her baba kept trying to encourage her by saying, "It won't be too long now." But she was so tired and hadn't had water in so long; her mouth was as dry as cotton, and it only got worse by the minute. They walked past more death and destruction for some time, painting a new picture of their city in their minds. As they got closer to the outskirts of the city some dead still lay among the wreckage; then, farther out, there was just a lot of dirt and some trees.

After walking for she didn't know how long, she started feeling dizzy. It was probably the lack of water, but she didn't want to complain. A few more steps, then her legs got weaker, shaking with every step. Looking back on the situation, she didn't remember passing out or how long she was gone, but she awoke to the sounds of a baby crying. The smell of smoke and dirt overwhelmed her senses. She opened her eyes to find Baba at her side and looked up at his face, wondering when he had started to look so old.

"Where are we?" Her throat still dry, it sounded more like a frog croaking.

"We made it. You had a fainting spell, but I carried you the rest of the way. You'll feel better once you get some food in you."

He could tell she was still out of it, so he brought her a bottle of water and helped her hold her head up as she gulped it down. It was the best thing she had tasted in a long time, and she had to keep herself from drinking the whole thing at once. She couldn't keep her hands from shaking.

Baba pulled the bottle away. "You don't want to make yourself sick. If that stays down, then I'll bring you bread." He laid her back down on a pile of lumpy rugs and put one of them over her.

"Rest yourself. We're safe here," he said, but there was something in his voice that made her feel like he wasn't telling the truth.

She didn't want to lie back down. She wanted to know where she was and wanted to see this new place that they would call home. Voices from outside poured in past the canvas material. Amal looked around the little, ragged tent that was barely holding itself up; this would be her home until they found a new place to stay.

"I don't want to lie back down. I want to look around."

Baba shook his head. "You'll have plenty of time for that later, but now you need rest." He stood hunched over and walked toward the entrance of the tent.

"Where are you going? Don't leave me!" she pleaded, desperately wanting to get up from her resting place.

"Relax yourself. I'm just going to get more water. I'll be back." And with that he was gone.

Amal felt scared. She didn't want to be left alone in this strange place, but she had to calm herself. Panicking made her nauseous, so she just lay as still as she could and continued to look around. Her circumstances were depressing, to say the least. They had nothing but the dirty clothes on their backs, and they were living in a tent that had been patched several times over, it seemed. She lay there and thought of her sister, Jannah, and her mama, but the task proved to be too painful. She closed her eyes against the sadness, and despite the crying of an angry baby in the background, she fell into a deep sleep.

She dreamed she was walking barefoot in a spacious field of tulips. The sun filled the sky and radiated orange and pink rays that warmed her skin as they glowed and illuminated the tulips. They were as soft as paper under her fingertips. She knew she was dreaming and that she would wake up to her living nightmare, so she enjoyed the beauty and solace that her mind gave her. She would sit in this field until she woke up, but until then she stretched her limbs toward the sky, smiling to herself. Birds sang her their sweet songs of freedom. She lay back and felt the warm grass around her.

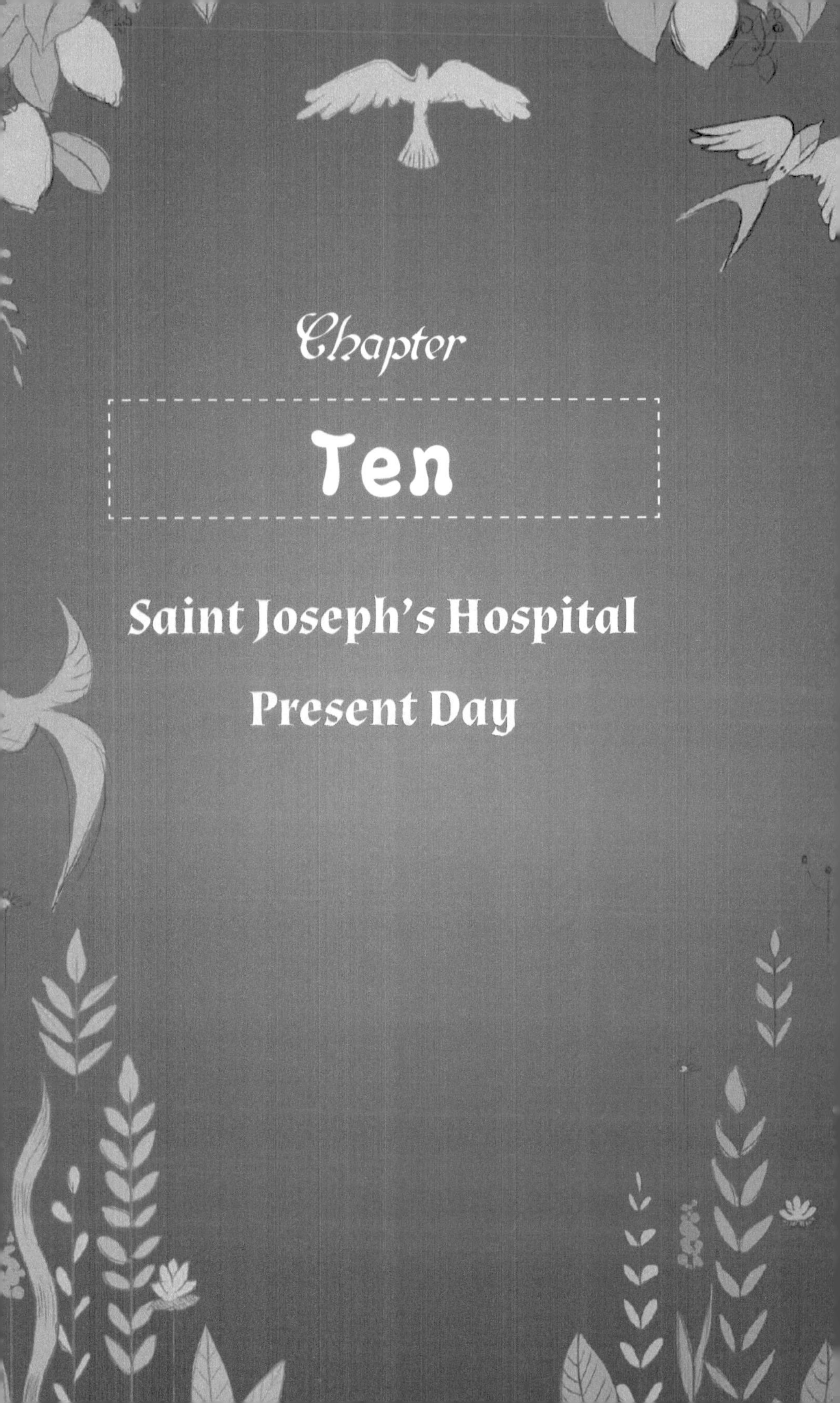

Chapter

Ten

Saint Joseph's Hospital

Present Day

Amal heard a flurry of voices and sounds around her, some yelling commands. She wasn't sure where she was, but didn't have the energy to open her eyes. Sounds of hurried footsteps and a familiar voice reassured her that everything would be okay, and she felt someone holding her hand. This person's skin was warm and pleasant. There was something about this touch that made the other noises, which filled her ears like the hum of angry honeybees, quiet themselves. Then she felt some strange movement before she passed out again. She had become familiar with this place of unconsciousness and was most comfortable in this plane of nothingness. Nobody could hurt her or make her sad. She was her own person here, in the darkness of her mind. Numbness was the best feeling in the world when everything hurt so much.

She awoke to the familiar sounds of beeping. The room was dark, but Amal knew she was in the hospital. The smell of disinfectant, the steady beeping, and the ticking of a clock accosted her senses. Opening her eyes, Amal searched the room to find she was alone. Her body was bruised, very sore, beat up, and tired in more ways than one. Her ribs burned when she breathed, so she tried not to take deep breaths. Shallow breathing wasn't much better. Every muscle in her body burned with the memories of what her body had been through, what *he* had done to her. Amal didn't know how long she had been here. Maybe it was a day, maybe a week, but she knew she was in the same hospital that she had been in before. Strangely that brought her a mild sense of comfort. How long she would be here this time she didn't know, but all that mattered was that she was safe now.

The bed and her blankets were warm, making her sleepy, but she didn't want to sleep anymore. She was tired of that. There was an IV placed in her vein, probably to reduce any pain. They were numbing her physically and mentally so she wouldn't feel a thing. Amal knew it was Ann's hand she felt and wondered if she was safe and okay.

A flurry of scrubs walked into the room, and that was when she saw her. Jackie was standing with her back to her, changing the names on the dry-erase board. Amal almost cried seeing her standing there as beautiful as she was the first time she saw her. When the nurse turned to see Amal sitting there, looking at her, with her little back straight in the pea-green hospital gown, she had to stop herself from grabbing her and hugging her until she couldn't breathe.

"How's my favorite patient?" the nurse asked Amal.

"I'm good!" Amal half said and half croaked it out.

"I'm so glad to see you! They took you away before I had the chance to say goodbye, but here you are now."

Amal smiled her usual bright smile. For the moment she forgot about the terrible place she used to live, forgot the beatings, being starved, and treated like a slave. There, in that moment, she was just glad that she was here now with her favorite person.

The next few days went by in a blink. Some lady with Social Services came by, asking questions of her previous living situation, and though she was scared, she told the truth. Amal told her of the horrible things that had happened and how she was used like a slave and never saw the inside of a school. The social worker was a nice woman who apologized profusely for what Amal had been put through and assured her that her foster mother would be brought to justice. Percy was currently in jail awaiting a trial and sentencing for the sexual abuse of her and Ann. She was glad that he wouldn't be able to hurt anyone else.

She played checkers with Jackie and went to her appointments with Amelia, where she was encouraged to explain her abuse in detail. She didn't want to think about the horrible woman or her boyfriend; it made her sick to her stomach. But what sickened her more was the thought of suffering again in another home. Amal could tell that soon she'd be thrown into another strange family with an evil foster mother and abusive boyfriend. The visits to Amelia's office, no matter how well meant, were a constant reminder of her bad luck. Her sessions with the therapist did little to calm her troubled spirit.

Fortunately, Nurse Jackie was a glimmer of sunlight in the gloomy clouds she'd found herself in. Amal wished she could live in the hospital forever, but deep inside her heart, she knew that the day would come for her to say goodbye again and forever. The day did come in due time.

It was a cold Saturday with a hint of rainfall in the air. Amal had just had her lunch and fallen asleep on the hospital bed after taking some pills. The pain of the abuse seemed to have subsided, but the nightmares grew stronger each day.

"How is the headache?" asked Nurse Jackie, placing a palm on her forehead.

Amal opened her eyes and smiled. "Not feeling really good. I still see him in my sleep," she replied.

Nurse Jackie nodded. She knew very well the trauma young children–victims of abuse–tended to cope with every day. It was her job to tend to them, to make them feel safe. However, seeing these helpless children constantly reminded her that real monsters roamed this world and she could do nothing about it. This thinking alone made her extremely furious.

Amal saw the flash of anger in her eyes and said, "Don't worry! I'll be fine."

As soon as she said this, Mr. Wright drifted in with his usual disinterested demeanor. Amal gasped on seeing him, ready to bolt away. She forced herself to breathe, but it seemed a dark entity had taken hold of her chest.

"Hello, Amal," greeted Mr. Wright with a cold voice. "We found you a new home. A great one."

"No!" Amal cried, holding tight to the nurse's hand. "Please don't let him take me."

Nurse Jackie frowned thoughtfully and whispered something to the social worker. He sighed, shrugged, gave the nurse a small traveling bag, and exited the room.

"Look, Amal," Nurse Jackie began, "I'm sure you're gonna love it where you're going this time. Don't worry. I'll pay you visits. I promise."

The nurse opened the traveling bag and brought out a blue polka-dot dress. Amal stood up and gave the dress a cold, hard scrutiny. Everything felt like déjà vu. But she was determined to survive–she owed it to Baba to live, and she owed it to Jannah to find a life in America. Yet she thought as she walked out of the hospital, *the outside world is so scary.*

Within minutes she was looking out the windows of Mr. Wright's black sedan as it swept down the streets. The passing tall buildings, shimmering streetlights, and rich ambiance of the city did nothing to excite her. With tears brimming in her eyes, she missed Ann and wondered what kind of life awaited her on the other side. And as she went deeper into her thoughts, the cold hands of sleep and the pills she had been given before she left came to embrace her. In her dreams, she heard that familiar banging on the door.

And one onerous voice was screaming, *"It's me, Percy. Just let me in. It's raining like hell out here!"*

Chapter

Eleven

Monroeville, Alabama

Present Day

Amal awoke hours later on a comfortable bed that was rich with the scent of fabric softener, inside a strange room that smelled like lavender. She groggily brushed off cold sweat from her brow and sat upright. She blinked hard and swore she saw something out of the corner of her eye where the light was the brightest. She tried to strain her eyes to see, but she was startled when it got up and moved quickly out of the room.

"She's awake!" it yelled as she heard thumps of footsteps from beyond the walls.

Was she in a house with people? It all seemed very confusing, and her head felt weird.

"Stop all that hollering! You're going to scare the poor girl."

She heard a female voice come echoing into the room from somewhere in the house. More thumping from far away; then it started to get closer.

Bracing herself for whomever was coming through the door, she willed herself not to be afraid. The knob turned slowly, and the white door gently swung open, revealing a small brown-skinned lady in a bright floral dress. She was holding a tray with a bowl of something that smelled wonderful. Amal couldn't remember the last time she had eaten. The tiny woman took small, delicate steps toward the bed and smiled down at her kindly. Her cheekbones were the highest she'd ever seen. She placed the tray down on the dresser beside the bed and sat down on the edge of the bed. She put a hand to the girl's forehead and shook her head, pleased with the temperature.

"Hello, sweetie. I know you're probably wondering where you are," the woman spoke, never taking her eyes off of her. "You've been asleep for a while. We almost thought the worst, but I'm so glad to see you up and looking so alert. Your fever seems to have gone down as well."

Amal just stared down the multiple blankets that surrounded her. The woman seemed to wait a moment for her to speak; then, when the silence grew too long, she spoke again: "My name is Barbara, but everyone calls me Aunt Bobbie. You can do the same."

Suddenly the door creaked, and Amal caught the sight of a girl maybe a little younger than herself, peeping through the doorway. She was the same color of brown as the tiny woman, with long black braids going down her back with lavender ribbons at the top of each one. Her dress was lavender with little yellow flowers. Ruffled socks and yellow Mary Janes decorated her feet. Her eyes were a captivating pale brown, almost like Amal's sister's. Tears came to Amal's eyes thinking of her, so she looked down.

The woman, having followed Amal's eyes to the door, spoke, "That's Kenya. She's eight years old."

Once Kenya heard her name she walked in and exclaimed, "I'm almost nine!"

Smiling, Barbara agreed, with a chuckle that made Amal want to laugh. "She's been watching over you the whole time. Wouldn't leave unless she needed to eat or go to the bathroom. She wanted to make sure you were going to be alright."

Amal looked up at Kenya and gave her a small smile and dropped her head again. There was silence again until Barbara spoke.

"Here I am, talking away, and your soup is getting cold." She tested it with her pinky. "Oh, it's still warm!" she said and handed it to Amal.

"Come on, Kenya, let the girl eat in peace." She stood up, grabbing Kenya's hand. "I know that this is all new to you and you may be scared. I don't know what you've been through, but I just want you to know you're safe here, and if you need anything at all, just call me."

Barbara and Kenya walked to the door, still holding hands, and left. Seeing them hold hands made Amal think of her own mother. She pushed that memory down as a single tear dripped down her cheek, and grabbed the spoon to eat her soup. Once she ate her fill, she lay on her back in the bed, listening to the sounds of the house. She could hear faint voices and sounds coming from outside.

A light breeze blew through the window, waking Amal out of a sound sleep. She was greeted with the same smell of lavender. She couldn't remember falling asleep, but sometime after she ate she must have. All Amal remembered was closing her eyes for a second. That was all, and here she was, in the same room. She thought maybe she had been dreaming of meeting the nice woman and little girl, but as she looked around the dark room she was surprised to find it had been real.

In the dim lighting she was able to fully look around. The room was small and tidy, with a dresser against the wall to her left, facing the bed, which was the largest bed she had ever slept in. To her right the lace curtains blew with the wind. She listened to the stillness around her. After she was sure she gathered the blankets in her hand and slowly swung herself to the edge of the bed. Her body was still sore and her head spun, but curiosity won in the end, and she placed her feet on the floor. The room swirled around, her making her lose her balance. After she steadied herself, she opened her eyes and noticed a mirror on the other wall. Taking careful steps, she made her way to it and looked at herself. Even in the darkness she could see her bruises and how tired she looked. Bringing a hand to her face, she pushed the hair from her forehead and then ran it through her black hair, which had been combed while she was asleep. Her scalp felt warm under her fingertips. Then Amal noticed her eyes; they seemed so different, like they didn't really belong to her. These were not the eyes she was born with; they were new. It was like looking in the faces of those trapped with her on the sea. They were hollow, and it scared her so badly she couldn't look anymore. She rubbed her eyes furiously, trying to change them. They weren't hers and she didn't want them. Amal wanted her eyes and her life back. She didn't realize she was crying until she felt the breeze caress her wet cheeks.

She walked back to her bed and sat down, when dull pain shot through her pelvis and crotch. She felt raw and hurt down there. The thought of Percy sneakily swept into her brain, threatening to bring back the memory of the terrible things he did to her. She threw herself under the covers and cried until she heard the faint sound of singing. She stilled herself and listened closely, but still couldn't make out the words or where they were coming from.

Leaving the bed, she looked down at the gap at the bottom of the door to see a faint light. She tiptoed as well as she could, given the circumstances, and placed an ear to the door. It was coming from out there. She was scared, but the song sounded so nice she wanted to listen. As quietly as she could, she cracked the door. Thankfully it didn't creak, and she began tiptoeing out into the hall. Everything but the door across the hall was dark, and as she looked back and forth she couldn't make out much detail but that along the left side of the hall were three other doors and down the right were one door and a staircase to a floor below. She tiptoed a few steps until she was at the partially open door. She could see the nice, older lady sitting on a stool next to a small white bed, and nestled inside was a sleepy Kenya. The room was small and painted bright purple. She couldn't see much, but she wanted to hear the song. She closed her eyes and listened, though it was toward the end:

Thula thul, thula baba, thula sana,

Thul'ubab uzobuya, ekuseni.

Thula thul, thula baba, thula sana,

Thul'ubab uzobuya, ekuseni.

Kukh'inkanyezi, zi-holel' ubaba,

Zimkhanyisela indlel'e ziyak-haya,

Sobe sikhona ka bonke bashoyo,

Bayathi buyela. Ubuye le khaya.

Thula thula thula baba,

Thula thula thula sana.

It was the most beautiful thing she had ever heard. She didn't need to understand to feel the love this lady had for Kenya. After the song was over Amal was going to return to her room, but something stopped her in her tracks.

"Aunt Bobbie," Kenya said.

"Yes, darling?"

"What's wrong with that girl? Why doesn't she talk? I thought if I was nice to her, she'd be my friend, but I don't think she likes me at all."

Barbara reached over and smoothed out the bed sheets. "It's not that she doesn't like you. She just not used to us yet, but I think she'll come to like you pretty soon."

That answer obviously wasn't good enough for Kenya, as she seemed to be considering something.

"Really?"

"Have I ever lied to you?"

"No, ma'am!" said Kenya, smiling as bright as the morning sun.

Amal didn't listen to the rest. She just made her way back to the room, shut the door quietly, and climbed back into bed. *Does she really want to be my friend?* As Amal was overcome by the ever-familiar feeling of sleep, she made a pact with herself that she and Kenya would be friends.

Amal awoke and turned toward the nightstand near the bed; it said 5:00 a.m. She wasn't sure what time prayer came in around here, but she got up and crept down the hallway to the small bathroom. She wondered if she would be in trouble for not waking up sooner. She had a hard time washing for prayer, but she finished and quickly went back to her room. She took a towel from the bathroom to use as a scarf, and just as she finished the sun began peeking through the curtains. Folding her prayer scarf and placing it on the dresser, she decided to get a little more sleep, but she heard commotion from downstairs. She eased her way to the door and heard the signs of the lady and the little girl downstairs. Remembering what she had promised herself the night before, she hurried back to the bathroom to find folded clothes on the side of the sink, with a note that read: "I didn't know what color you like, so Kenya picked them out for you. We hope you love them!" At the bottom Kenya had signed her name. She held the note to her heart, with tears stinging her eyes. These clothes meant more to her than anything she had ever been given. It was a pink light-weight sweater dress with a cream ruffle around the collar and matching pink tights. She blushed when she saw the new pink cotton panties lying on top. In the all-white, tiny bathroom the clothes stood out, but in a good way. She held the dress up to find a tag still attached. Had they spent money on her? She couldn't tell because the numbers were scratched out, but she would find a way to pay them back.

After a nice hot shower, she felt like a new person. After using all the things that were left for her, she exited the bathroom, leaving her dirty clothes in the hamper. The bunny slippers on her feet felt as fluffy as clouds, though she was walking on hard wood. She strolled past the place she slept and stood at the top of the stairs, with her heart thudding in her chest. The smell of food traveled up the stairs to her, luring her toward it. She took each step one at a time, holding the railing for dear life. The bottom floor was very open, and she could see the entire first floor from the third step. The living area was to her right, and the dining area to her left, and the kitchen to her upper left. The walls were painted a sandy brown, with various paintings on the wall. It seemed to have taken a lifetime to get to the last step, but she finally made it.

She took a deep breath as she heard Kenya and Barbara singing together. Their voices made her happy, and she wanted nothing more than for them to keep going, so she quietly sat at the table and waited with her ankles crossed and a pleasant smile on her face. There was a huge portrait near the entrance to the kitchen of an older woman who looked a lot like Aunt Bobbie, with feathers in her hair and a solemn expression. The picture captivated her, making her feel as though she knew the woman just from looking in her eyes. She was so engrossed in the photo that she hadn't realized the singing was over until they walked in. They both stood in shock when they finally saw her sitting at the very end of the table. She smiled as pleasantly as she could, while her heart hammered in her chest.

"Good morning," Amal said politely as the two took her in.

"Hello! Look, Aunt Bobbie! She's up!" Kenya bounced up and down.

"Yeah, I see! Praise the Lord! Looks like today is going to be better than I thought!" Aunt Bobbie smiled lovingly at Amal. "You're just in time for breakfast. I made grits, eggs, and toast."

"Raisin toast! My favorite!" Kenya added as Bobbie put her plate in front of her.

"Thank you for cooking. I appreciate it," Amal said, sounding more like an old woman than a twelve-year-old girl.

"No need to thank me. I wasn't going to let you go hungry," Bobbie added with a chuckle.

Amal looked at the plates of food as Aunt Bobbie placed them on the table. She took in the smell, savoring every scent. It had been so long since she'd had a decent meal. They had fed her at the hospital, but the food was terrible.

She watched as the woman and girl took their seats at the table and bowed their heads before looking up again. Kenya immediately went for the toast as if someone were going to steal it from her. Aunt Bobbie, finally noticing that Amal hadn't made her plate, regarded her curiously. "Are you not hungry?" she asked.

"I am. It's just . . ."

"What is it, baby? Would you like something else? I'll make you whatever you'd like."

"No, the food is fine. I just . . . How much can I eat?" Amal asked shyly.

Bobbie had to fight the sinking feeling in her stomach, and when she finally found her words, she asked, "How much can you eat?"

"Yes, ma'am."

"Baby, you can have as much as you like whenever you want, okay?"

"Okay. Thank you." Amal turned her attention to her food, feeling relieved and thankful. By the time Amal made her plate, Kenya had already finished and was sitting at the table chatting away. Bobbie stared at Amal, watching her get her food before excusing herself to go to the bathroom. She stayed in there for so long, Amal worried if something was wrong. She hoped she hadn't done anything wrong. Once Bobbie returned to the table and took her seat, Amal kept glancing up at her to see if she was angry with her. She showed no signs of being mad, but Amal would apologize either way.

After breakfast was eaten, Bobbie and Kenya cleared the table, then shooed Kenya away. Amal stood to leave, but the pretty brown lady sat at her spot at the table and asked Amal to join her. She wasn't sure why, but she thought to herself, *Here it comes.* This was where she would learn who these people really were and what they expected from her. Her heart dropped, but she kept her eyes on the woman and pulled a chair out, taking a seat.

"I didn't mean to offend you by asking about the food."

Bobbie looked taken aback by what she said. "You didn't offend me."

"So you're not mad at me?" Amal asked cautiously.

"No! I don't have a reason to be angry with you. I just wanted to talk to you."

Amal breathed a sigh of relief. *So she isn't angry with me. Then why does she want to talk?* she thought.

"I'm just glad that you're finally awake. You scared all of us."

Amal didn't feel like she had been asleep for long, but apparently she had been.

"I just wanted to know if there was anything you wanted to ask of me. Is there anything special that you need? I go to the store about once a week, so just let me know."

Amal sat stunned. Her whole time here, in America, no one had cared about what she wanted. Everything was decided for her. Yet this kind woman was going to go out of her way to make her comfortable.

"Thank you, but I don't need anything. You've done enough," Amal said.

"Well, do you have any questions for me? Do you know where you are?"

Amal realized that she didn't know where she was. "I have no idea where we are."

"You're in Monroeville, Alabama. We're in the middle of the country, so there aren't any fancy buildings or shops. We don't have much out here, and it's always quiet, but it's also very beautiful. We get a clear view of the stars at night. I'll have to take you out one night so you can see them."

Amal thought of seeing a sky full of stars while being serenaded by the night. She couldn't wait. She didn't know why, but her eyes kept moving to the large portrait on the wall.

"That's my mother," Bobbie said, nodding her head toward the painting.

"She's beautiful," Amal said.

"She was mean, but I guess when you have twenty-three children you'd be a bit grouchy too." Bobbie laughed; then she asked a question she wished she could take back. "Do you have any siblings?"

Amal's face dropped immediately. She pushed back from the table and walked upstairs. Bobbie held her breath until she heard the sound of a door close.

Twelve

Monroeville, Alabama

Present Day

Amal couldn't stop thinking about her family and the life that had been taken from her, wishing she had them back. She would give anything to go back in time, but knew she couldn't. Her heart hurt, and her chest felt as if it were going to cave in two. When Ms. Bobbie asked if she had any siblings all she saw was her sister's dead body and her father holding her. It took everything in her not to run away. A scream dared to break free from her mouth, so she just got up and went to the room she'd become familiar with. It was dark out, but she had the curtains open, staring out at the night as she sat on the side of the wooden bed. Her body felt heavy, and she felt as if she could sleep forever. She rubbed a hand over her eyes, and the tears began to fall; soon she was sobbing.

Baba! Mama! Please come back! Please, God, please give them back to me! If I'm being punished for something, please forgive me!

She was sobbing so hard she didn't hear the door open or feel the bed move as Kenya sat next to her. Reaching an arm out, Kenya held Amal as she cried.

"It's okay. It hurts right now, but it gets better," Kenya said sweetly, soothing Amal by rocking slightly.

"How do you know? How will it be okay?" Amal gasped through her tears. "I''s never going to be okay! Never!"

Kenya reached and put a hand under Amal's chin. "Look at me. I promise it's going to be fine." Kenya gave a slight smile. "And I know because I used to hurt in the same way you are."

Amal sniffled hard. "Really?"

"Yes," she said as she wrapped her arms around Amal once again.

"How does it get better?" she asked.

"By talking about it and letting good people love you," Kenya said, still rocking Amal like a baby.

Her crying had stopped, but it started up again. "No one can love me! Not with the way I am," she cried.

Kenya, without skipping a beat, said, "I love you and so does Bobbie. We love you a whole lot." Kenya kissed Amal lightly on the top of her head and spent the next few hours telling Amal her story.

Kenya was born to a mother who was a crack addict and a father who was a heroin addict. She spent the earliest part of her life in various crack houses. Although she didn't remember much of the beginning because she was only months old, she remembered having to walk on floors that were riddled with trash, human feces, and needles. Her first memories of her mother were of her running through the neighborhood naked and of her father being so high he would fall asleep leaving Kenya unattended for hours. She was only three the first time her mother sold her for drugs. At five, when her mother left a "customer" in her room, it was then that Kenya had enough and fought the man. For days she wandered the streets alone, through various neighborhoods, until someone saw her and called 9-1-1. After a few months in a foster home, she met Aunt Bobbie and had been with her ever since.

Amal was shocked but didn't move a muscle or interrupt. The story had touched Amal in some strange way. She looked up at Kenya, who had tears streaming down her round cheeks from recalling the nightmare. Amal brought her nightgown up and wiped her face. Kenya smiled in thanks, and Amal smiled back. They sat hugging each other until Kenya yawned long and slow.

"Do you feel any better?"

"Yeah, much better."

"Good!" Kenya said, and as she got up to leave she added, "You don't have to be sad by yourself anymore. If you ever need someone to talk to, come talk to me. Okay?"

"Okay."

"Good night."

When she reached the door, Amal stopped her. "Kenya, can you stay with me? I think I got enough room here."

Kenya smiled and ran toward the bed and jumped in. They lay facing each other in the dark, barely able to see each other. Kenya's body radiated a comfortable warmth that made Amal feel safe, and she had a sweet smell to her, as if she were a piece of candy. Amal tried to pick out the girl's features in the dark but couldn't.

As Kenya's eyes fluttered closed and her breathing pattern deepened, Amal found herself falling asleep, but right before she closed her eyes she said, "I love you too, Kenya and Ms. Bobbie." She wasn't sure if she heard it, but it didn't need to be heard. Amal would show them.

Chapter

Thirteen

Aunt Bobbie

Present Day

She tossed and turned in bed, which was odd for her since she was usually up at sunrise cooking, washing, and working in her garden. By the time the sun went down, she was normally exhausted, but this time was different. She had only slept for an hour or so when she found herself awake and looking up at her ceiling. She felt as though she didn't need to be in bed just yet and decided she would go read for a few. *That should calm me,* she thought, and pulled the covers back and put on a big, fluffy house robe and slippers. Just as she began moving toward the door, she heard something. Though it's true she was old, she was far from crazy, so she left her room with the intent to figure out what was going on, and preparing to fight if need be.

The hall was quiet when she first came out, despite the sound of hushed voices. The house was dark and still around her. She could see the curtains gently blowing at the end of the hall. Cool air swept through the house, giving off the damp smell that comes before rain. The voices were still constant as she took a few steps to find Kenya's room empty. The voices were coming from Amal's room, but that couldn't be right since the child hadn't spoken a word in days. Still, she pressed her ear to the door and listened to their conversation. She felt a warmness in her chest when she realized what was going on. Kenya was doing what Bobbie had tried to do and failed. It didn't make her upset. Girls that age needed each other, and from what she heard, she couldn't have been happier. Removing her ear from the door, she made her way back to her room and shut the door. She was in complete darkness, standing with her hand still on the knob, smiling. *Maybe everything will be okay,* she thought, and slid back into her warm bed with the words Kenya had spoken running through her thoughts: "I love you and so does Bobbie." Kenya had never been wrong in her life. She did love the girl, every bit of her.

Amal
Present Day

Last night was the first night that she'd felt safe with anyone other than her family. She and Kenya nestled in the bed together like two baby birds until Kenya woke her up to announce that Amal was no longer allowed to stay in the room during the day.

"There's so much we can do! Bedrooms are for sleeping, and I've had enough sleep and so have you."

She went to the closet, which Amal had no idea had been fully stocked. *When did they buy these things?* she thought. As soon as Kenya picked something out, she rushed Amal to the bathroom and stood outside the door while she showered. After she scrubbed and smelled of roses and something else she couldn't place, Amal got dressed. The dress was a hot pink with white polka dots and a bow tied in the front. She slid on her house shoes and brushed her teeth. After she was done she opened the door, signaling that she was dressed and ready.

Kenya pushed past her, as it was her turn to shower and dress. Amal sat on the cool wood floor in the hallway and ran her fingers through her hair and tried not to think too much. Before long, Kenya emerged in a brown-and-pink dress similar to Amal's.

Kenya looked at Amal. "When's the last time you had your hair done?"

Amal couldn't remember the last time it had been done. She had just been leaving it down or in a tight braid. Back home, her mother had done her hair in the mornings. They would sit on the side of her bed, and her mama would slowly comb through it while humming to herself.

"I don't remember."

"Well, I guess we have to do something about that. Come on," Kenya said, pulling Amal to her bright purple-colored room. It was small, but just right for the two of them. She had a dresser and a small white vanity that was just the right size, with a mirror. Her room matched her vibrant personality, with lots of color everywhere. Amal sat down in front of the vanity, secretly glad she had washed her hair. She looked at her face in the mirror and immediately felt ugly. She still had a light tracing of bags under her eyes that looked dull and lifeless. Immediately she felt like she couldn't keep looking at herself in the mirror, so she looked down.

"How you want it done?" Kenya asked, gently dragging the comb through Amal's hair.

"I don't know. Just a braid, I guess."

She started at the end and worked her way up, like Mama used to do. It felt so good that Amal became so relaxed she could have fallen asleep. Kenya sprayed something on her hair that smelled of fruit-flavored candy, and then Amal understood why Kenya smelled so nice.

Once she had detangled the roots, she began to work in Amal's hair with quick fingers. She began humming, and

Amal closed her eyes and listened. It sounded like the song that had been sung when she first got there. She wanted to ask what it meant, but she didn't want Kenya to stop humming. The song soothed her soul as she thought of her country and the faces of all the people she knew, the lost ones, ran like a flip-book through her memory. All those years seemed so distant now, as if they had been lived by someone else and Amal were just listening to a story about them. Her family, friends, and neighbors, who had made her life so enjoyable for years, were now gone, but she had their memories.

She remembered her baba being so upset after her grandmother died that he didn't sleep or eat for days. Mama, desperate for some help, had called his brother, and Amal would never forget what he had said: "If she were here, do you think she'd be happy with how you're behaving? No! She may be gone, but we have to keep living." So, right there in Kenya's room, she decided that she would keep living in honor of those she had lost, and take each day as it came.

"Done!" Kenya announced, clearly happy with her work.

Amal was almost afraid to look up, but Kenya tilted her chin up with her finger until she was eye level with the mirror. It had been a while since she'd felt pretty, but looking in the mirror now, she felt like a princess. Kenya had done her hair up in a braided crown. Amal's black hair shined from the oil she had put in her hair with careful hands. She had even put a few flowered pins in the front. Amal smiled brightly and thanked Kenya. She jumped out of the chair and hugged

Kenya until she squealed that she couldn't breathe; then she laughed.

"You're funny. One minute you're down in the dumps, and the next you're happy and jumping around."

Amal laughed. "I'm happy because of you. Thank you for being so kind to me," she said as tears streamed down her face.

"No, no!" Kenya said as she wiped Amal's tears. "Let's stay happy. No crying." She hugged Amal.

"You know, you look kind of like Frida Kahlo."

Amal pulled back from her a bit. "Who?"

"Nobody," Kenya laughed.

Fourteen

Amal

Present Day

Amal couldn't remember the last time someone had done something for her and hadn't expected anything in return, but here it was different. She felt at home as they sat cross-legged on the floor and Kenya explained how to play a card game called Old Maid. Amal kept getting distracted. She looked round at all the knick-knacks on the tables and shelves. There were stories behind all of them, and she hoped to hear them soon.

"Are you even listening to me?" A voice interrupted her thoughts, and she looked up to see Kenya looking irritated, at her.

"I'm listening, but it still makes no sense to me!"

Kenya sighed hard at Amal's response.

"Maybe we can play something else until Bobbie gets up."

"Can I ask you something? Why do you call her Aunt instead of Grandma?"

Kenya stacked the cards with a tap on the coffee table. "I tried, but she said it made her feel like an old lady."

She looked up at Amal, and as soon as they locked eyes, they laughed. Bobbie was nothing like an old lady. Amal didn't know how old she was, but guessed she didn't look her age at all. Her smooth skin and high cheekbones had probably fooled a lot of people. Uncertain if it was okay to ask, she was dying to know how old Bobbie really was. After their laughing spell, they both decided to try the game one more time. As Kenya told her the rules of the game again, Amal decided she kind of liked the mystery of not knowing Bobbie's age.

Bobbie

Present Day

Bobbie woke up at 5:00 a.m. every morning. She had a ritual that she never deviated from. She made her bed, showered, dressed as brightly as possible, combed her silky black curls into submission, and headed downstairs, where she would start a pot of coffee. Today was no different. When she passed Amal's door and found it still closed, her heart sank a bit. She had thought for sure Kenya's words would help, but she might have been too optimistic. She descended the stairs one step at a time. Her hip gave her issues from time to time, but today was a good day. Reaching the last step, she almost stumbled when she saw Amal and Kenya playing a game in the small living room. Kenya heard her first, looked up, and smiled her normal wide, toothy smile.

"Good morning, Aunt Bobbie! Look who's up!" Kenya pointed at Amal, proud and happy to have someone to play with.

A lump caught in Bobbie's throat, and she almost couldn't speak. "Yes, I see!" Tears stung her eyes.

Amal turned to smile shyly. "Good morning."

The room was so full in that moment that the whole place seemed brighter. She noticed Kenya's face change to a questioning glance, and Bobbie realized she had been staring for too long. "Anybody want pancakes?" she asked.

Kenya clapped happily, and Amal just smiled before looking back down. Bobbie took that as a yes and went into the kitchen to get busy. Since today was special, she decided to make blueberry pancakes.

Amal
Present Day

Amal wanted to run and hug Aunt Bobbie when she saw her. She wanted to tell her she was sorry for the way she had acted, but instead she just smiled at her and sat in place, hoping Bobbie would read through her smile. It seemed to take her a moment to get herself together, but when she did she excused herself, and minutes later the smells of breakfast wafted through the house. She and Kenya took their places at either side of the table. There was a white crocheted tablecloth, with the dark wood of the table peeking out from underneath through the little openings. Amal ran her hand over it, feeling the texture and the groves of the fabric, her skin catching the fabric ever so slightly. She could tell the tablecloth was handmade. Each and every stitch was delicately manipulated with care.

"You like that?" Amal looked up to see Aunt Bobbie standing with a plate of pancakes stacked high and oozing blue in spots and steaming hot.

"Yes, ma'am, I do. Did you make it?" Amal asked as Bobbie set the pancakes on the table.

"Yes, I did. I'm a part of a crochet group here. We have a little something at the church once a week, where we all get together, talk, and make things. Sometimes we donate to different places, like hospitals and nursing homes."

Bobbie walked back into the kitchen and came out with plates and forks before going back to get her coffee; then she finally sat down.

"We make little things like blankets and hats for babies or warm things for the homeless during the winter months." She stopped to take a bite of a pancake and chewed carefully. After swallowing, she added that it was what kept her going, other than her garden and Kenya.

"Could I come?" Amal asked. "I mean, if that's okay. I don't want to cause trouble."

Aunt Bobbie cocked her head to the side in a curious manner. "How could you cause trouble?"

Now Amal had her full attention, and as Bobbie looked at her, Amal was able to take in the older woman fully. She still couldn't tell how old she was, but Amal was amazed at how gorgeous she was. Her skin was flawless, and she didn't have a wrinkle in sight; just smooth brown skin.

Amal cleared her throat nervously. "I mean, not on purpose, but I know I'm not Christian, so I don't want to make it uncomfortable for anyone," Amal said, looking down at her lap.

"Child, you couldn't make anyone uncomfortable. See, the way I see it is, you believe in doing good and staying away from bad things, so that's all that matters. Doing good and being a good person. You think I'd let you in my house if I thought otherwise?" The question was so blunt it made Amal look up, but when she saw Bobbie smiling she relaxed. "The ladies would love to meet you. I've already told them a lot about you. How about we have a small get-together here and you can meet them for yourself? Then, if you want to join, we can go from there. Deal?"

The idea of a party made Amal tingle with excitement. "Deal! What about you, Kenya?"

Kenya was in front of Amal, shoveling pancakes into her mouth as if they were going to run away. Looking up after swallowing, she said loudly, "Nope! It's so boring."

Aunt Bobbie laughed a little. "Well, I guess that's that. Enough talking. Let's eat!"

After breakfast, they cleared the table and washed the dishes. Amal dried and Kenya washed. The normalcy of cleaning up after a meal made her feel at ease. The kitchen wasn't a big space; just big enough to fit a few people comfortably. The appliances were a mix of colors, with no two things alike. A ray of warm sunlight beamed in through the small window over the sink, shining down on a few sprouting plants in plastic cups.

"Girl, you're supposed to be washing dishes, not the floor!" Bobbie's voice filled the room.

Amal looked over to see suds everywhere and Kenya's arms deep into the metal sink, splashing about.

"I'm a sea monster!" Kenya shouted, and made burbling noises, flapped her arms about. Suds went flying around the kitchen, splattering across Amal's face. Bobbie ran over to lift Kenya up on her hip. "You can't trap me! I'll eat you alive!" Kenya said, still flailing her arms as Bobbie tried to stop her.

Aunt Bobbie didn't have the heart to keep at it and broke out into laughter. Amal found herself laughing as well. She still didn't know how she had gotten here, but all that mattered in that moment was that she was happy. This place was safe, and she almost felt like she belonged in that little kitchen. The feeling was like finally coming home after a long trip. She sighed and felt the sun's rays spread across her skin like a warm blanket.

Chapter

Fifteen

Amal
Present Day

It escaped her, how she hadn't noticed the backyard, but through the huge window in the dining area was half an acre of land dedicated solely to growing plants. When Bobbie came down from her room in her gardening outfit, which was an old long-sleeved dress, pink boots, and a tan sun hat, and opened the door, Amal was in awe of the beauty that was contained within the plain wooden fence.

Aunt Bobbie loved to garden, and one could definitely see that by the many plants she had grown and how large they were. There was something special about her hands. It seemed like she could probably plant anything and it would grow without a problem.

The wind blew slightly, catching the wind chimes and sending a lovely melody into the air that smelled of damp soil and greenery. This yard was something out of a fairytale. A small, shaded porch led to a cobblestone walkway that wove through the middle of rows of huge plants and ended at the base of a huge magnolia tree, where a rope swing hung under the tree's huge blossoms. The cobblestones had been painted with little dots in different colors. Each rock was different in its own way, yet they were equally beautiful. Kenya promised to climb the tree with her after she was done picking weeds. Aunt Bobbie asked if she wanted to help, but Amal was afraid she would do something to hurt the plants. She didn't want to do anything to take away from the beauty of the place. Bobbie said that was nonsense, but she was still tentative.

Aunt Bobbie hummed happily as she tended the lush green garden. Amal looked up as she heard her name;

Bobbie was waving for her to come to her. She quickly made her way over to where she was knee deep in tomato plants, pointing at a little bird pecking around happily. It was a beautiful red color with a black line around its beak. She wasn't sure if it was male or female, but she remembered reading somewhere that the brightly colored birds were male, as it helped them attract mates. He hopped around as if he was completely comfortable with their presence.

"Isn't he gorgeous?" Bobbie asked.

Amal smiled and shook her head. "Yes, ma'am, he is! I love the color of his feathers."

"I think that's a cardinal. He's probably looking for bugs or worms to eat. Look at him hop around."

Suddenly the bird took flight and gracefully landed on Amal's shoulder. He turned to look at her, cocking his head to the side, and hopped in place a few times. It startled her slightly, and that made Bobbie smile brightly.

"Looks like he's taken a liking to you. Animals tend to see us for who we really are, so that must mean you've got a good heart."

Amal looked at her face, trying to look past her words. *Me? A good heart?* she thought. Amal's smile dropped as she thought about that.

Aunt Bobbie seemed to notice and said, "You know, when I was your age I had some terrible things happen to me. Some really bad things that should never happen to children. And sometimes when bad things happen we think it's got something to do with us. It took me a long time to realize something."

With the bird still perched on her shoulder, Amal asked, "And what was that?"

Bobbie turned to her plants and snipped a few dead leaves here and there before answering. "I finally realized that I wasn't the bad things that people did to me. No matter what happened to you, you're still a good girl." She turned to look at Amal, the brim of the sun hat shading her milk-chocolate skin. "You know that, right?"

Amal didn't feel the tears come, but when a teardrop plopped on the dirt below, she brought a hand to her cheek and felt the wet trails her tears had left. The bird flew off, and she watched him fly away until he was nothing but a dot in the sky.

Bobbie took off her gloves and pulled her in for a hug. "It seems the only thing I can do is make you cry," she said.

That sent a pang of sadness to Amal's chest. This woman had been nothing but nice to her, and all she had done was make her feel bad.

"No, you don't make me cry," Amal said.

Bobbie used the sleeve of her bright dress to wipe away Amal's tears. "Sure seems like it."

Amal looked up at her face. "My baba, my dad, he used to call me Little Bird. He said I used to bounce around like that when I was little. When I saw the bird, it reminded me of him." Bobbie shook her head as if she understood. "I love being here and I'm happy. I just can't help but think about my family."

Amal hadn't heard Kenya walk up, but in a soft voice she asked, "Your daddy, what happened to him?"

Amal was sobbing now. "He's dead. They're all dead."

Bobbie
Present Day

Night came quietly but quite sooner than Bobbie had expected. Before she bathed the girls and put them to bed, Kenya had demanded her bed be put in Amal's room. "Just for a little while," Kenya had said. She had to admit she was relieved the girls had taken to each other so well. Maybe Kenya could help Amal.

The house was quiet around her. The only thing that could be heard was the ticking of a clock that had been given to her by a friend. She slid her swollen feet into fluffy blue house shoes decorated with a bow and made her way down the hall. She peeked in at the girls, both sleeping peacefully. The moonlight bathed their skin in a sultry blue glow. Crickets sounded outside, and frogs chirped happily. She watched the rise and fall of their little chests and thought about her other children, adopted and biological.

Ever since Bobbie was a little girl, growing up in Alabama, she had loved caring for children. They seemed to flock to her. People thought it was funny when strangers' children would take to her without even having to say a word. She got her experience from taking care of her many siblings. Her mother was a small Native American woman with a beautiful spirit and a quick temper who had twenty-three children by the time she was forty. Bobbie got her height, body shape, and quick temper from her mother and her rich brown color and warm personality from her father. Her mother died at the age of forty-two, leaving Bobbie to care for her siblings with the help of her father, but when he passed away she was completely alone and had no choice but to seek help from extended family. Their family had to be split up, and she was left to take care of two children at the age of ten, relying on her gardening skills to feed them until she found employment elsewhere. They stayed in public housing until Bobbie woke up and found the husband of the woman who ran the business, in her bed. She ran out and took nothing but the clothes on her back and her siblings. The woman she was working for offered to house them as long as she paid rent and they didn't cause trouble. For years, she did housework as a maid and took in ironing or sewing. Soon she met her husband, and he built the house she was in now, and they spent the remainder of their married life here.

A sudden creak in the wood snapped Bobbie to attention. She left the girls' room looking for the noise and was reassured that it was just the house creaking. She straightened the couch cushions and did some light cleaning up until everything was to her liking. She loved her home and how quiet it was. After making her last rounds downstairs, checking the locks on the doors and windows, Bobbie slowly scaled the stairs and went back to peek in on the girls, who were still sleeping soundly. She smiled to herself and shut the door, walking back to her room in darkness. She lay in bed counting her blessings until she fell asleep.

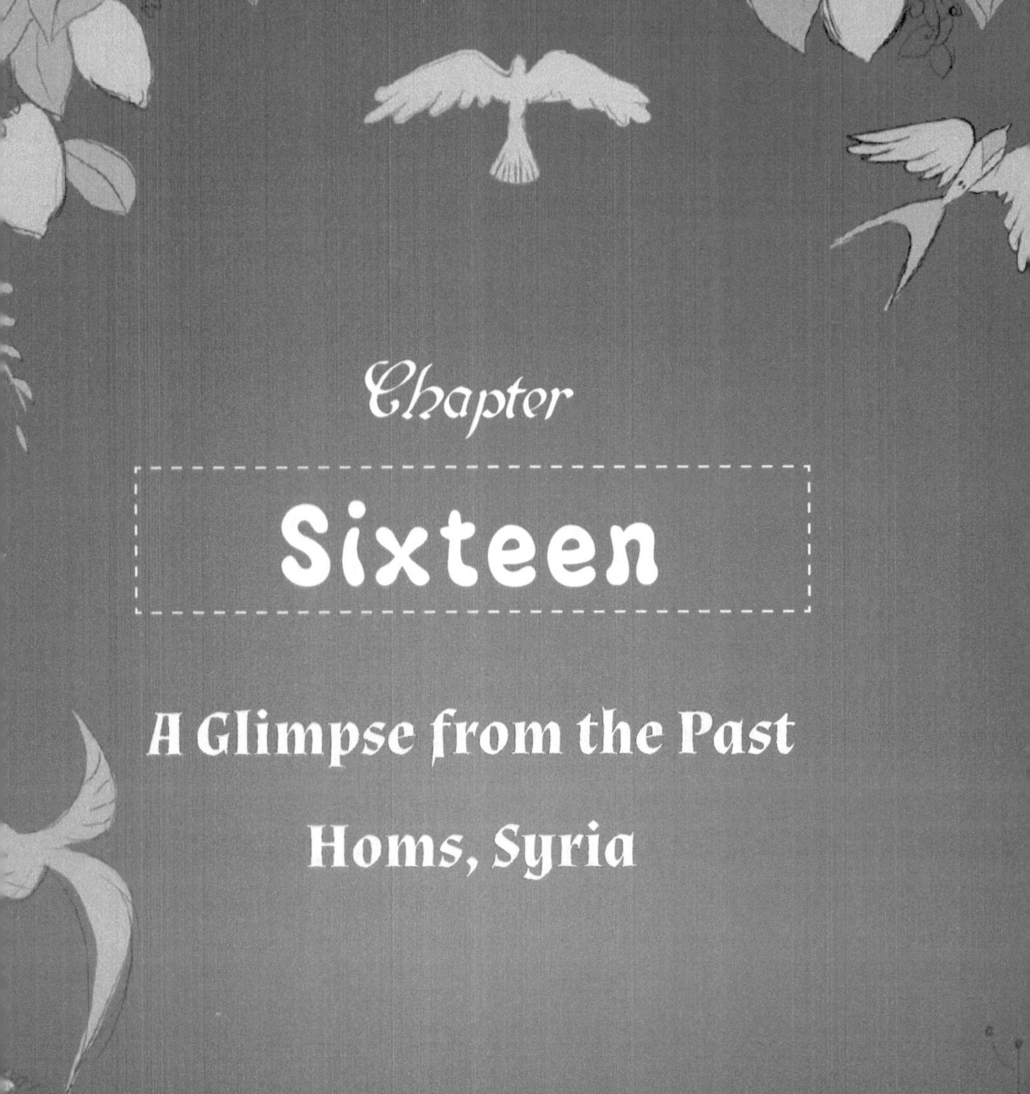

Chapter

Sixteen

A Glimpse from the Past

Homs, Syria

The sounds of destitution and the smell of human feces hung over the air in a thick cloud. Being in the tent couldn't even keep the smell down. Amal's father told her four people had died yesterday. There were no funerals and no one mourned them. Life just went on. They just buried them and kept going.

She sat on a pile of rocks on the outskirts of the camp, watching the kids play. She was having to survive off a few bites of bread and water, and the hunger was giving her a headache that didn't want to go away. She rubbed her empty stomach as it protested. The men at the camp did what they could to hunt, but always came up short. The food went to the children first, but there was never enough.

"Come play with us."

She looked up and saw one of the children standing in front of her, holding out a dirty hand to her. She was so pained she couldn't speak, and she rubbed her stomach, hoping he would understand.

"It hurts less when you don't think about it."

Amal looked the boy in the eyes and could see a familiar hollowness in them that everyone at the camp had. They had been broken, mentally, physically, but they tried to hold on spiritually. The old man who had lost his wife to sickness was always trying to remind everyone of their religion. "God has a plan," he would say. Amal sometimes wondered if he was right or if he was completely out of his mind. *Where was God when my sister died, and where is he now?* she thought.

She took the boy's hand and stood, slowly walking to their homemade play area. They were playing soccer with a ball made of plastic bags. She kicked the ball a little but couldn't keep up. Hunger slowed her down and made her clumsy. Eventually she ended the game and made her way back to her tent. She wove through the dusty pathway with her head down, walking past tent after tent. Without warning, the ground shook and then came an ear-splitting boom. Her heart beat out of her chest as she screamed and took off running for the only safety she knew. She kept running and was almost there when she was grabbed by someone. She wiggled, screamed, and fought with everything she had.

"Calm down! Calm down!" the voice said.

She turned to see her baba. She wrapped her arms around him and wept into his chest. "I hate this! I just want to die!" she sobbed.

"Don't say that! Don't you ever say that again!" Her baba grabbed her by the shoulders and shook her.

"When is help coming? Has everyone in the world forgotten us?" she asked, looking into his eyes, waiting for an answer.

"The world may have forgotten us, but God is always with us! Always!" he said through tears, and pulled her into his arms again.

The bomb hadn't hit the camp, but they were close enough to feel the effects. They were lucky, but what if it had been closer? Since then she stayed indoors most of the time. She would only leave when her father would press her.

He wanted her to go out and enjoy her day, regardless of their circumstances.

It had been five days since she'd eaten. Her dad had tried to find food, but failed. They were reduced to eating dirt and grass. Military vehicles patrolled but never stopped to help even when the children would chase after them, screaming and begging for food. Amal's father was out with a few of the men, trying to find food. She sat on a rock praying for something, anything, because she didn't know how much more of this she could take.

Thinking back on the situation, maybe if she hadn't been so hungry she wouldn't have done it, but then all she could think of was getting food. As she was used to seeing military vehicles, she didn't think anything of it when one stopped in front of her. Dust flew as the vehicle came to a stop. The window rolled down and a guy with short black hair and shades called to her.

"Hey, little girl!" he said. Amal looked up nonchalantly, too hungry to care. "You hungry? I know where you can find food."

"Really?" Amal replied hopefully.

"Yeah, just hop in and we'll take you."

"I have to ask my baba first. He'll be worried if he can't find me."

"Don't worry, you'll be back before then. Come on," he said as he held out a bottle of water. She grabbed the bottle and hopped in without thinking. It would only be a ten-minute drive, he said. When she got in and saw all the men, she knew for a fact she had made a terrible mistake. She panicked as she tried to get out. They laughed and the driver sped off as she screamed for help. A man with a black shirt held her as a man with brown hair tried to take off her clothes. She kicked and screamed, but it was no use. The man who was trying to take off her clothes put a bag over her head. She gasped for air and strained against him, trying to free a hand to tear away the bag. She saw blurry visions of the men moving around her as they cackled like demons. Sharp fingernails dug into her arms and legs. The more she fought, the more out of breath she became, until everything went black and there was nothing but pain and laughter. The last thing she heard was the voice that had offered her food telling everyone they would get a turn.

She didn't know how long it had gone on, but she awoke in her tent with a woman praying over her. Her warm hand lay on Amal's head. She could hear her father's angry voice outside.

"Don't move, sweetie," the woman said, when she realized she was awake. The woman gave her a weak smile. Her brown scarf was draped loosely around her head. "Do you remember anything?" she asked.

Amal saw flashes of the men's faces, felt the heaviness of their bodies on hers, the feeling of hands around her neck. Their laughter rang in her ears still, but she shook her head no.

"Something very bad happened to you, but you're okay now. Just don't move. I'll get your father." The woman gave her one last sad look before leaving Amal alone.

Chapter

Seventeen

Louis

Present Day

The night was young, and the music played loud and smooth. Jazz, booze, and cigarette smoke filled the air. He tapped his shiny black shoes on the floor, in time with the music. Louis was going to enjoy himself tonight because it was his last night in New Orleans. No one could know, especially not Bobbie, why he was coming home. She would be disappointed, and he couldn't do that to her. She would be happy to see him, and he wanted to keep it that way. He was running out of funds quickly, as he drowned himself in liquor and women to ease the pain and disappointment he held within himself, leaving no other option but to go back home.

He was deep into the swing of the music when a beautiful woman with caramel skin, in a sparkling sequined red dress walked up to him and asked him to dance. They went out on the floor and got caught up in the music, like flies in a spider's web. Their movements were hypnotic. She seemed to know every move he was going to make and matched it. The night was truly theirs.

Louis wanted his last night there to be special, so they danced until the music stopped and the bar closed. Then he invited her to his place, which was a small loft above a coffee shop a couple of blocks down. She paid no attention to how messy his dwelling was; besides, she wasn't there for that. She was fierce and quick, pushing him to the nearest flat, cushioned surface. When their bodies met their movements mimicked the way they had danced. They were synchronized, working together until the ending came; sweet, rhythmic, and powerful. He was almost sad when he had to leave her there, but his bags were already packed and in the trunk of his car, so after sleeping for a few hours he dressed quiet-ly, leaving a note and a few bucks for her to get home, and promptly made his leave. He wove through the streets until he turned and was speeding down the vast expanse of high-way before him. He felt better the farther away he got from his failure.

He lit a cigarette with one hand as he held it tightly between his lips. This would be his last one, and he would savor it. Bobbie wouldn't allow any such nonsense in her house, and he wanted to respect her wishes. He puffed and tapped his finger in time with the music that played on the radio. "All Along the Watchtower" by Jimi Hendricks was one of his favorites. He took in a deep breath of fresh air before filling his lungs with more smoke. Thinking how ironic that was, he laughed a little to himself.

Amal
Present Day

All she could hear was the beating of her heart and the sounds of water and screams. They were so loud they made her insides shake. She put her hands to her ears and yelled, "Stop! Stop!"

Suddenly the ground began to shake. "Amal! Wake up! Wake up!" She opened her eyes in shock to find herself in her bed, with Kenya looking at her. "You were having a bad dream! It's okay," Kenya said as she rubbed Amal's shoulders as if she were trying to warm her up.

"I'm okay. Thank you for waking me up," she said, giving Kenya a weak smile. Lying back down, she felt her back covered in sweat and cool to the touch.

Kenya moved back to her bed. "You were saying stop. Do you remember what you were dreaming about?"

Amal thought of the dream. Images of the raft flashed in her mind. She pushed them back and said, "No, it was probably nothing."

Kenya didn't seem convinced but didn't push the subject. "You know, if something bad happened to you, you can tell me. We're friends, right?"

Amal turned onto her side, facing away from Kenya. "You want to be my friend?" she asked.

"Sure! I love being around you! You make me happy!"

Amal turned and, smiling at Kenya, said, "Then we're friends!"

Kenya shushed Amal. She started to ask why, but stopped before she said anything. There was a flurry of voices coming from downstairs. Amal could pick out Bobbie's voice, but there was someone else.

"Who is—?" Amal began to ask, but Kenya cut her off and screamed, "Louis is here!" She ran to the door and downstairs, leaving Amal alone in her bed. Her heart raced and she wasn't sure why. *Why am I frightened? If Bobbie and Kenya are down there, it's okay*, she thought, but the deepness of the voice made her sit still. She braced herself when she heard hurried footsteps on the stairs. It was Kenya, who paraded in the room wearing an oversized hat that looked silly with her long white cotton nightgown and braids.

"You wanna meet Louis? Come on!" Kenya raced downstairs again, and Amal got out of bed slowly, not sure if she wanted to meet him. She made it out into the hall and tried peeking through the railing, but she couldn't see. All she could hear was Kenya talking and the guy laughing.

As she slowly descended the stairs a deep voice said, "Well, well. Is this Miss Amal?"

She looked up to see a tall man with skin like Bobbie's. He was slim and wearing dark-washed jeans and a blue shirt. His legs looked like noodles. He smiled big and bright as he sat next to Kenya.

"She's a little shy, so leave her alone. Come here." Bobbie motioned for Amal to sit on the chair next to her. Not knowing what else to do, she walked over and sat down, feeling safe with Bobbie near.

"This is my boy, Louis. He's nice. Don't worry about him," Bobbie said, holding her hand.

Amal took a quick peek up to find him looking at her, but there was no danger in his presence, just kindness, so she gave a small smile and looked back down. If Bobbie liked him, then he was okay, but she didn't have to trust him.

Kenya and Aunt Bobbie seemed enamored with him. Amal watched as Kenya smiled up at him, listening to his every word, and laughed at funny things he said. She wasn't paying attention and wanted to be anywhere but there, silently wishing he would leave soon. Then she glanced at the door and saw a large cluster of bags and knew he wasn't leaving. Would she have to share a house with him? She wanted to run back upstairs but was stuck next to Bobbie.

"So what grade are you in?"

She thought he was still talking to Bobbie and Kenya, but when she felt their gazes on her she looked up to see him looking at her again. Her thoughts went back to her school in Syria, her teachers, and afternoons spent with her sister helping her with homework. She pushed away the thought and answered quickly, "I don't go to school anymore."

"But she will soon. She's twelve, so she'll be in the sixth grade," Bobbie said.

Amal looked at her, dumbfounded.

Bobbie must've read her thoughts, and so said, "Yes, you

will be going to school. You have to. You don't want people to come throw me in jail, do you?" She smiled, and Amal quickly shook her head no.

"Will I be with Kenya?" Amal asked. Her heart beat fast in her chest. She was just now getting used to being here, and now had to think about school in a country that she knew nothing of other than from movies and TV.

"You'll be going to the same school, but you won't be in the same classes. You'll be fine, though. From what I've seen, you're a smart girl." Bobbie rubbed Amal's back.

Tears stung her eyes, but she willed herself not to cry. She suddenly felt small. After sitting for what seemed like hours, her brain buzzed with the new information that she would be going to school in America. The whole thing seemed strange.

"Look at the time! It's almost eight o'clock. Who's hungry?"

"Me!" Kenya and Louis answered at the same time, making Kenya giggle.

"I said it first!"

"No, you didn't!"

"Yes, I did!" They bickered back and forth.

"Now, don't start that mess! It's too early in the morning for all that fussing," Bobbie interrupted, with a hand on her hip, making both of them shut up.

"Sorry, Mama, but she started it," Louis said, poking out his bottom lip.

"No, I didn't!" Kenya yelled.

"I don't care who started it. I'm finishing it. Hush! I'm going to cook." And with that she disappeared into the kitchen to do what she did best.

Aunt Bobbie must've caught wind of how Amal was feeling and so called her to help in the kitchen. Amal watched as Bobbie went about her normal routine. Her petite figure in another flowered print dress floated around her as she opened cabinets and retrieved ingredients to prepare the food. Amal pressed her small body against the flat side of the fridge. She could feel the coolness on her side.

"I hope you're not worried about school. I know you just got here, but maybe it'll help–you being around kids your own age."

Amal closed her eyes and sighed.

"It's okay to be nervous. It'll be alright."

Amal looked at Bobbie for reassurance. "You promise?"

Bobbie smiled and said, "I promise," then went back to cooking.

After breakfast was cooked and eaten, she sat on the weather-worn wooden swing outside under the fragrant magnolia. She was dressed in a pale-green sundress with no shoes. Any other day she would've been happy, but since Louis had arrived, Amal felt forgotten. It wasn't the first time, and she was sure it wouldn't be the last. She lifted both legs in unison, swinging herself slowly. The sound of the back door opening made her look up to find Aunt Bobbie in her sun hat and gloves.

"Why aren't you inside with Kenya?"

Amal shrugged. "She's playing with Louis."

"And you can't?" Bobbie asked. Amal fell silent and looked at her feet. Bobbie nodded to herself, then began clipping at a vine with bean pods on it. "The party is going to be Saturday. Well, it's not like a party; it's more like a get-together, maybe. I've told all my friends about you, and they can't wait to meet you. They seemed impressed by the fact that someone your age would want to learn to crochet."

Amal could see her mother in her head as clear as day, with a crochet project in her lap. She always seemed to be trying to figure out some new pattern or caught up in making a blanket for someone's baby shower. The idea of her being close to learning the craft gave her comfort.

"I can't wait to meet them either. My mom loved to crochet," she said without thinking. "Really? Did she ever make you anything?" Bobbie asked.

"A few sweaters, slippers, and a hat that was lopsided."

Amal thought of the hat and smiled. Her mother had been so proud of herself for learning a new pattern, only to find that it didn't fit. Amal had tried to squeeze her head in it anyway, trying desperately to keep her mother from feeling bad.

"I miss my mama," Amal said after a brief silence.

"I'm sure you do, sweetie. So it's just you? You have no other family?" Bobbie asked.

Amal remembered the sound of the bomb and how the ground had trembled under her feet; a vision of panicked people and the smell of smoke and death assaulted her senses. She shook her head to clear it away. "No, it's just me."

Bobbie said, "That must make you feel lonely."

People used the word *lonely* as if that word could really describe the despair she felt on a daily basis. She had lost everything she loved. She often wondered why she was still here.

She shook her head. "Yes, very much so."

Aunt Bobbie put down her clippers, satisfied with her work, walked over to where Amal was sitting, and attempted to sit on the ground next to her, but her hip gave her a hard time. Amal jumped up and offered her the swing, and she found a nice spot on the ground and sat before Aunt Bobbie.

"I just want you to know that no matter how lonely you feel you will always have me and Kenya. I even think Louis is fond of you, and he just met you." She smiled and continued, "I know I'm not your mother, and I won't pretend to be, but I consider you as one of my own, and I'll always care for you. I just wanted you to know that."

It brought tears to Amal's eyes that she couldn't control. *She loves me? How can this woman love me?* She thought of what those men did to her and how it had made her feel so dirty and shameful. When she looked into Bobbie's deep brown eyes she saw sincerity there, so she didn't say anything. When Bobbie pulled her into a hug, she accepted it and sat on Bobbie's lap, embraced in her arms, until sunset. Neither of them wanted to move a muscle.

Chapter

Eighteen

A Glimpse into The Past

Homs, Syria

A strange pain throbbed between Amal's legs as she lay in the tent. Her father appeared, opening the zipper slowly, as though he thought she might be sleeping and he didn't want to disturb her. When he peeked in she noticed his eyes were red, as if he had been crying. He moved over to her and grabbed her tiny hand in his.

"I'm so sorry for leaving you. This is my fault." His voice broke as he fought back tears. "I'm so sorry. So sorry." He squeezed her hand and shook his head. "May Allah forgive me. I should've been here."

She looked up at him, and it broke her heart. He thought it was his fault, when it was really hers. If she hadn't gone looking for food, it wouldn't have happened. She should've just waited for her father. It wasn't long before they both were crying. Neither could find the words for how they felt. His guilt overcame him. She had never seen her father look so vulnerable and helpless. It scared her. She used to think her father could do anything. He was like a superhero in her eyes, and seeing him now, in his sorrow, humanized him. Finally he lifted his head and ran his palm across her forehead and cheek.

"It wasn't your fault, Baba. It was mine! I should've never gone looking for food! I'm sorry!"

"You have nothing to be sorry for. You only did what you thought was right, Little Bird. You were hungry and you went looking for food, but that didn't give those men the right to do what they did to you. They are to blame, not you, my sweet girl."

"But . . . ," Amal sniffled.

"Listen to me! Don't blame yourself for those men's wrongdoings! I failed you once; I won't fail you again. I've heard some people talking about leaving and going to America on a boat. We have nothing left here, and no one here wants us. Maybe you can find a good life there. There's no war, no fighting. You can be happy and safe there, Little Bird."

Her head swam with the new information. "But you will come with me, right?" she asked.

"I will. Now go back to sleep."

She closed her eyes and dreamt of nothing but blackness. It felt like she had only been asleep for a moment when her father finally woke her.

"It's time!" he said, handing her a bag with bread and the little water they had left. He shook her by the shoulders after she stood, looking into her eyes. "I need for you to be alert."

Gunshots erupted in the distance, making Amal jump. "Baba, who's shooting?" They could now hear screaming and the sounds of people running. Her heartbeat quickened. "What is going on?" she asked.

Her father shook her shoulders again. "I need you to pay attention. There are bad people out there, and we need to leave now. Don't worry. Just follow me!" There were more gunshots, but these sounded closer. Her father grabbed her hand. "I know you're in pain, but I need you to run. If anything happens to me, you follow the road to the water.

There are people there waiting for us in a boat. You go with them!" He grabbed her hand before unzipping the tent.

"What are we supposed to do, Baba? What's going on? Why won't you answer me?" Amal cried. Deep sobs shook her shoulders.

"Hey! Hey! There is no time for crying! Do you want to die?" Amal shook her head no. "Then stop asking me questions and do as I say."

She was in shock—at first because of the gunshots and screaming, but now because her father had never spoken to her in that manner, so whatever was happening must be serious. Amal gulped down tears as he blew out the oil lamp and pulled her through the tent opening. It was pitch black when she emerged from the tent, but a faint red glow filled her vision; as they ran she saw that part of the camp had been set ablaze. They ran through crowds of screaming people. In the dark she could make out the bulky, dark masses of military vehicles. *So they're shooting us down like animals. And for what?*

They began walking, keeping a fast pace. Amal trailed behind her father so closely she was on his heels. A few people began following them, as if they believed the girl and man knew something they didn't. Suddenly a large vehicle drove up beside them and turned to stop in front of them. It happened in seconds. The gunfire sounded like thunder. Her father grabbed her and lay on top of her, trying his best to shield his daughter from the rounds of ammunition. She lay beneath her father until she heard the vehicle drive away. She didn't move for a while, as she expected her father to get up when it was safe, but he never did.

"Baba, it's okay. They're gone." But she got no answer. "Baba?" She pushed against his weight until she rolled him off of her, calling "Baba?" Then she shook him.

She strained her eyes trying desperately to see. She shook him again, and something damp came off on her hand. She didn't need to be told it was blood; it was just something she knew. She jumped when he roused a bit, making a faint moaning noise. "Baba, come on! We have to go! You're bleeding and we have to get you help!" He smiled at her as if he hadn't heard a word she said. Even in the dark, she could see his bright teeth; some were stained with blood.

"I love you, Little Bird," he said, reaching a hand up to caress her cheek. Then it fell beside him and he didn't move again.

"Baba, please! Come on! We have to go! Please wake up!" she sobbed. She shook him and pulled on him until her arms were tired. She laid her head on his chest and cried. "I can't do this without you. Please wake up!" she cried.

A group of people ran past, reminding her of what her baba had told her: "Go to the water."

She reluctantly got up, saying a silent prayer for her father's soul; then she ran. She ran until her worn shoes split and her feet were bloody and torn up. She didn't stop until she could smell salt water, and sure enough, waiting on the dark shore was a small boat. She stood on the shore for a moment looking back. This place used to be her home. Her family had lived and died here, and she was about to leave everything she knew to go to a place she had only seen in movies. She wiped away the bittersweet memories of her home, knowing she could never go back. She turned and walked to the boat. A man handed her a life jacket, and she found a place on the cramped raft, where she sat feeling nothing but the coldness inside her.

Bobbie

Present Day

In the days leading up to the party, she busied herself with chores. Bobbie didn't like having anyone over unless her house was completely clean, which used to drive her husband crazy. She moved furniture, dusted, cleaned windows, and waxed the wood floors. The girls helped her with the smaller chores, and Louis did the heavy lifting. She had been surprised when he arrived on her doorstep days before, and knew something was wrong even though he wouldn't say it. One thing she had learned being a mother of eight, then a foster mother of six, was to let them come to you first. Once her kids were grown, she'd learned to let them be, and when they felt like they needed her help, they would ask for it. She'd made the mistake of butting into her eldest daughter's life uninvited, and she wouldn't do it again. As much as Bobbie wanted to ask Louis why he was home, she didn't.

As a child and teenager, he had made so much fuss about becoming an artist, and despite her protests, he held on to his dream. She wasn't trying to crush his spirit, but she had bigger dreams for him. Aunt Bobbie wanted him to be a doctor, but when she brought up medical school, he would bring up art school. They argued until his gradu-ation day. After seeing him walk across the stage in his cap and gown left her in tears, she let him be. He had picked some famous art school in New Orleans, and he couldn't wait to go. His leaving for school had left a hole in her heart so deep it ached constantly. She wondered how he was and what he was doing so often, it was all she thought of. He sent her pictures and called twice a week, but it didn't help cure the pain that came with loneliness, and hearing his voice just made it worse. *Is he really okay?* she wondered. And she began to sink into depression until Kenya came. Kenya brought her out of herself, and soon she felt whole again.

Now, as she watched Louis for any signs of anything wrong, Bobbie hadn't noticed anything big, but she could tell he was hiding something. The way he lowered his eyes when he spoke to her, never making eye contact for too long, was enough to let her know. But she wouldn't push it; she would wait until he was ready to tell her.

Amal

Present Day

The party was set for the next day, and Amal was all nerves. She tried to imagine the faces of the women she would see and hoped they would be as nice and welcoming as Bobbie had been. Her new friend Kenya had forgotten about her—her life seemed to revolve around Louis now, and wherever he went, she went. Amal wanted nothing to do with him, and she surely didn't trust him. The only good man she knew was her baba, and she would like it to stay that way.

The afternoon was comfortably warm; the sun fell over her bare shoulders like a silk shawl as she hopped from one rock to another, admiring the different designs. "One foot, two feet!" she said repeatedly to herself as she bounced off each rock. One was gold with pink, the same pink her sister had loved. It brought back fond memories of her family and of a certain day in particular.

Everything around her was washed in happiness. She awoke to the smell of incense burning and the sounds of children laughing. Her new dress was spread across the end of her bed. It was a sea of pink and green spilling off to the floor like an unkempt flower bed. Little flowers adorned every inch of the dress in different colors with green vines separating and adding order to the beautiful chaos. Her mama entered the room, looking at the dress on the bed as if it was her life's greatest work.

"Assalaamualaikum! Eid Mubarak, Little Bird!" she sang, her sweet voice warming Amal's insides. Her mom was a swishing blur of pink and cream. Amal giggled as her mother walked the invisible catwalk in the middle of the room. She made the most serious face she could muster, walking and twirling past stuffed animals and dolls, her tiny feet making little thudding noises on the wood floors. Amal clapped and her mother picked her up from the bed, swinging her around. Amal laughed until she was red in the face, before her mother put her on her hip and took her to the bathroom. She quickly bathed Amal, then lifted her out of the water and wrapped her in a fluffy towel, then took her back to her room. The fluffiness of it was comforting, as she loved to be wrapped in blankets, no matter the temperature. They made her feel safe. Her mother lifted her up again and in a voice that wasn't hers said,

"Amal? Amal . . ."

She looked up to find Louis standing against the huge magnolia. "You alright?" he asked, smirking slyly, making Amal blush hard as she realized she was daydreaming. "I just came to check on you. I looked out here, and you were just staring off into space."

Amal looked at Louis, shielding her eyes from the sun. "Yes, I'm fine. I was just thinking." She hadn't had a good look at him before, but he was handsome. He was a lot taller than she had thought. He had a closely shaved beard and wavy black hair.

"About what?" he asked; the smirk on his face was like he'd heard a joke but didn't want to be the first one to laugh. It made her feel a strange warmness in her cheeks.

She blushed hard. "That's none of your business. Where's Kenya?" She quickly redirected her focus, but she couldn't help but roll her eyes.

"She was tired so she's taking a nap. What's with the attitude, little lady?"

'Little lady'? Did he just call me that? Where does he get off thinking he can call me little lady? she thought. Heat began to rise in her chest and her heart raced.

"Attitude? I don't have an attitude!" she said sharply, with a hand on her hip.

"I didn't mean it like that! I was only kidding!" He put his hands up in the air like he was surrendering.

"Well, it's not funny. Ever since you came, she's been ignoring me. I don't have any friends. Kenya is my friend, and you can't have her!" She heard the words coming out of her mouth, but hadn't meant to say them. *Am I jealous?* she thought.

Louis sighed and shook his head as if coming to an agreement with himself. "I'm sorry. I'll have a talk with her when she gets up." He pushed off the tree and began to walk toward the door, but stopped with his back to her. "By the way, all she talks about is you," he said, then made his way into the house; the screened door slammed shut behind him.

Amal stood there stunned. *Kenya hasn't been paying any attention to me, and he expects me to believe that?* She'd had friends back in her homeland, but none of them had been as important to her as Kenya was. She loved her energy, and it never failed to make Amal happy. Her kindness was that of a mother. She had never met anyone like her or Aunt Bobbie before. Maybe she had been mean to Louis, but she couldn't help how she felt, and she decided after a few moments under the tree that she would go apologize to him. She turned around and walked toward the back door. The cool air from the inside blew straight into Amal's face as she walked into the house.

"Amal! Is that you? Come in the kitchen!" Bobbie's voice called from the kitchen.

"Yes, ma'am!" Amal said, dusting off the bottoms of her feet before walking to the kitchen. From the doorway she could see Bobbie in a blue apron stirring something in a pitcher.

"You ever had pink lemonade before?" Bobbie asked as she stirred the contents of the pitcher, making rhythmic thuds.

"What's pink lemonade?"

Bobbie took the spoon out to taste, then threw the long wooden spoon in the sink. Reaching into the cabinet above, she got out two glasses and then ice from the fridge.

"This . . . is pink lemonade," she said as she handed Amal a full glass. The ice danced around the top of the drink in smooth circles.

"Bismillah!" she whispered, then took her first sip. The sourness of the lemons and the sweetness of the strawberries made Amal's mouth water and her cheeks pucker. She loved it and downed the rest in two gulps. Wiping away the remnants of the drink with the back of her hand, breathing hard, she smiled at Bobbie, who wiped the top of her lip with the bottom of her apron.

"So I guess that means it was good?" Bobbie asked jokingly.

"It's more than good! Can I have more?"

Bobbie poured more in her cup, then got another from the cabinet. "Here, take this to Kenya."

Amal scaled the steps carefully so she wouldn't spill the drinks. When she got to her room the door was cracked, so she just pushed it open with her feet, only to find a sleeping Kenya. She looked peaceful. As she moved closer, Amal could she her chest gently rising and falling. She decided that a nap didn't sound too bad and made her way to put the drinks on the nightstand between her and Kenya's beds, but before she could get there, Kenya popped up, growling like a wild animal. The shock alone almost sent the drinks flying, but Amal steadied herself and managed to only spill a few drops on the floor.

"Are you crazy? You almost made me drop these!"

Kenya took one look at Amal and started laughing. She laughed so hard it made Amal laugh.

"You are crazy!" Amal exclaimed.

After their laughing fit was over, Amal took a seat on the side of her bed. "I just came to bring you some lemonade."

Kenya took the glass from Amal and thanked her. They both drank lemonade and talked until the drinks were finished and their stomachs were sore from laughter.

Trish
Present Day

You never know how much you have until you have to pack it up and shove it in the back of a car. Trish was standing at the back of her old lime-green Cadillac trying to decide what to keep and what to leave behind. She didn't have long to decide because he would be home soon. The sun made her brown skin glisten, and she was sweating under its intense glare. She brought her hand up to smooth out her hair, forgetting that even the slightest amount of pressure made her scalp cry for mercy. She winced and slammed the trunk closed with a thump and stood out front for a moment, just staring at her house, taking a last look at it.

Her ridiculously high heels clicked on the pavement as she sashayed toward the driver's side of the car, opened the door, and sat with a grunt. She would have to invest in some looser clothes if she was going to be living with her mom again. Trish slammed the door and pulled out a tiny mirror from her purse to check her makeup. Once she was satisfied that her bruises were barely noticeable, she put the mirror away and started the car. Within minutes she was out of the neighborhood she hated, driving past shops, schools, and churches, weaving through familiar streets until she got to the interstate. She thought of turning back, but she just pressed her foot on the accelerator harder and willed herself to keep going. If she returned, she knew he would kill her this time. Every time her mind brought up memories of the night before, she would press on the gas a little harder.

She didn't remember how it started. How did arguing turn to light slaps and light slaps turn into closed fists, hair being pulled, and her face being slammed into the wall, leaving a spot she couldn't get out; a spot that would always remind her of pain and sadness?

PTSD was what her doctor had told her she had, among other things. At the time Trish had thought it was funny and laughed. When he had asked why she was laughing, she'd simply looked at him, smiled ruefully, and said, "Nothing."

That clean-cut middle-aged white man with his perfect credit score, nuclear family, perfect teeth, and cookie-cutter house would never understand Trish or her problems. Everyone was just names and labels he gave out at will until it was time for him to head home to the wife and kids. She saw him every other week in his stiff khaki pants, polished shoes, and brightly colored shirt and tie. Every week he expected her to talk, but her day-to-day was always the same: wake up, clean, cook before Randy came home, and pray to God he hadn't been out drinking. She tiptoed around him all the time, doing everything the way he liked, but she didn't know why she even tried. Nothing was ever good enough for that man, and when she messed up—let's just say he was quick tempered on a good day. Trish felt like a prisoner in her own home, as he dictated every move to her. She hadn't even been out on her own since they were married at eighteen, and now, as she sat behind the wheel, the roar of the engine seemed to fill her with courage she didn't know she had. As she adjusted in her seat, Trish winced through the pain from last night's beating. In about three hours she would be safely tucked away in the backwoods of Alabama. When she was younger she hated being so isolated, but God, was she looking forward to it now. He wouldn't be able to find her there, and that was Trish's focus the rest of the way.

Chapter

Nineteen

Amal

Present Day

As the day was nearly over Bobbie, Kenya, Amal, and Louis sat on the front porch watching the sunset. The sky was the color of a blazing fire, orange with hints of pink and red. They were all quietly watching the sky change before them when Louis abruptly rose to his feet and went inside. Amal cut Kenya a confused look, but didn't say anything. He returned moments later with a large bag and sat in the same spot. He opened the bag, revealing paints and a small canvas.

Kenya leaned over to Amal and whispered, "He likes to paint. He's really good at it. He went to school for it and everything. Isn't that right?"

Amal just rolled her eyes and kept watching the sky. She tried to pretend she didn't care, but she had to admit she was curious. He got busy mixing colors and running a pencil along the square piece of white fabric on wood.

She looked at Kenya, who smiled at her knowingly. "You can go watch. He doesn't mind."

Her curiosity won again, and she whispered, "I'll go if you go."

So she and Kenya rose to their feet and dusted off their dresses and made their way to where he was sitting. He happily sketched away, almost oblivious to their presence. He was like a machine, perfectly drawing his surroundings. Amal couldn't wait to see what he would do next. They almost didn't notice the sound of a car driving up and parking until Amal heard a door slam and looked up. Bobbie rose to her feet, trying to see who was there, but Amal could see perfectly. A woman walked up the driveway in a tight black dress that barely covered her thighs and bright red shoes that where extremely high. She didn't know how the woman was walking in them, but she did so gracefully. Her hips swayed from left to right seductively. She wore her hair in a short pixie cut, and her lips were painted the same red as her shoes. Big-framed sunglasses that were way too big for her covered half her face.

"Hey, Momma! Don't act like you don't remember me!" she shouted playfully.

"Trish?" Louis said, then jumped from the porch and took off in a run toward her and wrapped her in a hug. He lifted her off the ground, making her laugh.

"I'm glad to see you too! How's my favorite little brother?"

After he put her down she held his face in her hands, looking him over. Amal watched Bobbie walk over to the pretty woman as if she were in a trance. The woman wrapped her arms around Bobbie.

"I missed you so much, Mama," Amal heard her say, and the feeling of abandonment crashed into her like a thousand turbulent waves. In that moment she felt lonely, lost, and devoid of love. She tucked her hands behind her back and looked at her dirty feet on the porch. Tears fell in big drops and mixed with the dirt on her feet. So many fell she was sure her feet would soon be caked in mud.

"Excuse me, little miss!" She looked up to see everyone walking toward her. The woman was arm in arm with Louis and Aunt Bobbie. Kenya skipped along after them. "I know you heard me pretty girl."

It hadn't occurred to Amal that the woman was talking to her until she saw her looking right at her. The closer she got, the prettier she got, and Amal could see how much she favored Aunt Bobbie. They were like twins. She wiped her eyes quickly, not wanting anyone to know she was crying.

When the lady made it to the porch, she held out a hand. "My name's Trish."

"I'm Amal," she said, then shook hands.

She was so beautiful and she smelled so lovely, like something she had never smelled before. She imagined some expensive exotic flower growing in the depths of the rainforest; the harvesters' native to the area making a dangerous trip to pick the flower at the exact time it blossomed to extract all of its wonderful fragrance to share with the world.

"Amal's a very pretty name. What does it mean?" the woman asked as she sat on the edge of the porch, like she was a little girl. Amal sat down next to her and Kenya followed.

"Amal means 'hope.'"

"Hope," Trish said thoughtfully. "And it's Arabic, right?"

It surprised Amal that she knew. Smiling brightly, she said, "Yes! How did you know?"

Trish smirked slyly and brushed off her shoulder. "I got it like that!"

"Oh please!" Louis said, sucking his teeth.

"Don't be a hater!" Trish said, flashing her million-dollar smile. "I think me and you are going to be friends. You wait and see!" Trish nudged Amal with her shoulder.

Amal and the others sat out on the porch and talked until it was time for dinner. They all filed inside one by one, the smell of Aunt Bobbie's food luring them inside.

"So what's this?" Amal looked at the main dish with a questioning glance.

"It's meat loaf, sweetie," Aunt Bobbie said as she set the table.

"You don't know what meat loaf is?" Kenya asked as if she thought Amal had broken some unspoken rule of living in the south.

"It's just ground beef with egg, some oatmeal to keep it together, spices, and tomato sauce. You bake it in the oven, and that's it—meat loaf!" Bobbie said, adding big bowls of mashed potatoes and mixed vegetables to the table.

She didn't really understand what it was, but she knew Aunt Bobbie could cook very well, so she ate her food happily next to Kenya. They would lightly bump the other's foot under the table and laugh in between bites of the yummy dish. Nobody but Aunt Bobbie noticed that Trish wasn't eating.

"Are you alright?" Aunt Bobbie asked. "If you want, I can make you something else."

Amal looked across the table to Trish to find the plate in front of her untouched. She sat with a solemn look on her face. She was like a different person from the bubbly woman she had talked to earlier.

"No, Mama, I'm fine. I'm just not hungry. Everything looks good though, Mama." Bobbie cut her a sharp look but didn't say anything, and the room was filled with silence.

Louis chimed in to break the silence, "Did anyone tell you about the lunch we're having tomorrow?"

"Oh really? And does it have something to do with Miss over here?" Trish smiled playfully at Amal while talking.

"I'm joining the crochet group!" Amal added, as she was happy to see Trish smiling again.

"Really? It's not often someone your age would want to do something like that. I think that's cool. I know a few stitches, but I can't make anything."

Trish refolded the napkin in her lap and placed it on the table. "When you learn how, let me know; I'll pay you to make me a few things," she said, giving Amal a wink and a smile before disappearing upstairs.

After dinner Louis helped her get the bags from her car. Amal had never seen luggage so colorful—bright pink, yellow, and turquoise with white polka dots—and they were all filled with stuff. Aunt Bobbie was over the moon to have her children back in the house. Amal wasn't so sure about Louis, but she could tell that she and Trish would become friends. She loved her energy and bright smile, even if her clothes were really tight.

When all the bags had been brought in, the night resumed as usual with conversation, bath, and bed. Kenya and Amal were tucked into their beds and left to think about the events of the next day. Neither of them could sleep, and they lay talking in hushed voices.

"So where are you from?" Kenya asked with a yawn.

Amal didn't want to think about her home, but she didn't want to be rude. "I am from Homs, Syria. It's a long way from here."

"But how did you end up here?"

Suddenly the memories of the night she fled with her father flashed in her brain. "It was bad there, so I fled on a boat with other people, but I don't quite remember how I got here."

Kenya turned on her side to look at Amal. "How bad was it? You mean, like a war? I learned about war in school, but I've never met anyone who was in one."

Amal sighed. "Yes, it was like a war. A lot of bombing and shooting, people dying and getting hurt." Amal could see her father lying on the ground that night when the sound of gunshots filled her ears. She didn't want to talk anymore, so she pretended to be asleep.

"Do you miss your home and your family?" Kenya asked, but Amal didn't answer and kept pretending to be asleep, hoping Kenya would fall asleep soon. Amal missed her home tremendously, but she knew there was no going back. As she started to drift off to sleep, she heard Kenya call her name a few times, but she didn't answer.

Amal

A Glimpse into the Past
Lost at Sea

The night she left was surreal. It was as if she were in a movie. When she got to the boat, others tried to join them, but there was no room. They watched as some of the ones who were left behind wept, and a few just stared as if they could see their fate before their eyes. Amal looked at them as she floated away, staring, until the people were nothing but tiny specks on the shore. The atmosphere was something out of a horror movie.

The water was icy cold and as black as ink and looked thick, like tar. Amal tried not to envision all the sea creatures below her, lying in wait. Knowing the only thing that was there to protect her was the flimsy lifeboat. The craft, which was packed with people, seemed to strain under their weight. Shivering as a gust of wind chilled her to the bone, Amal wished she had a coat or something to keep her warm; her clothes were threadbare and torn in several places. The woman that was sitting closest to her must've seen her shivering, as she handed her a piece of rectangular cloth to wrap herself in.

Amal smiled in thanks but quickly noticed the woman was no longer wearing her hijab, but when Amal tried to hand it back she just shook her head and said with a wink, "I'm sure the Almighty will let me get away with it, just this one time."

Amal was overcome by the kindness the woman had shown her. She was just some girl that no one knew, yet the woman had removed her own hijab just for her. Amal made a mental note to buy her a new one when they got to wherever they were heading.

Little Bird

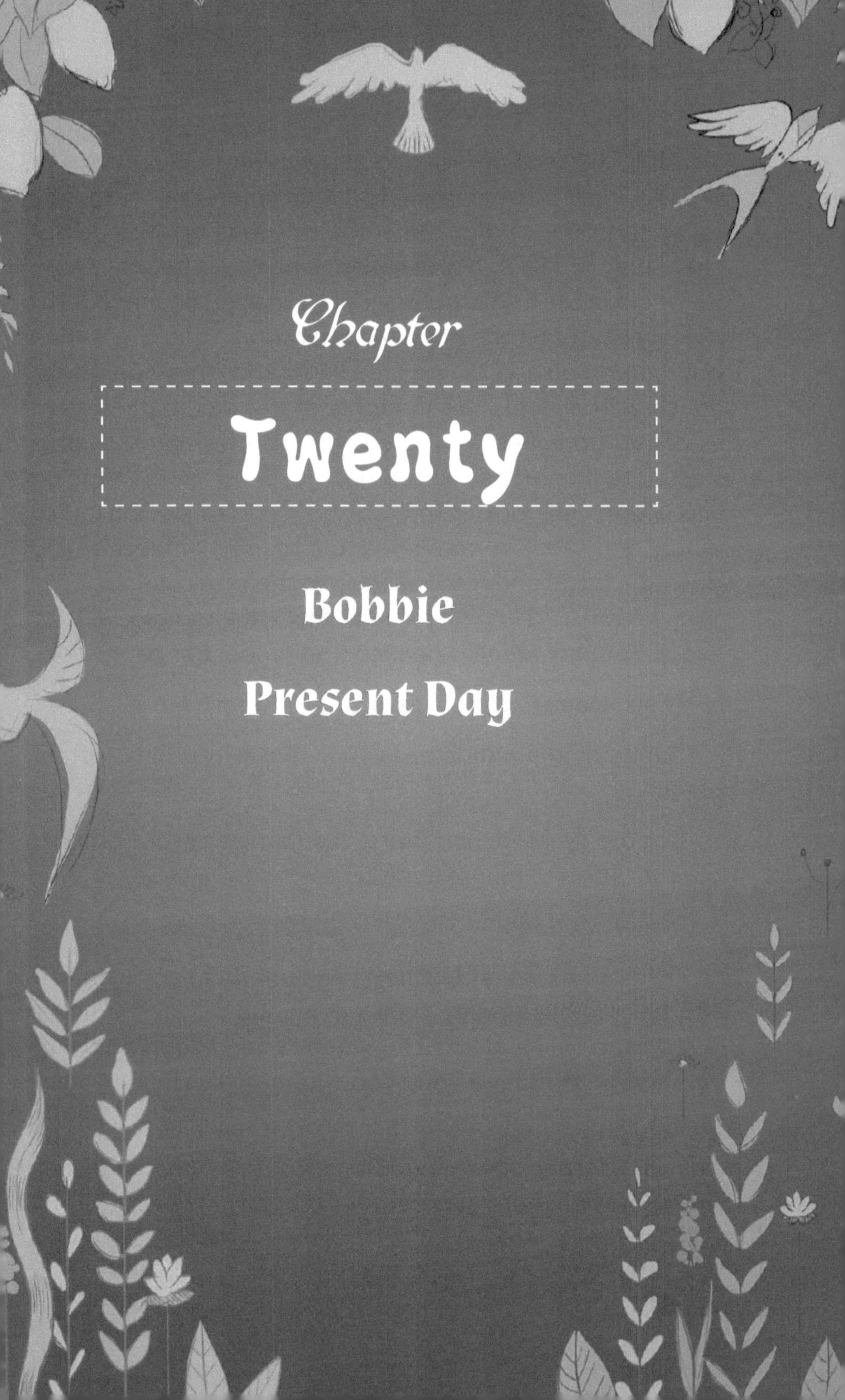

Chapter

Twenty

Bobbie

Present Day

After cleaning the kitchen and washing the dishes, she made herself a cup of tea and sat down on the couch. She loved this time of night when no one was up. Sometimes she'd pray or talk to her husband. If he could hear her now, he would laugh and probably call her crazy. She missed that man. Feeling that the lights were far too bright, she turned out the kitchen and dining area lights and curled up on the couch with a book, but thoughts of the day made it hard to concentrate. She wondered why Trish was back. Bobbie was more than happy to see her, but she knew something was wrong. She looked so tired and her eyes just looked so empty and sad. She could hear the thumps of feet coming down the steps, and she looked up to see Trish coming down. She was dressed in pink pajamas that were too big, with no socks. Her pink toenails peeked from under her pants legs.

"Can't sleep?" Bobbie asked, making Trish jump.

"Oh, Momma! I didn't see you! You scared the crap out of me."

Bobbie grunted. She didn't like that crap word one bit, but she chose to ignore it this time.

"Sorry, Momma."

Trish came over and sat next to her mother. As she looked into her mother's pretty brown eyes, she reached a manicured hand over and laid it on Bobbie's hand, rubbing it with her thumb. "How have you been, Momma? I've missed you."

As Bobbie looked into the eyes of her child, she saw sadness—despair, even—but she tried to hide it with her smile. She held her daughter's hand tightly in hers.

"What happened? Why did you come back?"

"Nothing. I just missed you, is all. It's been a while since I've seen you." Trish gave a weak smile.

Anger ignited in Bobbie's chest, and she had to fight it back. The one rule she had given her children growing up was to never tell a lie. If they told the truth, no matter how bad the situation was, they wouldn't get punished.

Looking at her daughter angrily because she knew she was lying, she said, "You must think I was born yesterday. Don't lie to me, girl! I haven't seen you in years, and all of a sudden you're back. I'm not angry because I haven't seen you, but I know you're lying to me."

And with that, Trish broke into tears.

Bobbie wrapped her in her arms like she used to when she was little. "Please tell me what's wrong."

But Trish couldn't speak through the tears she had been holding in for so long. She just shook her head.

"Please talk to me. I can't help if you don't tell me what happened. Did he hurt you?"

Trish tried to answer but she couldn't.

"Sshhhhhh, it's okay. It's going to be alright," Bobbie assured Trish. "You're here now. You're okay." Bobbie held her daughter's hand tightly in hers. They spent the next few hours talking about nothing in particular. Though it was only small talk, it seemed to calm her daughter, so she let the situation go. After years of not seeing each other, it was a breath of fresh air to Bobbie, who missed having little conversations with her daughter. When Trish was growing up, she had followed her mother everywhere she went. Bobbie had loved her little companion and had come to depend on her company—that was, until she'd met Randy. Trish had been in love, but Bobbie hadn't trusted him.

She had a hard time falling asleep after her talk with Trish. So the guy who was so sweet to her in the beginning turned out to be a monster. No matter what her daughter said or didn't say, she knew that Randy had been beating her. As she lay in her bed staring up at the ceiling, silently praying and trying to make sense of it all, she felt like a bad mother. It was her job to keep her kids safe, but she couldn't even do that. All that time, he had been pretending. Smiling in Bobbie's face only to go home and abuse her daughter behind closed doors. She could tell that Trish had some scars and bruises. Makeup never hid everything. She would never be able to get them out of her memory. As she faded into sleep she thought of all the ways she would kill Randy if she saw him again.

Amal

Present Day

It was 2:30 a.m., and Amal tossed and turned in her sleep. She sweated profusely, making her hair and nightgown stick to her moist skin. Her muscles jumped and her head shook back and forth as she dreamt.

Greedy hands held her down while one was over her neck. She tried to scream and kick, but she couldn't move. Massive hands with fingernails like claws ripped her clothes to shreds. Over her own fear and muffled cries she heard laughter come from the twisted faces of bloodthirsty demons. Once her clothes were off, they took turns with her, each man taking a bit of her soul with him until she felt hollow. Tired of fighting, she lay still. She knew there was no escaping. The monsters beat and abused her until she felt nothing. They tore out her innocence, piece after piece, then devoured it. She felt sharp teeth ripping her flesh with ease. Her body went limp with pain.

Bobbie

Present Day

The sandy seashore spread out as far as the eye could see. The water was so clear you could see through it to the fish that dwelled within. She walked on the shore hand in hand with her husband. Her small hand inside his huge one as they walked without words, they enjoyed each other's company. That's how their relationship was. They could talk about anything and everything, but they also loved quiet times together when no one had to say anything.

A light rain fell from the fluffy blue clouds, but they didn't run for cover; instead, they kept walking.

Bobbie often had this dream, and she cherished every moment of it. This was the only time she got with her husband, and she enjoyed it.

She looked up at him and smiled, but he didn't smile back. His face turned from content to frightened, and he yelled, "Wake up and go to the kitchen!" She looked at him with confusion written all over her face. "Why? What?" But before she could ask again he grabbed both her shoulders and shook her. The scenery changed suddenly, going from bright and sunny to dark. A storm was moving in, and a bolt of lightning hit the water. He yelled in unison with the thunder so loud it shook her to her core, "Wake up!" He shook her...

. . . And she jumped out of bed, awake before she even realized it.

Her legs moved without her knowing, until she was bounding down the stairs toward the kitchen. Amal was standing in the middle of the room with her back to her. She sighed with relief, thinking that the girl just wanted a glass of water or maybe a snack.

"Sweetie, why are you up? Come on, I'll take you back to bed." She walked over and gently grabbed Amal's arm, only to feel something warm come off on her palm. She looked down at her bloodstained hand in horror. Amal turned to face her, tears running down her face, and dropped the knife on the floor into a pool of blood that was slowly collecting around her tiny feet.

"I didn't mean to do it. I didn't mean it. What's wrong with me?" Amal's eyes rolled in the back of her head, and Bobbie caught her just before she hit the ground.

"TRISH! LOUIS! SOMEONE CALL 9-1-1!"

Amal

A Glimpse into the Past
Lost At Sea

If Amal had to guess, she had been on the water for a few days, but she wasn't quite sure. She was sunburnt, hungry, and sick. They lost a few people along the way. Some went crazy and had to be thrown overboard, a few threw themselves off as they didn't have any other means to kill themselves, but some just passed away. She hated that they had to be thrown over and not buried properly. They always said prayers for the deceased either before or after they were thrown over.

At only twelve years old, she'd seen so many terrible things, she didn't know if she could come back from it. Her appreciation for life was dwindling fast. She started out being afraid of death, but now she wished she'd just die and get it over with. The lady that gave her the scarf to keep warm with was the only reason she was still in her right mind. Her name was Hala, and she and Amal would chat when they had the energy. Hala liked to talk about her family but mostly about how life would be when they got to where they were going. Hala went on and on about it. Amal suspected she was trying to lift their spirits, and she appreciated it, but Amal had lived through too much to care. She doubted they would make it off the boat, which looked even worse than it had when they first began their journey.

Before the storm, there were only six of them left. The boat swayed up and down, making Amal nauseous, but she had nothing to throw up. Her lips and mouth were as dry as the desert, and her skin continued to burn as the sun bore down on her. She couldn't remember how long they had been on the boat. Was it a week or just a couple of days? She didn't know and, frankly, she'd stopped caring. No one said a word; they were all just as tired and dehydrated as she was. Every few minutes someone would moan or cough, but that was it.

Amal had never thought this would be the way she would die, though death wasn't something she had thought of much, but here she was, awaiting her time. She imagined what the angel of death would look like. *Will I be afraid when he comes for my soul?* The brief sound of thunder rumbled, snapping her out of her daydream. Clouds started rolling in slowly, giving her a terrifying feeling in the pit of her stomach. They would never be saved. There would be no happy endings for them. It was all over. The sky went from light blue to black in minutes, and the wind kicked up around them, making the boat sway even more. Amal looked up to the sky and felt overcome with helplessness. It was all over for them. The storm would be the end of their journey together. As the sky rumbled and the boat shook, all the fight she had in her disappeared. When the wind began to blow, the waves started to reach dangerous heights. Soon the rain beat about her head and shoulders. Something told her that it was the end for them. Her life and her journey would end there. With the realization that this would be the last of her life, she looked up to the sky and yelled, "Mama! Baba! Jannah! I'll be there with you soon!"

Bobbie
Saint Joseph's Hospital
Present Day

Bobbie sat resting her head on the wall behind her in the waiting room. Trish sat next to Bobbie reading and trying to pretend she wasn't as worried as her mother was. Every time Bobbie saw a doctor, she jumped up and kept replaying the night and what had transpired. *How did it come to this? I should've paid more attention to her.* The self-blame went on and on. The room was stark white, like the rest of the hospital, with a tacky green line down the center of the wall. It smelled like cleaning products and illness. She didn't know if it was the coffee or the smell that was turning her stomach. *What is taking them so long?* She checked her watch, and it said 4:24 a.m. It had been almost an hour and a half. She took a few deep breaths to slow her heartbeat.

"She'll be fine." Trish put her book down to calm her mother. "I don't understand a word I'm reading! I wish they would come tell us something, anything!"

"Me too," Bobbie said. She laid her head back in the same spot, trying to get as comfortable as possible in the chair, when a doctor came in and extended a hand toward her. "Hi. I'm Dr. Santos."

She and Trish quickly rose to their feet, shaking his hand. "I'm Barbara Bralev, and this is my daughter, Trish."

"And you're her . . . ?"

"I'm her foster mother and this is my daughter."

"It's nice to meet you both. Now let's get down to business. She did well in surgery. We had to reattach some tendons and stitch muscle back together. She lost a lot of blood, though, so we gave her a transfusion."

Bobbie shook her head absorbing everything he said.

"It's good that you found her when you did, but I have to ask: these look like self-inflicted wounds. Do you know if she was depressed or if something happened?"

Bobbie pressed her lips into a thin line. "She's been through a lot. Her family's gone. I'm all she has—we're all she has." It was as if speaking the words made everything more real. Blinking away tears, Bobbie added, "I was all she had and I let her down."

Dr. Santos put a hand on her shoulder. "You can't be there all the time. Sometimes things like this happen, but it doesn't mean you failed her. The best thing for you to do now is to love her, and we'll be here to help her get better, okay?"

All she could manage to say was, "Okay." Dr. Santos had stepped back to leave when Bobbie asked, "Can I see her now?"

The doctor shook his head no. "As I said, she lost a lot of blood and had to be taken to the ICU, where she's resting and being monitored. When she gets more stable, we'll call you back. You look tired. Go home and rest. Everything will be fine."

She had made the mistake once; she wouldn't do it again. She planted her petite frame in a chair and promised not to move until she knew for sure that Amal was okay.

"Come on, Ma. Go ahead and go home. I'll even stay if you want."

Bobbie rolled her eyes and folded her arms.

"Mama, don't act like that. You need to rest."

Bobbie didn't move a muscle. "I'm not going anywhere. I'm staying right here. I don't want her to wake up and find I'm not here."

Trish shrugged. "Okay then. I guess we're camping out here for a while."

Chapter

Twenty-One

Bobbie

Saint Joseph's Hospital

Bobbie had never been this anxious before. She paced the floor waiting for the doctor to tell her she could go in and be with Amal. Trish tried but failed to keep her calm. After two hours, she couldn't sit still anymore, and just before she was going to march up to the nurses' desk, the doctor came back.

"Mrs. Bralev, she's stable enough for you to go sit with her. She isn't awake yet, but just give her some time."

Bobbie and Trish grabbed their things in a hurry and followed the tall man down the hall until they stopped in front of a door. He gave it a gentle push and led them in. Bobbie could feel her heart beating in her chest, keeping time with the machines beeping and the faint sounds of breathing. Amal had the room to herself, which Bobbie thought was good, but she wasn't prepared for what she would see next. The doctor opened the curtain, and there lay Amal under several warm blankets. She looked so small, pale, and fragile. Her normal bright glow had been blown out like a candle in the wind. Bobbie wouldn't have known she was alive if she hadn't seen the steady rise and fall of her chest. The smells of hand sanitizer and rubber gloves were in the air. Bobbie gathered her dress and sat next to Amal's limp figure as she breathed heavily from beneath the pile of thick blankets keeping her warm. Bobbie searched for her small hand under the pillow, then brought it to her lips and kissed it, resting her cheek on the back of her tiny palm. Against the light skin of Amal's hand, Bobbie's skin shined like melted milk chocolate.

"I'm going to be right here when you wake up," she said as she smoothed a hair from Amal's forehead. "I'm not going to leave you here alone."

Amal

Saint Joseph's Hospital

Slowly the fog in her head began to lift as Amal heard the sound of a familiar voice that called her out of her sleep. When she opened her eyes, she found herself in a hospital yet again, but something felt different. Her arms burned and she couldn't move them. Still, the familiar voices kept talking as if she weren't there.

"Bobbie!" she called weakly, and before she knew it, both Bobbie and Trish were in the room.

"Praise the Lord, she's up!" Bobbie yelled, and Nurse Jackie ran in after them. She smiled sweetly when she saw Amal looking at her.

"I'm starting to think you keep getting sick so you can come see me, kid." Jackie smiled at her, while Aunt Bobbie was beside herself in tears. "They've been here this whole time, waiting for you to wake up," Nurse Jackie said matter-of-factly. "Why don't you both go and get something to eat, or maybe coffee, and I'll watch my favorite little patient?"

Trish grabbed her mother in a hug and kissed her cheek. "Come on, Mom. Get some food." And Trish ushered Bobbie out before she could argue with her.

"I'll be right down the hall! I'll be right back!" Bobbie called over her shoulder while leaving.

Nurse Jackie sat on the edge of the hospital bed, her weight shifting the mattress, making Amal's arms hurt. She winced before she had the time to play it off. "I'm sorry! I didn't mean to hurt you." Jackie said, moving to a safe part of the bed.

"It's fine. Why can't I move my arms?" Amal asked.

Nurse Jackie pulled back the sheets to show restraints on her wrists. "We had to tie you down just in case you tried to pull out the stitches in your sleep. We'll take them off as soon as they start to heal up, love." Jackie took the sheet and covered her arm back up, being careful not to hurt Amal. It was quiet for a few moments before Nurse Jackie broke the silence: "Are you going to tell me what happened?"

"What do you mean?" Amal asked, looking down.

"You know what I mean. Why did you hurt yourself? You can tell me."

Amal thought about what had happened and to be honest she didn't fully understand why she had done it, so she just shrugged.

"Hmmm," Nurse Jackie said before getting up. "Well, you're going to have to talk about it sooner or later. You have people that love and care about you. You remember that. I have to go make my rounds, but I'll be back when I can."

Amal turned her head to look out the small window that was to the right of her. She knew she had people who loved her, but she didn't know why or how they could love her. Later Bobbie and Trish came back with Kenya in tow. Kenya and Amal played a game of I spy after Bobbie covered her in kisses, then tentatively sat back and watched Amal's every move, like a mother bear watching over her cubs. Amal willed herself to be as normal as possible around Bobbie and even Kenya. She didn't want either of them to think anything was wrong, but she couldn't help but feel down. Her mind was so foggy that she had a hard time keeping a single thought.

Over the next few days, her trips to see Amelia were the only times she felt safe enough to say how she actually felt. She was tired in a way that sleep couldn't fix, and felt awful, but she was hopeful that the feeling would go away soon. Each day she woke up feeling worse than she had the day before. It got so bad that she stopped eating and talking completely. She was there physically, but her mind was elsewhere. It plagued her with thoughts of her past. The memories weighed heavily on her mind, making it hard to think or do anything else.

The sun was setting as she sat on the side of her bed, looking out the window. She saw cars and people walking back and forth. Kenya had stopped coming, as Amal just didn't have the energy to socialize. Bobbie came, but she generally just sat on the side of her bed and sang to her. She loved Bobbie's deep, sultry voice. It made the hurt go away. But today she was alone.

She looked down at her feet, wiggling her swollen toes. Her mama used to draw on her feet with henna. Beautiful flower designs had decorated her feet and legs. She missed tracing them with her finger. She thought of the way her mama would laugh when she ran a finger over her foot. Tears came to her eyes, but this time she didn't fight them; she let them flow freely. She cried and cried, until the front of her hospital gown was wet. There was a light knock on the door, and before she could wipe away her tears, Bobbie stood before her with a straight face. She had a white plastic bag in her left hand.

"I know I can't help you. The only person that can is you," Bobbie said, getting a paper towel from the bathroom. She came back and gently wiped Amal's face. "I love you, and I'm going to help you as much as I can, but you have to help yourself. I'm willing to fight with you, but you have to put in the work as well, and if you can't talk to me, then talk to the doctor. Talk to someone. You have to get all that hurt out of you because if you don't, it'll eat you alive." Bobbie placed the bag on the side of the bed next to Amal. "I'll be here with you through it all. We won't let this beat you," Bobbie said as she slid the bag to Amal.

Sniffling, she looked down at the bag and opened it. Inside the bag were many balls of bright, colorful skeins of yarn and a brand-new crochet hook and a book. She pulled the book from the bag, being careful not to hurt her arms. It read, *"The Beginner's Guide to Crochet."* The cover showed a pretty blanket.

It was all so nice that she couldn't help but smile. "Thank you!" Amal said, grateful for the gift and holding her arms up for a hug.

Bobbie gave her a warm hug and kissed her cheek. "We'll get through this together. Okay?"

Amal shut her eyes to contain the new tears that threatened to break free. "Okay."

It was around 1:00 a.m., and Amal couldn't sleep. She looked to see Bobbie sleeping peacefully on the couch in the corner of the room. Amal didn't want to wake her by turning on the TV, so she dug through the bag and got the book out with the little light she had coming from the bathroom. When Amal cracked the book open, she felt her world expand around her in the tiny hospital room. She had forgotten how much she loved reading until now. She read the first couple of pages and looked at the pictures, running her fingers along the shiny pages. She read the book from front to back, taking in all the information it had to offer. She learned about the different stitches and how to do them, but she wondered if she could execute them with the way her arms felt. She reread the book until the sun came up.

She read the book so much that during a session with Amelia, she asked, "I've seen you reading a book. What's it about?" Amelia had her hands around a cup of fragrant tea as she sat, slightly reclined, in her office chair.

"It's about crocheting," Amal answered.

"So you're thinking of taking up a hobby? I think it will be good for you to do something like that. It may make you feel better about yourself and give you something else to focus on. Have you started anything yet?"

"No, I haven't. I've just been reading it," Amal said, rubbing her hands together. Her cuts had started to heal so they itched like crazy. She thought she would go nuts if she couldn't scratch soon.

Taking a slow sip of her tea, Amelia placed it on her desk. "Well, what are you waiting on? You have the materials. You'll never know what you're good at until you try." Amelia smiled her bright white smile, her red lipstick framing her perfect teeth.

Amal couldn't help but think that maybe she was right. Maybe she could be good at crocheting, and if she wasn't, at least she could say she had tried. As she walked back to her room, she thought of all the colors of yarn she had. She debated with herself on which she should use first. She wanted to use the pink, but it was so pretty that she didn't want it to run out. Growing up, Amal had never had a favorite color. She loved all colors equally, but with the yarn it was different. Each color seemed to compete with the other, making the plastic bag they were in look out of place.

When she got to her room, Bobbie and Jackie were talking over coffee, the little Styrofoam cups tucked between their hands. Small plumes of steam danced above the rim of each cup.

"There she is!" Jackie said. "How was your appointment?"

Amal sat on the edge of her bed. "It was okay."

Bobbie shook her head and asked, "Did you talk to her like we talked about?" With both of them staring at her, she felt like she was under scrutiny. "Yes, ma'am, I did. She thinks me taking up a hobby is a good idea."

"It is! I can't wait to see the first thing you make! Bobbie was telling me about your interest in crocheting," Jackie said, then took a sip of her coffee.

"She's got lots of pretty colors in that bag there. I can't wait to see what she makes, either," Bobbie agreed.

"Well, I have your number now, so I can call and keep up with you, little lady. If that's okay with you, Amal?" Jackie asked.

"Of course it's okay! I would love that!" Amal said, beaming at the idea of being able to talk to Jackie.

"I'll give you mine so you can call me anytime you'd like."

Amal was over the moon. She had missed her friend, and now she would be able to call her whenever she wanted.

As Bobbie slept quietly in a chair on the other side of the room, she let out small puffs of air as she exhaled. Night had thrown its dark veil over the sky as Amal held the crochet hook clumsily in her right hand and looped the yarn around her fingers the way the book told her to. Amelia's voice repeated in her head: *"You'll never know until you try."* She had picked out the softest of the yarn in a bright, vibrant neon-green shade. It took her a few tries, but within an hour she went from making a slip knot to making a row of chains about a foot long.

"I did it!" she exclaimed, waking Bobbie out of a sound sleep by accident.

"What's that, sweetie?" she asked sleepily.

"I made something, Aunt Bobbie! I made something! See?"

Bobbie smiled, still hazy with sleep. "See? I told you. I knew you could do it."

She went back to sleep almost instantly, but Amal was ecstatic; she had done it. She was so happy with herself. She spent the rest of the night making chains, not realizing how long she had been working until the white line of sun came up, painting the sky bright pink. She rubbed her eyes; now she was feeling sleepy, but she looked down at her work and smiled. She had made a massive chain, twice as long as she was. And though it wasn't as fancy as the things she had seen in the book, she felt like she had made the best thing ever. Right then, she felt what real happiness was as she curled up with her creation in one hand and a crochet hook in the other and fell asleep with a smile on her face.

She dreamed that the sun was high in the horizon, but the sky was decorated in ribbons of different colors—pinks, purples, greens, and reds—in waving lines separated by solid, thin lines of black. There was a tree that at first glance looked like a regular tree, but as you looked more closely the bark swam around the tree in hints of brown and shimmering gold. The ground was warm beneath her bare legs, and she found she was wearing a dress that was the brightest pink she'd ever seen. Her hair hung down her back like a bridal veil. Around her lay skeins of yarn, tons of it, in different colors, and in her hand was a magical crochet hook. It was crystal and white but also had an opal shine to it. She could feel its warmth and wanted nothing more than to let it unleash its magic, but she couldn't stop staring at it. She grabbed a skein of yarn and began to crochet. A shimmering blanket began to appear, changing colors as it got longer. She grabbed one skein after another, adding different colors and textures to the blanket. The more she crocheted, the longer it got, until it covered every inch of the ground. When she was done she lay down and looked up at the sky with the magic blanket covering the ground around her as it emitted its own warmth and glow.

Chapter

Twenty-Two

Amal

Saint Joseph's Hospital

She woke up early Wednesday morning with yarn on the brain, but it would have to wait. Today she was going home! Amal still didn't understand what had happened to her that night, but she did feel much better. Her arms had healed quite nicely and only hurt a little, and the pills they gave her lessened the sadness. She rose from her bed and went to the bathroom, humming a lighthearted tune. Bobbie was gone when she woke up, but she was around somewhere. Amal grabbed her bag and went back in the bathroom to take a quick shower and dress. It took her a little under five minutes, and she was getting dressed in the comfortable pajamas Bobbie had bought for her. They were lavender with little kittens drinking milk and playing with balls of yarn. She was still trying to think of ways to repay Aunt Bobbie, but she had known her long enough to know she wouldn't accept any repayment in the form of cash, so she would make it up to her in hugs.

She left the bathroom thinking of her crochet book and all the things she was going to teach herself, when she saw the silhouette of a man in the doorway. She gasped and looked up to find an older man, probably in his sixties, with dark brown skin and a head full of gray hair, dressed in khaki pants and a red shirt that had been lovingly ironed. He smiled with his lips together, making wrinkles form around his eyes. He held his hat to his chest.

"Hello there, miss. I'm sorry if I frightened you. I'm Henry." His voice made her calm down instantly.

She straightened her back and smiled back at him. Something about the man made her feel comfortable. "Hi. I'm Amal."

"It's so nice to meet you, miss. I've seen you before, but I don't think you remember me. I've come to give you a ride home. Bobbie's already in the truck waiting on you. Are you ready to go?" he asked.

"Yes, I'm ready. All my stuff is here." Amal held up a full plastic bag.

"I can take that for you if you'd like," Henry said.

"Oh no! I've got it. It's not heavy at all," Amal said, but he took it from her hands anyway.

Mr. Henry was a true gentleman. He opened doors for Amal the whole way down to the car, making her feel like a princess in kitten pajamas.

When they got outside, Bobbie was waiting in the passenger seat of a red pickup truck. She waved happily at Amal when she saw her. Bobbie had changed and was in another one of her overly flowered dresses with a wide-brimmed sun hat that sat atop her curls. "Hey, baby!" she yelled. Amal could see the shadow of a smaller person in the back, who she guessed was Kenya.

"You ready, Miss Amal?" Henry asked as he opened the door to let her in. Amal was excited to finally be going back to Bobbie's home. She missed the comforts of her little room and the beautiful garden. She imagined herself sitting under the magnolia and crocheting until her fingers hurt.

She slid in next to Kenya, who gave her a big hug, and they were off. She could tell they were getting closer to the house, as the scenery changed. Buildings turned into trees, and trees turned into acres of fields and winding dirt roads.

She held her bag to her chest as she enjoyed the view. After about a thirty-minute drive, they finally turned onto a single dirt road that led to a long driveway, and before long they were in front of the house. Amal noticed a few cars out front, but she didn't pay them much attention. Something about the house made her feel at peace. It wasn't much to look at; it was just a tiny white house. But it was the people that she shared the house with that made it special. This whole time she hadn't noticed that Trish wasn't there. She had been a permanent fixture in her room at the hospital. She had fluffed her pillows and watched over her when Bobbie needed sleep.

"Where's Trish?" she asked as the truck rolled to a stop.

"She's in the house getting some things together. You just noticed she wasn't here?" Bobbie asked teasingly.

"Yes, ma'am, I did," Amal answered, smiling a bit.

"Silly girl," she laughed. "Now, Henry, come help me down out of this truck. You know my knees are bad!"

"Yes, Bobbie, I'm coming." Henry said, going as fast as he could, until he was right beside her. She held out her hand and exited the vehicle in a regal fashion, as if she were the queen, which she was in her own way, and her home was her castle.

Henry came over and opened the door for Amal. She had to be careful not to bump her arms. She jumped down with a thud, and Kenya came tumbling down to the ground after her. Bobbie held out a hand to both of them, and they walked hand in hand to the front door. Amal looked around at the little house and the plants in front of it. The house and the yard truly were a testament to Bobbie and her magic hands.

They climbed the steps to the house. Bobbie dropped Kenya's hand and knocked before opening the door, and Kenya let out a nervous laugh, which Amal thought was strange.

Why would she knock at her own door? And why is Kenya laughing?

But she didn't have time to process the thought before she heard people yell, "SURPRISE!"

Amal jumped back before Kenya pulled a spray can out from behind her back and shot silly string all over her. She was shocked, but Bobbie held her hand tight as she smiled and laughed a bit. The whole living room had been decorated with pink balloons, streamers, and a huge sign that said, "Welcome Back."

"Is this for me?" Amal asked as she walked in, trying to get the string out of her hair.

"Of course it's for you!" said a lady who was holding a box with the shiniest pink wrapping paper and the biggest bow she had ever seen. Trish stood beside her smiling. The woman stepped forward to introduce herself. "Hi, I'm Hattie Mae, but you can just call me Aunt Hattie."

Hattie was a tall, medium-built woman with a head full of hair that was done up in a tidy bun that sat gracefully on the top of her head. She was several shades darker than Bobbie, and she was just as beautiful. Her features were sharp. If you didn't know her, you'd probably think she was mean, with the way her face was set, but Amal could tell she wasn't.

"We've heard so much about you from Bobbie. She told us you were having a rough time, so we thought we'd throw you a little party," Hattie said. She was wearing a hot-pink-and-brown skirt suit with matching pink heels.

"Thank you. I really appreciate it. I love everything," Amal said, fighting back tears.

"No need to thank us! We love a good party, don't we, girls?" Everyone murmured in agreement; highly decorative hats bobbed up and down.

"I told you things would get better," Bobbie said, slightly squeezing Amal's hand in hers. Bobbie led her to a chair that Amal hadn't noticed. It was against the wall and was decorated with balloons, and the wall behind it was covered in huge paper flowers and letters that spelled out "Princess." It looked like it had taken forever to do. Bobbie placed a silver crown on her head and told her to sit down.

"These are the ladies from the group. Let me introduce you." From where she was sitting, Amal had a good view of all who were there. A group of six older women stood before her in bright, colorful clothing; some had matching hats that were covered in flowers. The smallest lady of them all stepped up and, in a tiny voice that she could barely hear, said her name was Viola. Viola was the eldest of the group, and she seemed very shy, but she didn't dress like it. Her outfits did the speaking for her. She wore a bright tropical-blue sundress that swiped the floor when she moved.

Her face was so round that when she smiled her cheeks pushed her eyes shut. She quietly said she was the founder of the group and how happy she was to finally meet Amal. Then came Tullie: She was about the same height as Bobbie, but her skin was the color of coffee with a lot of creamer in it. She wore a flowy green skirt that was to her ankles and a long-sleeved blouse with a huge rose pattern all over it. Her glasses were perched on the very end of her nose; the frames were rose gold, which set off her green-and-brown eyes. She was a ball of energy and joked that if Bobbie wasn't careful, she'd take Amal for herself. She also said how happy she was to finally meet Amal. The last three stepped up at the same time. One look at them, and Amal knew they were triplets. Augusta, Bama, and Pascagola were the first triplets she'd ever met.

"I'm the oldest," Pascagola said with an air of importance that made Amal want to giggle.

"You are not!" Bama interjected. "She thinks she is so important just because she happened to come out before us, but she's just full of sh—"

"Bama!" Bobbie yelled, cutting her off from finishing her sentence.

They were dressed in skirt suits of the same style but in different colors. Pascagola was in purple and lavender, Augusta was in yellow and pink, and Bama wore gray and teal. Each wore matching hats as well, with bouquets of flowers positioned on the tops of them. They were the same shade of toasty brown, but Bama was the tallest of the three. Each of them had completely different personalities, and when they talked she felt like she was a part of a TV show or movie, as they bickered back and forth a lot.

When Aunt Hattie finally broke them up, she laid the huge box in Amal's lap. Amal had never gotten something so big before, and she didn't want to open it. She would've been happy just looking at it, but they all insisted, especially Kenya. She took her time opening it, as she didn't want to tear the paper too much. She opened the box and peered inside to find that it contained a bunch of smaller packages, which were wrapped individually. Amal looked up, not believing that she was getting gifts.

"These are from all of us. Open them! Open them!" Kenya impatiently egged her on.

Amal took out the first package she put her hand on and began to unwrap it. She could see pink plastic peeking out as she ripped it open until it was fully revealed. It was a set of crochet hooks with pink grips. "That was from Bama." Amal looked up, smiled, and thanked Bama, who smiled back.

The next one was wrapped in purple paper. She tore at this one more urgently than the last, revealing clothes. Amal unfolded everything and realized it was a skirt suit like the one Hattie was wearing but in her size. She looked up at Aunt Hattie and could tell by her smile it was from her.

"I do hope it fits, dear. I'm sorry, I didn't know your size."

"Thank you! They're so pretty! I don't know where I'll wear it," Amal said, still holding it up and looking at it.

"I guess we'll have to throw another party so you can wear it," Aunt Hattie said.

Suddenly Amal jumped up from her seat and ran up the stairs, right into the bathroom, to put everything on. When she came out and marched down the stairs everyone cheered and fawned over her, their new little friend.

"You look like one of us now!" Hattie said, but Aunt Bobbie said that something was missing and went into the hall closet and came out with a round box. She opened it, revealing a hat. She placed it on Amal's head and ran to find a mirror.

"Now you're a proper little southern lady," Bobbie said. Amal looked at herself in the mirror. She hadn't felt this good about herself in a while. It took her a few seconds to take herself in, but once she did she put a hand on her hip and posed. She did look like a proper southern lady, and she loved it.

After the food was eaten and everyone said their good-byes, Amal lay in bed thinking about her day. She was beyond exhausted, but she couldn't stop smiling. She had met some of the nicest people today and couldn't wait to see them again.

"Did you really like your party?" Kenya asked.

"Yes, I loved it! It made me feel good."

Kenya seemed to think about this for a while before speaking. "See? I told you."

Amal, curious as to what Kenya meant, rolled on her side to look at her. "You told me what?"

"That people love you, silly. Even people who didn't know you did all this just for you." What Kenya said hit her heart when she realized what she was feeling, and she did feel loved.

"You know what? You're right. I don't understand why, but people do love me, and I want to thank you for helping me see that. You're a good friend." Amal rolled on her back and counted the dots on the popcorn ceiling.

"Thanks. I'm not trying to be mean or anything, but I have something to say." Kenya's serious tone made Amal roll over and look at her.

"Go ahead."

"Now you know people love you, so don't do that to us again."

Amal furled up her eyebrows. "Do what?"

"Hurt yourself!" Kenya leaped out of bed, clearly angry. "You almost died! We had to watch you the whole time. I didn't know whether you would come home or not. You have people that love you a whole lot, so you think about that the next time you think about hurting yourself!"

She looked Amal in the face with tears of pain in her eyes. Amal got up and walked toward Kenya until she was right in front of her.

"You're right. I'm sorry. I didn't mean to do it, and I really don't understand why I did it, but I'll never do it again."

Kenya let out a deep breath as though she were a balloon deflating. "You promise?"

Amal held out her pinky. "I pinky swear." They both smiled and locked fingers before climbing into their beds.

Twenty-Three

Monroeville, Alabama

Present Day

When Amal opened her eyes she glanced at the clock. It was only 2:00 a.m., but she was wide awake. She couldn't remember any dreams, if she had dreamed of anything. She quietly threw off the covers, slid her feet into her slippers, tiptoed toward the door, grabbed her bag of yarn, and made a beeline to the bedroom door. Quietly shutting the door behind her, she was immediately bathed in the stillness of the night. Trish and Louis had taken Kenya's room. She could hear soft breathing coming from that direction, and Bobbie's door was shut. She was the only one up. Holding her bag to her chest, Amal glided noiselessly down the stairs and tiptoed until she got to the back door. She slid it open as quietly as she could and waited to hear if she had woken anyone up. Nope, I'm good, she thought as she eased her way out of the small opening into the backyard.

The night was magical, to say the least. Fireflies swam through the air in time with the croaking of toads and the chirping of crickets. The stone pathway was lit with small lamps and wove its way right to the base of the tall magnolia. She removed her slippers on the porch and hopped barefoot from one stone to another until she was finally face to face with the magnolia. She didn't know why, but she felt as if she were intruding on something special, so when she reached the tree she spoke: "Excuse me, Miss Tree. Your branches and flowers are so lovely. May I have a seat?" She waited a while before she sat down on one of the large roots that peeked through the dirt. As she settled into her spot, a large blossom fell into her lap, and she took that to mean the tree was okay with her being there.

She said a quiet thank you and tucked the flower into her hair before empting her bag into her lap. The colorful yarn tumbled out, covering her thighs in a wash of colors. It flowed like a river of soft wool across her legs and her white nightgown. She found her crochet hook among the mass of fibers and positioned it in her hand. Since the "accident," she'd had a hard time holding things the right way, but that wasn't going to stop her. A light breeze blew, agitating the wind chimes. She closed her eyes and took in their melody until it was over and she found herself enveloped in the night's symphony once more. It was warm and her cotton nightgown clung to her back, but she wasn't moving anytime soon. She searched her small stash until she found some yarn she liked. It was called Cotton Candy and was a mix of blue and pink supersoft wool.

After positioning the yarn in her hand the right way, she began to crochet. She made a chain that was as long as she was. In the moment, she was calm and focused. All the pain she'd been through melted away. It was just her in this ethereal place. Bobbie's backyard was heaven to her. She heard everything and nothing at the same time. Sitting on the root of the tree, she was home. This was where Amal was meant to be.

Bobbie

Monroeville, Alabama

There was so much on her mind that she had a hard time staying asleep. She was happy but fearful at the same time. Happy because her girl was finally home, but fearful because she didn't know what would happen next. Things seemed so peaceful, and she wanted them to stay that way. But she wasn't a fool, and she acknowledged the fact that life didn't always cooperate. During Amal's hospital stay, she had prayed so much it became second nature, almost like breathing. Amal was home and seemed to be better, but she'd never forget what the doctors had told her. Amal had an emotional disorder from everything she'd been through, and she would more than likely be stuck with it for the rest of her life. Every day would present its own challenges, and Bobbie would need to learn more so she could better assist Amal through her struggles.

The house was quiet except for the light snoring she heard. She still didn't trust it, so she got up. She would just check the girls and go back to sleep. When she made it out in the hall, she saw that Amal's door was cracked slightly, and her heart leaped in her chest. She rushed to the room and swung the door open. She found Kenya asleep, but Amal was nowhere to be found.

Not again! she thought. She turned around and raced down the stairs as fast as her legs would take her. Amal wasn't in the bathroom or the kitchen. *Oh God! Not again!* She put her shoes on and ran out the front door, looking around wildly, and when she didn't find her there her instincts told her to look in the backyard. As soon as she slid the glass door open, she saw Amal under the tree, as pretty as a picture, with a flower in her hair, crocheting her little heart out. Amal seemed startled by the sudden noise and looked around, then smiled. Bobbie could feel her heart slow down. *She is alright, thank God. She is okay.*

Amal

Monroeville, Alabama

Amal had found her rhythm and was going at a steady pace when she heard a noise. It broke her concentration. She looked up and saw Bobbie standing in her pink robe and garden boots, staring at her weirdly. Amal just smiled, as she was happy to see her.

"Hey, Aunt Bobbie, look at me!" She held up her ridiculously long chain. Bobbie took a deep breath, then smiled back.

"You scared the daylights out of me, girl."

Amal thought about the past few weeks and realized what Bobbie probably thought. "I'm sorry. I couldn't sleep so I came out here. Isn't it lovely?" Amal hadn't realized that what she had done probably wasn't a good idea, but it was too late now. She made a note to remember to let Bobbie or someone know when she wanted to go outside.

"It sure is lovely out. You see why this is my favorite room in the house." Bobbie walked over and sat on the swing beside Amal. "Want me to teach you how to make a square?"

Amal nodded, holding her yarn and hook out to her. Bobbie shook her head no and went inside for a few moments and then came out holding a ball of yarn with a shiny hook sticking out of it. Bobbie came and sat in the same spot, placed the ball of yarn on her feet, and looped the free end around the hook. Amal couldn't help but notice how shiny her hook was. It had to be gold.

"You know, this was my momma's hook. This is the only thing I have of hers. It was the only thing I took."

"Do you miss her? Your mama?"

"Of course. Every second of every day. But she's always here with me. She's in the sky, the breeze, this tree. She's everywhere. That's what you have to remember. Your family is wherever you are. You keep them in your heart and your memories."

Amal thought about that for a moment, and some time passed before either of them spoke. When Amal looked at her, Bobbie had made a pretty long chain. "Now let me teach you how to add to what you have there." And that's how they spent the rest of their night. They crocheted and talked until sunrise.

***

Monday afternoon was hot and humid. This kind of heat made Amal sleepy. She lay on the floor of the living room, wanting to take a nap but not feeling like getting up. Right when she thought she had no energy to do anything, Kenya came downstairs and announced they were going on a long-awaited adventure through the woods behind the house.

"Kenya, it's too hot. Can't we stay inside?"

"No. We've been inside all day; plus I know where the lake is. We can swim and cool off." Kenya grabbed her hand and almost pulled her arm out of its socket. "Come on!"

So reluctantly Amal got up, and they left through the back door. As soon as the door was opened the heat rushed in, like wafts of heat from a preheated oven. She wanted nothing more than to close the door, lie down, and sleep, but Kenya persisted so she pressed on.

"Where do you think you're going?" Bobbie asked as they walked past her as she tended her tomatoes.

Amal secretly prayed she'd tell them to go back in the house.

"We're going exploring, Aunt Bobbie. We won't be gone for too long."

Bobbie stood up straight and winced with pain. "Okay, but you better have your butts back here before it gets dark. Be careful," she said and then went back to her gardening.

The wooded area behind the house spread out for miles. All Amal could see was trees. She wished she had put on pants, as bushes scraped her dress.

"Kenya, I don't think this is a good idea," Amal said, not wanting to admit she was afraid of getting lost. They walked until they got to an area where the trees were huge. She let herself imagine that fairies and trolls lived here. Her mama had read a book to her about an evil witch that lived in the woods. She lived in a creepy house and lured children into her home with promises of candy, only to cook and eat the children alive. Looking around, she hoped there was no witch in these woods, but as they walked she had a hard time thinking of anything else. *What would we do if there was a witch? Would she try to eat us?* she thought.

"Come on!" Kenya grabbed her hand, snapping her back to reality. She pulled her as they ran. A branch caught the end of her dress, ripping it, but Kenya was unstoppable. They ran until Amal could hear the sound of water. Only when they were standing at the river's edge did Kenya stopped running. "Take your dress off. We're getting in."

"What?" Amal asked, thinking she hadn't heard her correctly.

"We can't swim in these clothes. Take them off." Kenya stripped down to her underwear right there.

"Okay, but don't look," Amal said. She was shy about her body and didn't like the idea of stripping down in public, but Kenya gave her no choice.

"If you feel weird, just go behind a tree or something," Kenya said as she pulled off her shirt.

Amal looked around until she found the closest tree that she couldn't be seen behind and walked until she was standing behind it. She stood there for a few moments, trying to make herself do it.

"You done? Or do I have to come back there and help you?" Kenya yelled.

"I'm coming! I'm coming!" She stripped down to her pink underwear and undershirt, suddenly feeling too skinny and pale. She walked back, trying to cover herself with her hands.

Kenya saw her and laughed. "Girl, I ain't looking at you!" When Amal got closer, Kenya snickered. "This is good for you. You need some sun on that skin, you're so pale! Come on! Let's get in!" Kenya yelled excitedly.

"I don't know. I don't think . . ." Before Amal could finish her sentence, Kenya scooped up a handful of mud with a devious look on her face that told Amal she had better run. "Don't you dare!" Amal said, taking a few steps back. Kenya's smile grew wider as she stepped closer.

"What are you going to do if I do it?" Kenya asked, walking toward her friend slowly.

"I'm going to . . ."

"You're going to what?" Kenya asked. Every step backward that Amal took, Kenya matched.

Amal didn't wait for her to answer, and the chase was on. Amal turned and made a mad dash down the length of the river with Kenya on her heels, laughing like a mad woman.

"I'm going to get you!" she yelled. Amal and Kenya ran back and forth until they were dripping with sweat and panting for air. Amal was still running and screaming when Kenya's voice changed. "Can you hold on real quick?"

Amal turned to see Kenya bent over, and she didn't sound right. Something was wrong. Maybe the heat had gotten to her. So Amal made her way to her friend as quickly as she could.

"You okay?" Amal panted.

"Yes, I'm fine. I just needed a break. It's so hot out!"

Amal put a hand on her back. "I told you we should've stayed . . ." Before Amal could realize what was happening she felt something land on her head. She looked to see Kenya's smile going devious again.

"Gotcha!" And she took off running. Amal's head was covered in mud. Kenya would pay. She ran with everything in her and grabbed Kenya by the arm. They wrestled closer and closer to the water. Kenya was trying to push Amal into the water, and Amal was trying to push Kenya, until they both tripped, falling in the pleasantly cool water together. They laughed until their stomachs hurt; then Kenya swam to the middle of the river. Amal followed, trying to wash the mud out of her hair and ears.

"You're crazy, you know that?" Amal said, laughing.

"Yeah, I'm crazy! Crazy fun!" Kenya proclaimed as she crossed her eyes, then fell back into the water.

They spent the rest of the afternoon splashing in the water and enjoying each other's company, but when it started getting dark they came up on dry land, got dressed, and leisurely walked back. Amal was so tired that all she could think about was getting a nice hot shower and getting into bed. She would sleep soundly tonight.

When they made it to the back gate, they noticed Bobbie was gone. She was probably inside cooking. Amal's stomach roared at the thought of food. They took their shoes off and dusted their feet before walking into the house. The heat had completely dried them off during the walk back.

"Aunt Bobbie, we're back!" Kenya yelled. Amal wondered if Kenya knew how to whisper, before she heard the sounds of a familiar voice coming from the living room. He was sitting on the couch with his back to them. When Bobbie saw them she smiled. When the man turned, Amal's stomach dropped. It was Mr. Wright. Had she done something wrong? Was Aunt Bobbie sending her away? Her mind raced as she tried to remember if she had done something bad.

"Just the person we were talking about," Bobbie said. Mr. Wright gave Amal a tight smile.

"I've come to see how you are getting along. I see you're doing well."

"Yes, sir, I am. I really like it here." Amal looked at the man with pleading eyes.

"That's good. Very well, it was nice speaking with you, Ms. Bralev. I'm glad to see you're doing well, Amal," he said, making his way to the front door. Bobbie followed him outside, shutting the door behind them. It was only then that Amal could breathe; Aunt Bobbie wasn't sending her away. Her legs felt like jelly when Bobbie came back inside.

"That man is so dry. He wouldn't know a good time if it bit him in the behind," Bobbie said as she laughed to herself. "So how was your day? Are you hungry? I was thinking of making something quick since he came by so late."

Amal didn't care what she cooked. She was so overjoyed that Bobbie could've served handfuls of grass and dirt and Amal would've happily eaten it.

Later that night, Amal stood under the warm water of the shower trying to wash the leftover mud out of her hair. The shampoo smelled of pomegranates, making her homesick. She caught herself before she fell into a mood she couldn't get out of. She thought about her day instead and the chaos that had ensued at the hands of Kenya. She began humming some made-up tune. She could hear Trish and Bobbie talking downstairs. Trish was so loud that she reminded Amal of her baba. You had never known if he was upset or if he was just having a general conversation, because he was always yelling. Amal smiled thinking about her baba. It was easier to think about the good times than the bad ones, so she focused on the memories that made her happy.

Turning off the water, she hopped out and put on a cotton nightgown and slippers after drying off. It was hot so she left her hair wet. She felt the dampness of it cling to her back, and carried her clothes into her room to put in the hamper. She heard excited voices coming from downstairs when she was in the hallway, so she hurried down to find everyone crowded around the table. Kenya and Louis were sitting at opposite ends and were arm wrestling. Louis was clearly stronger, but he made out like Kenya was getting the best of him, which delighted her no end. He groaned and struggled as she squealed with delight. Bobbie and Trish were cheering her on. Trish abruptly turned to Amal and smiled.

"I got money on Kenya. How much you want to bet?"

Bobbie lightly hit Trish on the arm. "You know we don't do that gambling junk in this house, even if it is for play."

Trish shrugged and winked at Amal. "I got you next time," she said. And Bobbie hit her again. Trish laughed and began cheering.

After about a minute or so of Louis's pretend struggling, he finally gave out. Kenya stood in the chair, raising her fists to the sky, and yelled, "I am victorious!"

Everyone laughed before Bobbie shooed her out of the chair. "I don't need any more people in the hospital. My poor heart wouldn't be able to take it," she said, fanning herself dramatically. "Come on! Everyone off to bed! Good night."

Trish and Louis got up with Kenya and began heading upstairs. "You have a bedtime too?" Amal asked both of them.

Trish said, as seriously as she could, "As long as you're in this house, you do as you're told. I'm grown, but when Mama tells you to do something, you do it." She looked back at Bobbie after she said this.

Bobbie shook her head in agreement. "You're never too old to get punished around here."

Amal imagined Bobbie putting Louis or Trish in time-out, and she had to cover her mouth to keep her giggles in. Trish, Louis, and Kenya bid Bobbie a good night, each kissing her on the cheek, before going upstairs.

In the moment, Amal felt left out. Bobbie was their mother, and Amal felt like a guest intruding in a private moment. She dropped her head, said good night, and was about to scale the stairs when Bobbie called after her. "Where do you think you're going without giving me love?"

Amal turned around to find Bobbie sitting with her arms out. They looked so solid, but when she ran to hug her Amal felt the gentleness and love that was contained therein. Bobbie gave her a huge kiss on the cheek. "I don't know why you were trying to run off with my love." She held Amal close.

"I thought because they were your kids—"

Bobbie didn't let her finish. "You're my baby too."

Amal thought about this. "I just thought, because they look like you and I don't, that . . ."

Bobbie squeezed her tight in her arms. "You don't have to look like me or them to be my baby. You're my sweet baby, and don't you forget that. Now go to bed!" Bobbie sent her off with another kiss.

By the time she made it to her room, Kenya was fast asleep, clearly exhausted from torturing Amal during their day together. Amal listened to her steady breathing; it made her feel at home. She wrapped herself in her blankets like she was a caterpillar in a cocoon. Bobbie's words echoed in her memory as she drifted off to sleep: "You're my baby too, and don't you forget it."

"Hey, you!" Amal felt someone nudge her in her sleep. "Earth to Lady Bug! Wake up!" the person said in a hushed tone. Amal opened her eyes to find Trish standing over her.

"What?" Amal asked sleepily.

"I have a surprise for you, but it's going to take us a while to get there, so you're going to have to get up now."

Amal didn't know what was going on or why Trish was waking her up, but she swung over to the side of the bed and looked at her clock. It was 7:00 a.m. on a Friday morning. *What is so important that I need to be up this early on a Friday?* she thought, but she got up and went to the bathroom. After she washed her face she felt more human. Exiting the bathroom in a blouse and skirt, she went downstairs to find Bobbie had made them breakfast.

"So what's going on?" Amal asked, genuinely curious as to why she had been woken up so early.

"Trish wants to spend some time with you. She's taking you somewhere special," Bobbie said as she swept the floor.

"I thought we could use a girl's day out!" Trish came out of the kitchen, bubbly as usual, wearing loose-fitting clothes. Amal had never seen her in anything that wasn't skin tight, so she was pleasantly surprised by how nice she looked in them.

"Where are we going, though?" Amal asked.

"It's a secret, but trust me, you'll love it! It's going to take a few hours to get there, so you might want to bring something to pass the time." Amal immediately thought of her yarn.

"Should I wake Kenya up?" Amal asked.

"Nope! Today is just going to be you and me," Trish said. Amal was nervous. She had never been on a girl's trip before; only to sleepovers. And her mom or sister had always been with her.

After they finished their breakfast, Amal ran upstairs to grab her yarn bag, while Trish put on eyeliner and her huge sunglasses.

Trish

Present Day

"I'll meet you in the car!" Trish said, and about ten minutes later they were cruising down the dirt road that led to the highway. The morning was humid and very warm, so Trish cranked the AC all the way up. Amal's hair blew in her face. Trish giggled at the sight and turned the air down and passed her a pair of sunglasses, which were way too big.

"You listen to music?" Trish asked.

"Not really."

"Do you know who Beyoncé is?" Trish asked.

"Who?" Amal asked curiously.

"OH MY GOD! Did you live under a rock before this? You have to hear some of her songs. They get you in a dancing mood. No matter how bad I feel, I just turn this on and dance until my legs give out."

Trish pressed some buttons on her phone and plugged it into a cord that was attached to three pink speakers. Trish was right, and as soon as the music started playing Amal couldn't help but dance in her seat.

"See? I told you!" Trish said before she began singing along.

They went for miles, singing and dancing without a care, passing through city after city. Suddenly Trish grabbed her phone and pressed some buttons. The music kept playing, and that made Amal happy.

"We're going to make a little stop since we're making good time," she said as she turned onto an exit and made a left turn. They passed a huge building that Trish said was a mall. Amal wasn't paying attention to the music anymore, and sometime during the ride it had gone off. They weaved through traffic until Trish pulled off at a shopping center. It was a small cluster of businesses next to a McDonald's and a gas station. Before she could ask Trish why they were stopped, they pulled up in front of a store called Loops and Threads.

"This isn't the surprise, but I just thought we would stop here. Maybe you'll find something you like," she said as they got out of the car.

The sun was high in the sky now, beaming down on them and slightly burning Amal's skin. When Trish opened the door for Amal, she gasped. This place couldn't be real. It was a yarn store. She walked in slowly, taking in everything. They had every kind of yarn imaginable, wall to wall. A male voice greeted them as they came in, but Amal was too dumbstruck to respond.

"Well, hello, hello! What brings you lovely ladies in today?" the man asked cheerfully.

"She's new to crocheting, so I thought I would bring her in. This is a really nice place you have."

"Thank you. It's my pride and joy. So you say we have a new crocheter?"

That's when Amal looked at the man. He was probably in his fifties, wearing a bright sweater that looked handmade. "Yes. I just started," Amal said shyly.

"Well, aren't you just precious? Here, I normally charge for these, but I'll give you a few books. These talk about yarn types and come with patterns that are easy-peasy to do."

Amal looked around until she had seen everything, and with her hands full of books, she thanked Trish for bringing her.

"You didn't want anything?"

Amal hadn't come here with the impression that she would get anything, so she said no.

"Nonsense! Go pick something out," Trish said, not taking no for an answer.

"I think these things are nice, but I don't have money."

"Girl, no one asked you if you had money. I said pick something out!" Trish said as she put her hands on her hips.

It reminded Amal of Aunt Bobbie. She didn't move and just looked down. She didn't want Trish spending money on her. Trish got tired of waiting and went around picking out yarn that was obnoxiously bright.

"Here. You like these, don't ya?"

Amal couldn't lie. She loved them and shook her head yes.

"Then I guess we got what we came here for," Trish said as she walked to the register to pay for the yarn. Amal didn't even want to hear the total, so she walked off, pretending to look at some hooks.

When they were back in the car heading to wherever they were going, Amal kept her head down, the bag of new yarn in her lap.

"Why did you buy these for me?" Amal turned, looking at Trish, who had her eyes on the road.

"Because you like yarn and I like you. Plus you deserve them after all the shit you've been through." She smirked at Amal. "We're family now, and family does things for each other, so get used to it."

And with that she cranked up the music and a smile spread across Amal's face. They danced and sang until they were tired; then they turned the music down and Amal opened her bag of yarn. They were so soft and buttery that she had to stop herself from touching them.

After about an hour, Trish announced that they were close. Amal still had no clue where they were going until she saw the building. Masjid Taqwah of Birmingham, Alabama. Amal had to do a double take as she saw so many cars. She looked at the time, and it was around the time for the second prayer. Trish had driven her all this way to take her to see a masjid. Tears welled up in her eyes as she saw women in hijabs and abayas, some carrying children and some walking in together. There were people like her here. She couldn't believe it. Trish hadn't stopped the car before Amal took off her seatbelt and hugged her.

"If you hug me any tighter, you'll cut off my circulation!" Trish laughed.

"Thank you so much! You don't know what this means to me. This whole time I felt so lost, and now . . ." Amal couldn't finish for crying.

"Come on now! No more tears. We're going to be late. Prayer starts soon, right?"

Amal wiped her tears. "Yes."

"Then come on before we miss it!"

Amal and Trish followed the group indoors. The outside of the building was painted green and white. Amal wondered how they were able to keep the white so bright, but she didn't have enough time to dwell on the thought before she found herself inside the building. The entrance floor was shiny blue marble, and there were large white pillars along the walls. Shoe racks lined the faux mosaic walls.

"We take our shoes off here," Amal said to Trish, who was clearly awestruck at her surroundings. They removed their shoes and followed the blue marble floor to the entrance of the prayer area. Multicolored carpet, which had the same mosaic pattern as the wall in the entrance, ran from wall to wall. The smell of burning incense made the building feel warm and inviting. They took seats on the floor against the wall in the very back. Both of them looked around in awe, and for a few moments neither of them spoke.

"Where are the chairs?" Trish finally whispered.

"There are no chairs. We all sit on the floor. Only older people sit in chairs," Amal whispered back, not quite sure why they were whispering.

"Everyone here is so nice! They all speak and they don't even know us," Trish said while waving at a woman in a beautiful orange abaya.

"We don't need to know each other to speak. We're encouraged to treat strangers with the same kindness as we would a friend."

Trish nodded her head as though she understood. "Well, I love it!" She waved at a woman in black.

Not twenty minutes after they sat down a soothing male voice began making the call to prayer. Amal sat back and closed her eyes, breathing in the fragrant air. She felt his voice in every bone in her body and on every inch of her skin. The hairs on her arms rose up. When she opened her eyes, she saw Trish crying.

Amal nudged her with her elbow. "Are you okay?" she asked.

"It's just so beautiful," Trish said, wiping a tear that was running down her cheek.

When the sermon started, a man began speaking of charity and how it was obligatory for Muslims. He explained in great detail the significance of giving but also receiving.

Halfway through Trish leaned in to Amal and asked, "Where the heck are the men? I only see women here."

Amal giggled a little at the way Trish asked the question. It was like she was astonished that there were no men around. "They have their own area to pray. We stay separate," Amal whispered back.

"Oh!" Trish said.

The sermon was over in about thirty minutes, and then it was time to pray.

When everyone started to stand, Trish looked lost.

"It's just time to pray," Amal said reassuringly; then she walked over to a rack with white fabric draped over it, retrieved a scarf, and put it on.

She had walked back over to get in line when Trish said, "What about me?" before going to get one for herself.

"I'm sorry. I didn't know you wanted to pray," Amal said, helping her get the scarf on. They were huge and hung below their knees.

"Now what?" Trish asked.

"Time to get in line," Amal said, pulling her into the line. They got on the very end just in time for prayer to start.

After they prayed, Trish got caught up in conversation with a group of women whose clothes were draped over them and fluttered around them like the wings of butter-flies. Amal excused herself to go to the bathroom when she remembered she had forgotten to wash before prayer. While she was in the stall, she could hear the voices of younger girls, and she froze. A part of her wanted to go out and talk to them, but another part of her wanted to disappear. *They would never like me,* she thought. And before she could react one of the girls accidently opened her stall. "Oops! I'm so sorry!" she said after quickly closing the door.

The girl had seen her, so she had no choice but to go out if she didn't want to risk looking weird, so she flushed and opened the stall door. The group of girls was standing in front of the sinks, looking her way. She gave a quick half smile, then proceeded to wash her hands.

"Hi!" one of the girls said.

"Hi," Amal said, wanting to be anywhere but there in that moment.

"I'm Sara. I've never seen you around here before. You just move?"

"No, I'm just here visiting." The group of girls seemed to not like the idea of Amal having to leave. "My name's Amal."

"I like that name. My cousin's name is Amal."

Amal just nodded.

"These are my friends Rowan, Safa, Marwah, and Jawaher." They each said hi as they were introduced.

Amal took the group of girls in. Two of the girls were wearing abayas and hijabs; the rest were wearing skirts and long-sleeved shirts and hijabs. Amal heard the door open behind her, but didn't look. They smiled at whomever was coming in and brought their attention back to Amal.

"Nice to meet you, Amal."

"Nice to meet you too," Amal said, and looked up to see all of them smiling at her.

"Hey, since you're leaving, maybe we can exchange numbers?" the leader of the group said as more of a question than a statement. Amal was about to decline when Trish's voice boomed behind her.

"You sure can! Hi! I'm her sister!" Trish dug in her bag for a piece of paper to write the number on. When she found it, she wrote down the number and told the girls they could call anytime. One of the girl's mothers called them, and they made a prompt exit, leaving Amal behind holding the piece of paper with phone numbers on it.

"Look at you making friends!" Trish said teasingly.

Amal looked at the paper and wondered if they would really call. It would be nice to have more friends.

"Yeah. Thanks for giving them my number. I don't know why I get so nervous around people." Amal had never been shy, but recently she'd become more aware of herself.

"No problem! That's what I'm here for! Now come out! I saw a lady selling the prettiest clothes," Trish said.

It was around 4:00 p.m. when they finally left the masjid. They stopped at a Whataburger and got food. Amal loved the fries and spicy ketchup, so Trish got her a double order. After they ate and hit the road back home, Amal couldn't stop thanking Trish for surprising her today. She'd genuinely had a wonderful time.

They blasted music all the way back as they cruised down the highway. The sun began to set, and Amal watched the day turn to night. When they finally pulled into the drive-way, both of them were understandably tired from their trip. When they got inside, Bobbie and Kenya wanted to hear all about their day. Both of them took turns telling pieces of their shared story.

"Next time, I'm going too!" said Kenya.

Twenty-Four

Bobbie

Present Day

Mr. Henry took Bobbie to church every Sunday without fail, but since Amal's arrival, she hadn't gone. Since things had finally calmed down, she decided it was time to get back into the swing of things. She had ordered a few new Sunday dresses, with hats to match, from the Southern Miss catalog, that she couldn't wait to wear. Bobbie was from the old school where everyone dressed their best when they went to the house of the Lord, and Bobbie, being the mother of the church, kept the tradition going. The young ladies at the church knew what Bobbie would and wouldn't accept. She didn't believe in wearing casual clothes to Sunday service. One Sunday, a girl showed up in flip-flops, and Bobbie gave her the worst eye lashing she'd ever given, so naturally, the next time she saw the girl, she was wearing a pair of nice formal shoes and a dress that was past the knee. Mothers were said to use Bobbie's name when they wanted their daughters to dress appropriately. All they had to say was, "Mother Barbara's going to be there," and they would hurry to find something that Bobbie would approve of.

Bobbie put on a cobalt-blue skirt suit that was pressed as flat as paper. She removed the rollers she had set the night before from her hair, unleashing springy curls that she combed to make her hair wave and shine like glass. She sprayed on Chanel No. 5 and slid her feet into matching shoes before placing her hat on her head just right. She grabbed her purse, and as she headed downstairs, she heard Henry's truck pull up. Kenya was already downstairs and dressed. Having done her hair the night before, all she had to do was put on her Sunday dress and stockings.

"Should we wake Amal? Maybe she'll want to go."

Bobbie hadn't thought that Amal would want to go, as she wasn't used to that type of environment, and she was afraid to offend her and her culture.

"If she wakes up and we're gone, she might get scared," Kenya said.

Bobbie had to admit she was right. Though Trish would be here, she didn't want to make her feel like she had been left.

"Okay. Go see if she would like to go. I'll get Henry to wait."

Amal

Present Day

"Amal . . . Amal! Wake up!" She felt someone shaking her. She opened her eyes to find Kenya standing beside her bed in fancy clothes.

"What?" Amal asked, wanting nothing more but to go back to sleep.

"Come on! Me, Louis, and Bobbie are going to church. Come with us."

Amal hadn't showered let alone combed her hair. "I need a shower," Amal said.

"Don't worry about that. You can take one real quick. So you coming?"

Amal sat on the side of her bed, wiping the sleep from her eyes. She had never been to a church before, and the prospect of meeting new people was too exciting to pass up. "Sure, I'll go."

"Okay. Go wash up real quick, and I'll tell Aunt Bobbie."

Amal got off her bed and saw the pretty pink dress Kenya had picked out. She went to the bathroom and washed vital areas to ensure she wouldn't stink, and when she was happy she went back to her room to find Bobbie dressed in blue, sitting on the side of the bed.

"Good morning! Go ahead and get dressed. I won't look. After you're finished, I'll do your hair right quick."

She hurriedly put on the dress, stockings, and patent-leather shoes while Bobbie hummed to herself. "Done!"

Bobbie sat her down on the floor and got to work on her hair.

"I've never been to a church before."

"I know, sweetie. It'll be fine. You'll be with me the whole time."

"Are there kids my age there?"

"Yes, there are, and maybe you can make some new friends."

Bobbie pulled and combed until Amal thought she was trying to kill her. Once she was done, Amal looked at herself in the mirror. Bobbie had done her hair up in two braids and wove them together on top of her head. She put in the pretty pins Kenya had used when she did her hair the first time.

"Let's go!" Bobbie said, and in a few moments they were out the door.

Mr. Henry was waiting next to his truck with the doors open. Amal smiled when she saw him.

"Good morning, Miss Amal!"

"Good morning, Mr. Henry."

"It's such a fine morning, isn't it?"

Amal hadn't noticed, because she was rushing, but it was a fine morning. The weather was mild and the sun was shining bright. Her surroundings looked new and untouched. "Yes, it is Mr. Henry!"

When Bobbie was finally seated in the front, Mr. Henry helped Kenya in the back after Louis sat down; then it was Amal's turn. When she finally took her seat, she smoothed out her dress, not wanting it to get wrinkled. Henry slid in the front seat with more energy than she thought he should have, and they were off. She and Kenya counted cornfields and guessed at how tall they were, while Mr. Henry, Louis, and Bobbie talked. The way there was a nice ride, and Amal loved being out of the house and seeing the area she lived in. They turned down winding dirt roads without lights or street signs. Amal had no clue how they knew where they were going, but they did. Soon they started seeing people walking. All of them were dressed up and holding Bibles. They waved as they rode past until they were finally at the church. It was a tiny white building with a big wooden door. There were people parking their cars, walking in, and talking. Amal hadn't been nervous before, but suddenly she was aware of how different she was. *Will they accept me?*

She thought about just staying in the truck when Henry parked and Kenya said, "Let's go!"

Henry opened Bobbie's door first and helped her out, then opened the door for them. He held Amal's hand as she jumped down, her heart thudding in her chest as she looked around and saw who was there. Once a group of people saw Bobbie they began to walk toward her. Bobbie grabbed Amal's hand and looked down at her reassuringly.

"Is this the girl?" a woman in orange asked.

"Yes. This is my new baby!"

"Well, ain't she the prettiest little thing?" the woman said, pinching Amal's cheek and making her blush bright red.

Kenya laughed. "You're blushing."

"Leave me alone!" Amal laughed. "It's nice to meet you, ma'am," Amal said, shaking her hand.

"Oh, and so polite!" she said to Bobbie. "Honey, you can call me Aunt Sophie."

Bobbie held both Kenya and Amal's hands as she introduced Amal around to everyone. They talked until it was time for the service to start; then they began to file in. It took about ten minutes until they were finally seated. Kenya was on her left and Amal on her right in a seat right up front. Amal could see everything. The seats were long and wooden but surprisingly comfortable. The inside of the church was painted white as well, but the windows were beautiful stained glass. A large cross stood in the middle of a small stage up front with a stand and rows of seats behind it. A large group of women in purple abayas filled those seats in front; the cross and a man in a white abaya with a purple scarf with crosses on the bottom stood behind the stand. He said good morning to everyone, and everyone said good morning right back.

Amal looked around, taking in the scene. Everyone was dressed so nice and smiling like they were excited for what was about to happen. The man in white started by asking if there were any visitors and asked them to stand. Amal was confused, but she stood anyway. He thanked them for coming and told everyone to give the new ones a warm welcome. Everyone clapped, and then the visitors sat back down. Amal was happy to know she wasn't the only new person there.

Then the man started with the sermon. He spoke of love and forgiveness and how we have to forgive those who have caused harm. He explained that forgiveness wasn't for the other person, but for the ones who have been done wrong. He had Amal's full attention; the way he spoke had a way of drawing the listener in. He marched back and forth and spoke in a strange way that was like singing. It made her listen more intently.

Amal thought about her own situation and what had happened to her family. She hated the people who destroyed her life, and she wondered if she could ever forgive them. In her head she saw her house, her sister, her father, and those men as she pondered forgiveness. She thought about Percy and his evil girlfriend. What if she was hurting herself by not forgiving them for the things they'd done? She couldn't do anything about it, and as though on cue with her thoughts, the women began to sing, with their angelic voices sending shivers through her body. She was so moved by emotion that she didn't realize she was crying until Bobbie handed her a handkerchief and rubbed her back. She felt the women's voices deep within her soul. It was as though this were the first time she was truly hearing. It felt like they were singing for her. She didn't have the words for the way she felt, as she was overwhelmed by her feelings.

After the sermon, they had lunch on the grass outside the church. The atmosphere was relaxed and extremely social. Some adults were standing crowded together, and others sat on blankets on the grass, eating and talking. Bobbie had been whisked away by a couple of the women, so Amal watched some children about her age playing tag as she sat on a striped blanket with Kenya.

"You don't want to go play with them?" Amal asked, surprised Kenya wasn't running with them.

"I don't want to get my dress dirty. Plus I'm sitting here with you." She bumped Amal with her shoulder playfully.

"Well, hello there, young lady! How are you?" Amal turned to find Aunt Hattie standing with a hand on her hip. "Y'all better come give me a hug!"

Kenya and Amal ran to hug Aunt Hattie. She smelled of fried chicken and roses, as her perfume had mixed with the smells of cooking.

"How are you girls doing? You both look so cute!"

They told her they were fine, and after a short conversation, she was called away to start handing out servings of cobbler.

"Aunt Hattie makes the best berry cobbler. You want me to bring you some?" Kenya asked as she walked away.

Amal had no idea what cobbler was, but it sounded good. "Sure, I'll take some!" Amal said.

"Okay! I'll be back!" Kenya said.

Amal sat alone basking in the sunlight, still watching the kids play, when a blonde girl with brown skin came over to her. Her hair was shockingly light compared to her skin tone.

"I ain't never seen you around. I'm Willow."

Amal had to put a hand up to shade her eyes from the sun. "I'm Amal."

"What?" Willow asked loudly.

"Amal"—saying it a little slower so she could get it.

"What kinda name is that?"

Amal looked at the girl standing in front of her. "It's my name," she said, holding her head up high while looking her right in the eyes.

The girl raised her hands up in surrender. "I was just asking."

"And I was just saying." Amal didn't know why she felt the need to be firm with her. Amal knew she was the odd man out in this situation, but she wouldn't allow herself to be made to feel different.

"Willow, I think I heard your momma calling you," Amal heard Kenya say as she took her place next to her, holding two small bowls. Willow looked at both of them and walked away without another word.

"You okay?" Kenya asked Amal as she looked her in the eyes.

"Yeah, I'm fine." Kenya sat down and Amal followed.

"She can be mean at times. I won't let her bother you," she said, handing Amal a paper bowl. The smell of sweet berries and vanilla wafted up from the bowl.

It made her mouth water, and she dug her spoon in before saying, "What's her problem? I mean, why is she mean?"

Kenya wiped her mouth with a napkin, leaving a dark purple stain on the white square. "Sometimes her momma gets drunk and hits on her. She had to stay with us a while back because her parents got into a fight and both got locked up. Her aunt took her two sisters but wouldn't take Willow in because she causes a lot of trouble."

Amal looked off in the direction Willow had run.

"She pretends to be all tough, but she isn't. And she's definitely afraid of me, so she won't bother you."

Amal had eaten almost half the bowl. It was so good. She was stuck between wanting more and listening to Kenya when she asked, "Why is she so scared of you?"

Kenya put her bowl down beside her leg. "We were in the same class together last year, and she went on about how I was an orphan and how no one wanted me. She went on and on, and I was ignoring her until she called Aunt Bobbie a crazy old woman. Before I knew it, I was on top of her, punching her with both my fists. I got kicked out of school for a week, but it was worth it. I knocked two of her teeth out, and she's never spoken bad about Aunt Bobbie since."

Amal looked at Kenya, and she could still see the anger in her face as well as love. She hadn't cared what that girl said about her; it was only when she said something about Bobbie that Kenya got angry. Amal admired Kenya for so many things, but from that story, Amal learned more about her than she had in the past few months. When Kenya loved, she loved fiercely. As Kenya sat with both of her hands in fists, Amal smiled at her, and once she smiled back all the anger went away. Like that, she was the same silly Kenya she first met.

Amal looked at Kenya and, with a serious face, said, "I probably would've knocked her teeth out too."

Trish
Present Day

When everyone left for church, she finally had the house to herself, and she could relax. Other people had their ways of relaxing—some read books, some took hot baths, some ate chocolate—but the way she relaxed was by cleaning. She loved making things neat and tidy, so once everyone left she began her routine. She mopped the floors, dusted the furniture, and vacuumed till her heart was content. She would do anything to keep her mind off what was bothering her. It had been four, maybe five weeks, and her period hadn't showed up yet.

Before she left, she had already been a week or two late, but that wasn't the only thing that was bothering her. She was in the middle of cleaning the bathroom when she felt her phone buzz in her pocket. She dropped the mop and checked her phone. The caller ID said, "Unknown caller." She had been getting strange calls like that for about a week, and whenever she would answer, the person wouldn't say anything. She was beginning to get paranoid. *It's fine. It's not him.* One of the first things she did before she left was to get a new phone so he couldn't track her, but that wouldn't stop him. If he found her, she knew he would be mad enough to kill her. She tried calming herself down by picking up the mop and sweeping it back and forth in a meditative motion. *He doesn't know where I am. It's fine.* She would feel safer when everyone was home. Knowing they probably stayed after church for food, she finished mopping and then checked the doors to make sure they were locked. They always were, but she couldn't chance it. She was so paranoid that she half expected to see him standing in one of the windows, watching her.

After drinking several glasses of water, her bladder was full enough to pop, and she was ready to do what she needed to do. Trish dug the test out of her luggage and walked to the bathroom. Flipping the light on, she closed the door, locked it, and then opened the box and took out the instructions. After she was mildly educated on how to use it, she did it as quickly as she could and then placed the test on the sink. Her heart was lodged in her throat. If this thing said she was pregnant, she was screwed. What would she do? She had no job and was staying with her mother. There was no room in this house for a baby. She hoped it would be negative, that it was just stress that made her period disappear. The test took two minutes, and Trish paced back and forth in the hallway, her brain going ninety miles a minute.

When it seemed like two minutes had passed, she stopped pacing and stood in the doorway, willing herself to go look. Before she could convince herself to move, she heard commotion coming from downstairs. They were home. She quickly grabbed the test and ran for Kenya's room.

Chapter

Twenty-Five

Amal

Present Day

The smell of bleach assaulted their noses when Bobbie opened the front door and they all walked into the house.

"Trish's been cleaning," Kenya said.

"Good, we don't have to do it," said Louis, and he plopped down on the couch after kicking off his shoes.

"Boy, don't put your feet on my furniture!" Bobbie said, slapping his feet down to the floor. "You weren't raised in a barn!"

Amal ran upstairs to undress. When she got up there she saw Kenya's room door was closed. She started to knock so she could speak, but she changed her mind and went to her room. Once she was in a pair of jeans and a tee shirt, she came back downstairs, hoping Kenya would be up for going to the river. Trish was sitting at the table, looking out the window.

"Hey!" Amal spoke cheerfully, making her presence known.

Trish turned quickly, looking somewhat startled. "Oh hey, Lady Bug."

Amal could tell something was wrong. "Are you alright?" Amal asked.

"I'm good!" Trish tried to give her a smile, but instead she just looked tired. Then she turned her attention back to the window.

Before she could say anything else, she was interrupted by Kenya asking if she wanted to go outside.

"Can we go to the river again?" Amal asked.

"Sure! We can go rock hunting," Kenya said.

"Rock hunting?" Amal had never heard of such a thing and equated it to something American kids did.

"Yeah! It'll be fun."

Amal followed Kenya upstairs to her bedroom. "We need buckets," she said as she looked around. "There they are!"

She handed Amal a small orange bucket, and Kenya had a green one with a yellow handle. They were getting ready to head out when Trish rushed into the room.

"What are you doing in here? Get out!" Trish yelled.

"It's my room," Kenya whined.

Trish took a deep breath. "I know. I'm sorry." She slumped down on the bed. Amal wanted to sit next to her and make her feel better, but Kenya pulled her out of the room and shut the door before she got the chance.

"What was that about?" Amal asked. Kenya just shrugged and walked away.

Once they were finally outside, they walked through the woods until they got to the river.

"Okay, this is what we do. We find the biggest rocks from the edge of the river, and we collect them," Kenya said, instructing Amal as to what to do.

"Why are we collecting them?" Amal asked, clearly clueless.

"Just do what I say. You'll see later."

They spent the next hour searching for big rocks on the side of the river. Amal found some pretty big ones, and so did Kenya. When their buckets were almost full, they called it quits.

"What do we do now?" Amal asked.

"I'll show you when we get back."

They retraced their steps, and when they made it to the porch, Kenya told her to wait there. Amal stood holding a bucket full of large rocks, wondering what was going on. She didn't know if she should be excited or what. She leaned toward feeling weird about the whole thing until Kenya came back with her arms full of small bottles of paint and two brushes.

"We're going to paint them!" she announced, and dropped the armful of craft supplies on the porch before sitting down cross-legged. She put her hand on the spot next to her and motioned for Amal to sit there.

"You see all those painted rocks that make the pathway? I made those. I thought since you're my sister now that you'd like to make some too."

Had she heard her right? Had Kenya called Amal her sister? She sat down slowly, not sure what to say. "Your sister?" Amal's eyes were tearing up.

"Yeah! Duh! Bobbie claimed you, and when she does that there's no going back. You're one of us now." She smiled at Amal until she looked in her eyes and saw tears forming. "I wasn't trying to make you sad. Please don't cry!" She wrapped Amal into a hug.

"I'm not sad. I'm happy," Amal said through tears. "I'm glad that you think of me as a sister."

Kenya released her from her tight embrace. "Well duh, I think of you as my sister. You'd look like a weird brother," she said jokingly.

Amal laughed with her. "That's not what I meant."

"I know what you meant. I just wanted to make you laugh. You cry too much!"

"No, I don't!" she said blinking away tears.

"See? Big baby!" Kenya said as she poked Amal in the side.

"I am not! Anyway, show me what I need to do."

They spent the rest of their afternoon, and well into the evening, painting until dinner was ready and Bobbie called them in. Amal and Kenya's hands were covered in paint as they ate their dinner ravenously. Bobbie had to tell them to slow down. Louis cracked jokes as usual, but Trish wasn't her normal high-energy self. She just sat and picked at her food.

"You need to eat," Bobbie said to her. And without warning, Trish burst into tears.

Bobbie told everyone to leave the table because she wanted to talk to Trish alone. Amal didn't want to leave, as she felt the need to hug her. But she did as she was asked, and soon she and Kenya were upstairs playing a board game. Amal couldn't concentrate, though. She wondered what was wrong and wished she could help.

Bobbie
Present Day

"If I hadn't raised you, I would think you didn't like my food. Come here and tell me what's wrong," Bobbie said, looking at Trish, who got up from her place at the table and sat on the floor in front of Bobbie, laying her head in her lap. Now she was sobbing. "If you keep crying like that, you're going to make yourself sick," Bobbie said, wiping Trish's face with her dress.

"He hits me, Momma. I left because I thought I could get away from him. I know I should've told you, but I knew you would probably kill him. That man beat me every day since we were married. I didn't know what to do, so I just stayed. I thought it would get better, but when my period didn't come, I knew I had to leave. I'm pregnant and afraid."

As soon as Bobbie heard the word *hit*, she felt her blood pressure rise. Trish was right to think she would kill him, because she would've. There was no time for that now. Her daughter was pregnant and she needed her, so she just kept patting Trish gently.

"It's going to be alright. You're away from him now. You know I wouldn't let anything happen to you. If he dares step a foot in this house, I'll kill him right where he stands, but we don't need to think about that right now. You just told me that I'm going to be a grandmother! You're going to be a mother!"

"I don't know anything about babies, Mom. I have no way to feed or clothe this child. I have no home to keep him or her in."

"So we will make space here. You know your father left me a sizable amount of money when he passed, and as long as I'm here, you always have a place to stay. I told you that when you left. You can always come back here."

"Thank you. I love you," Trish sniffled.

"Me too," Bobbie said.

That made Trish smile a little to herself. When she was younger her mother had never been the type to verbally tell them she loved them, and she had to get used to giving hugs, but they knew she loved them by the way she went out of her way to make them feel it so they never had to question it. Whenever they would tell her they loved her, she would say, "Me too." Despite the situation, the answer was always the same. The only time she had told Trish she loved her was when she got married, right before she left. Sitting on the floor with her head in her lap, she felt loved, appreciated, and safe.

Trish and Bobbie said their good nights, and Bobbie went straight to her room and slowly kneeled before her bed. She let her knees settle in that position before she closed her eyes. She thanked God for keeping her daughter from being killed and bringing her back home. She also prayed for the baby, that the child would never have to endure what its mother had gone through.

Amal
Present Day

The day crept up on them slowly, turning darkness into light. The birds sang and flew among the clouds. Amal sat at her window wishing she could be a bird, even if it was just for a day. She wanted to know what it felt like to be completely free. She could go as far as her wings could take her, but after second thought, decided against it. She liked her life so far. Maybe she would fly around during the day, then come back to Aunt Bobbie's to sleep. A knock at the door stopped her in mid thought.

Trish poked her head through the partially opened door. "Can I come in?"

"Sure!" Amal was shocked to see her, but she was happy she wanted to come in.

Trish had been in an odd mood lately, so Amal had just left her alone. Trish sat down on the side of her bed. She was wearing a light-pink tee shirt and blue jeans that clung to her hips and thighs.

"I just wanted to apologize for yelling at you the other day."

Amal hadn't been mad about that. She had almost forgotten about it. "It's okay." Amal smiled.

"No, it's not. I had no right to yell. You see, I was trying to hide something," Trish said, her voice low.

"Oh! Like a secret? I love secrets!" Amal exclaimed. She was reminded of her sister and their late-night talks. Amal would sneak to her room, and Jannah would tell her things that she wouldn't tell anyone else. Amal had been the first to know when Jannah had a crush on the neighbor boy.

"You want to hear it?" Trish asked, scooting in close.

"Of course! I'm good at keeping secrets," Amal said.

"Okay, but only Momma and I know. You have to promise not to tell anyone."

Now Amal really wanted to know, so she sat on the bed beside her and slid in close, like she used to do with her sister. Trish cupped her hand around her mouth and whispered in Amal's ear.

Amal couldn't believe what she heard. She had to stifle an excited scream. "Really?" Amal said as quietly as she could.

"Yep. You're going to be an aunt."

Amal had to look at her to make sure she wasn't kidding, and she could tell by her face that she wasn't. "Do you know if it's a boy or a girl yet?" Amal asked excitedly.

"No, but I'll go to the doctor soon. You can come if you'd like," Trish offered.

"Yes, I'd love to come!" Amal gave Trish a tight hug and squealed.

"Cool! Now remember, it's a secret," Trish said, faking seriousness.

"I won't tell anyone," Amal said, her insides bubbly from the news.

Trish gave Amal's leg a pat before she got up to leave. "I'm going to go eat lunch. You want something?"

"No, thank you. I'm fine."

"You should go out instead of staying cooped up in this room. Go out to the backyard. Momma's out there, I think."

"I will," Amal said as Trish closed the door.

There would be a baby in the house. She couldn't wait until he arrived. She would help change diapers and play with him. They would get to go baby shopping and buy all those cute little clothes she'd seen at the store. She hoped it was a girl. She could dress her in pink and put bows in her hair. Amal was over the moon with excitement. Maybe she could make some stuff for the baby. All she could think of was her secret, and when she went to bed that night she dreamed she was playing with a chunky, smiling baby with no teeth.

Twenty-Six

Amal

Saint Joseph's Hospital

"So how have you been feeling? You look good!" Amelia sat behind her desk holding a cup of tea. She was in emerald green today. It looked nice on her.

"I'm good. I really like where I'm living. Everyone is nice," Amal said, feeling completely comfortable with her surroundings.

"That's good! How's your medication making you feel?" Amelia asked as she typed away at her computer.

"It makes my stomach feel funny sometimes, but I think it's working," Amal said.

"And no more hurting yourself?" This time Amelia looked up at her like she was her mother.

"Nope. Ever since I started crocheting, I don't feel like hurting myself anymore."

"I'm glad that you found a hobby that keeps you positive. So what have you made?" Amelia asked.

"Just a big rectangle. Aunt Bobbie says if I keep going, I'll have a nice lap blanket." The idea of having made something made Amal ecstatic. Amelia smiled at Amal without saying anything, and it made Amal feel weird. "What?" Amal asked, looking down at her scars, which were mostly healed.

"I'm just glad you found a good placement home. I was so worried after the first place you stayed."

Amal just smiled, not sure what to say. She could never forget that place and how badly she had been treated, but now she was in a place where she was cared for and even loved. She couldn't erase the memory of those terrible situations, but she could try to replace them with better ones. That's what Bobbie was helping her do. Being with her and her family made all the bad memories go away. For once, she was happy even though she had thought she'd never find happiness again.

When the session was finally over, Amal walked out of Amelia's office to find Bobbie and Mr. Henry waiting on her. While Bobbie read her Bible, Mr. Henry looked like he was about to fall asleep. As Amal walked closer she caught Bobbie's attention. She looked up and shut her book.

"Is everything alright?" Bobbie asked.

"Yes. Everything is good," Amal answered.

Bobbie and Mr. Henry stood and led the way out to the car. The ride back home was generally the same. Admiring the landscape always calmed her down. She imagined who might own some of the tiny houses she saw in the middle of huge fields of growing produce. She always knew she was close to home when the smoothly paved streets turned bumpy and dust flew around the vehicle. Mr. Henry would always say, "Hold onto your seats! It's going to be a bumpy ride!" Amal liked Mr. Henry and wondered why he and Bobbie weren't married. Maybe they would be soon. She made a mental note to ask Aunt Bobbie later.

It was scorching outside when they got out of the vehicle. After they survived the long walk to the house, they found Trish and Kenya at the dining room table, coloring pictures. The table was covered in crayons, markers, and colored pencils.

"Hey, Lady Bug. How did everything go?" Trish asked.

"It went well. We just talked, as usual."

Trish looked over at Bobbie as if to make sure it was true. Whatever was said in their silent exchange must've convinced her. "I'm glad to hear that everything is fine." Trish smiled.

"As long as I keep taking my medicine, I'll be okay," Amal said.

"Then we have to make sure you're taking it the way you should. No more scaring me, please."

As if on cue, Louis came in through the front door, carrying a large cooler that smelled strongly of fish. "Who's scaring who?" he asked, setting the cooler down on the floor.

"Boy, nobody was talking to . . ." Trish trailed off and got quiet before running to the trash can and throwing up. When she could get a breath in she asked, "What the hell is that in the cooler?" she yelled.

"Some fish I caught." He looked immensely proud of himself.

"Get it out before I get sick again!" Trish yelled, then gagged a few times. Louis just shrugged and took the cooler outside on the porch.

Aunt Bobbie brought Trish a towel to wipe her mouth, then a cold towel for her face. "Go lie down. You can come back down when you feel better."

"Want to color with me?" Kenya asked.

"Sure. I hope Trish feels better," Amal said as Trish slowly climbed the stairs.

"Aunt Bobbie will make something for her, and she'll feel better in no time—like she did for me one time. I had a virus and the doctor said it had to run its course, but Bobbie didn't listen. She went in the kitchen and mixed something up. It tasted terrible, but after about an hour, I was fine," Kenya said, waving her hands dramatically.

"Do you know what she gave you?"

"Nope. Even though I wanted to know."

Bobbie was mysterious like that. She loved taking care of children, gardening, and reading her Bible, but there was something magical about her. There was more to her than her garden and her big flowery dresses and church hats. Not to say that she was a witch, but something about her made everything wonderful. When she touched the seeds to plant them in the soil, lush bushes of vegetables and fruit sprang up, strong and delicious. If you were sad and she hugged you, all of it went away.

Bobbie

Present Day

The sun peeked through the tops of the tree, shining down brightly on the fish they were scaling and cutting up to cook for dinner. It had been a while since Bobbie and Louis had spent time together. She sat happily scaling the fish the way her mom had taught her. Louis had always been a natural fisherman. She could remember a time when he would go to the river with nothing but a stick and a piece of string and come back with a bucket full of fish.

Still keeping up her pace, she glanced over at him just for a second, taking him in. That was her boy, and God, did she love him, but she still felt like something was going on that he wasn't saying.

"You know I love having you around the house, but I was just curious as to when you'll be going back to school."

"I'll go back soon, Mom. I just needed a break." He cleared his throat and continued to clean the fish. His hands maneuvered the knife with ease. It took him seconds to gut and filet them.

"Have you got any friends there?"

"A few."

"Any chance I'm going to get any grandbabies soon?"

"Mom!" he yelled. His stomach flipped at what she was implying.

"I'm just asking. You're a handsome boy. I thought maybe you found a girlfriend."

"No, Mom. I've just been, you know, busy studying and stuff."

"Okay! I was just curious." Bobbie chuckled to herself.

She was old, but she wasn't dead. She would be a fool to think he wasn't fooling around with those loose college girls.

After they were cleaned Bobbie took the fish inside for frying. Cooking was her art, and in the kitchen, she was Picasso. A pinch of this, a dash of that, and the outcome was heavenly. She was taught to cook by her mother, who never used conventional measuring methods. She looked at seasoning or felt it in her hand and could tell if it was right or not. When the food was cooking, all she had to do was smell it to know what it needed or if it was just right. Her petite yet thick frame moved around the kitchen with ease and knew every corner and crevice of this room. Bobbie hummed as she seasoned the fish and shook the filets in mounds of cornmeal until they were completely caked in floury goodness. She eased the fish into the oil, which was another thing her mother taught her. Instead of dropping it in and making oil splash everywhere, she gently laid it in the oil until it was completely submerged. She loved the sound of fish frying. There was more than enough for all of them, so she decided on fish and grits for breakfast tomorrow.

Trish
Present Day

After dinner was when she started feeling better, so she made a mental note to try to keep something in her stomach during the day. She had offered to help Bobbie with the dishes, but the girls volunteered so Trish sat outside on the front porch looking out over the horizon. Patches of green landscape were covered in orange-and-red light as the sun set in its own time. She pulled a light blanket around herself, sighed, and, without thinking, put a hand on her belly. It was hard to believe there was a real person growing in there. While she went through the day, the little worm was growing limbs and developing so very quickly. Louis came walking through the front door, his long limbs swinging beside him, and he plopped down in a chair next to her.

"It's nice out, huh?" Trish asked.

"I guess," he said, unenthused.

"What's your problem? I'm surprised you're not painting right now."

"I don't feel like it."

"Why not? You're really good at it. You should go and get your paint. I'll be your muse," she said as she dropped her voice a few octaves and posed.

"Not right now."

If Trish had been looking at him, she would've seen him becoming visibly angry, but since she wasn't paying attention, she pressed on. "But I love—"

"Damnit! I come back and all everyone can talk about it school this, art that! I flunked out! Okay? Is that what everyone wants to hear? I am a failure!"

He was standing now with his hands at his sides in fists. His knuckles had gone white.

"I'm . . ."

"Don't say you're sorry. I'm the one that messed up. If anything, I should apologize to myself."

When he turned to go back inside he saw the door open, and standing there was Bobbie. He didn't know if she was mad, because of the blank expression on her face, but he didn't want to stick around to find out. He jumped down off the porch and walked down the driveway to the street, where she watched him walk away until he disappeared.

Bobbie

Present Day

It was past 2:00 a.m. and he wasn't back yet. She'd tried calling his phone, but she got no answer. She prayed as she paced the floor, thinking the worst, until she heard a noise at the front door. Bobbie's heart leaped in her chest when she saw Louis walk in. He looked tired and dirty, but he was alive, and that's all she cared about.

"Don't you ever scare me like that again! Where have you been? Are you okay? Do you want me to make you some food?" She was talking and checking him over and kissing him on the cheeks, all at the same time.

"So you're not mad at me?"

"Of course not. Why would I be? You made a mistake. So what? It's not the end of the world. Get up and dust yourself off. Don't wallow in your failure. I can't believe that you've forgotten that poem I taught you."

"No, Ma, I didn't," he said, but she began reciting it anyway.

> *Did you tackle that trouble that came your way*
>
> *With a resolute heart and cheerful?*
>
> *Or hide your face from the light of day*
>
> *With a craven soul and fearful?*

Oh, a trouble's a ton, or a trouble's an ounce,
Or a trouble is what you make it,
And it isn't the fact that you're hurt that counts,
But only how did you take it?

You are beaten to earth? Well, well, what's that?
Come up with a smiling face.
It's nothing against you to fall down flat,
But to lie there—that's disgrace.

The harder you're thrown, why, the higher you bounce;
Be proud of your blackened eye!
It isn't the fact that you're licked that counts;
It's how did you fight—and why?

And though you be done to the death, what then?
If you battled the best you could,
If you played your part in the world of men,
Why, the Critic will call it good.

Death comes with a crawl, or comes with a pounce,
And whether he's slow or spry,
It isn't the fact that you're dead that counts,
But only how did you die?

"I didn't forget the poem, but I love hearing it. It always cheers me up." He gave Bobbie a bright smile. It was then she knew she had her boy back. Her Louis was back.

"I keep forgetting you're just as hardheaded as me. Now go on upstairs and get a good shower and go to bed."

They said their good nights, and as she watched her son walk up the stairs, she could finally breathe a sigh of relief. She finally knew what was wrong. She could deal with this. After turning off all the lights in the house and making sure the doors and windows were shut and locked, she climbed the stairs as fast as her knees would let her, stopping at the top to listen to the sounds of sleep that echoed through the halls. The night was quiet, and she could hear no noise from outside. *It will probably rain tomorrow,* she thought as she shut her room door. Tonight Bobbie wanted to be comfortable, so she pulled out her favorite nightdress. It was billowy, like her other garments, but the fabric gave off a coolness. She loved the feeling of it on her skin, and when she slid it on over her head she smiled before curling up in bed under her favorite quilt. She didn't realize how sleepy she was, and before long Bobbie had drifted off to sleep, leaving the drama of the day behind her.

Chapter Twenty-Seven

Amal
Present Day

Amal awoke to the feeling of her stomach aching, and not a regular ache; this was something else. The pain radiated from her lower abdomen and up her stomach. She tried to roll over and go back to sleep, but the pain was relentless. After about twenty minutes of lying there wishing the pain away, she sat up, suddenly not feeling comfortable lying down. When she sat up she felt an odd sensation between her legs, a warm gushing. She panicked, thinking she had peed herself. She didn't understand how when her bladder wasn't full. Feeling the need to look down, she saw red on her white cotton nightgown, and she jumped up. *What am I supposed to do? Why am I bleeding?* she thought as she made a mad dash to the bathroom. She turned and looked at her nightgown to find a big stain of red on the back of it. She took it off and was standing in her underwear. *Nobody has hurt me, so why am I bleeding again?* She pulled down her panties and sat on the toilet just as another gush came, red and warm. She looked in the toilet in horror. She needed someone, but who could she ask for help?

She opened the drawer to find another set of pajamas and underwear. She folded toilet paper until it was about an inch thick and put it in her underwear. The first person she thought of was Trish. She had trusted Amal with her secret, so Amal knew she could trust her with this. She got up and, after making sure the toilet paper was in the right place, left the bathroom, moving noiselessly down the hallway until she got to Kenya's door, and then she froze. She thought of knocking, but she didn't want to wake up Louis. She took her house slippers off and turned the knob slowly; then she peeked in. Sure enough, Trish was sleeping peacefully on the bed and Louis was lying on the floor at the other end of the room. She waited a few moments before tiptoeing in. She would have to be as quiet as possible so Louis wouldn't wake up.

"Trish," she whispered. "Trish!" This time she shook her a little. Trish jumped up, looking around wildly, her curly hair in her eyes.

"Huh? What?" she said a little too loudly, still half asleep.

"Shhhhhhh . . ."

When Trish saw Amal she gave her a sleepy smile. "What's wrong, Lady Bug? Can't sleep? I don't have much room, but you can lie here with me." She grabbed Amal's hand, giving her a sleepy smile. Her hair looked like a wild animal had fallen asleep on top of her head.

"No! Something's wrong with me!" Amal said, on the verge of tears. Her stomach was doing jumping jacks as she stood there.

"What? What's the matter? You got sick?" Trish was now alert.

Amal was almost afraid to say it. "No, I'm not sick. I mean, I don't know if I'm sick or not."

"How do you not know if you're sick?" Trish asked, putting a hand on Amal's forehead.

Amal moved in really close and said as quietly as she could, "My stomach hurts here and I'm bleeding."

"You're bleeding? How?" As soon as she asked the question she understood and grabbed Amal's hand, moving out into the hall.

"You're bleeding from where?" Amal wrung her hands nervously as she stood before Trish suddenly feeling so small. "You can tell me," Trish said, putting her hands on Amal's shoulders. They stood there for what felt like hours until Trish broke the silence. "Okay. If you can't say it, can you write it down for me?" Amal hadn't thought about that and shook her head yes. Trish went back in Kenya's room and came out with a piece of paper and a pencil. "Here." Trish gave Amal the paper and pencil.

Amal stood holding the paper, not sure what to write. She looked nervously at Trish, who was waiting patiently for her to write something. She had to turn around and write on the wall; then she quickly gave the paper to Trish, not wanting to look at it. She shifted nervously as she watched her read it.

"Oh, sweetie! You got your period!"

"What's a period? I've bled before when I got hurt. No one has touched me again, so I don't understand," Amal said, trying to make sense of the situation.

"What do you mean, 'hurt you'? Someone hurt you and made you bleed down there?" Trish got closer to Amal, putting her hands around her face. Amal couldn't look her in the eye anymore, and Trish seemed to understand. "You don't have to tell me. It's okay. Come on."

She pulled Amal into the bathroom. The light seemed brighter for some reason. Amal stood in the middle of the room wringing her hands, while Trish dug through the small closet that was beside the door until she came out holding something that was in crinkly sounding paper.

"No one ever told you about your period, huh?" Amal shook her head. "Some people call it the curse, but don't you listen to them. It's a painful experience sometimes. You'll get more emotional than usual, but it's not a curse. You see, your period is what lets you have babies."

"Babies!" Amal exclaimed a little too loudly, so she covered her mouth.

"Yes. Your mother had one. That's how she had you," Trish said.

"Really?"

"Yes. Every female on this planet has one. How old are you?"

"I'm twelve," Amal said.

"Oh yeah, I got mine at your age. It's fine. Come, let me teach you about the wonderful world of pads," she said sarcastically.

Trish spent the next half hour telling Amal what she needed to do when her period came and what to expect. The more she told her, the better Amal felt about it. At least she didn't feel like something was wrong with her anymore. She was thankful that she'd live, but all this "period" stuff was too much for her. The idea of having to deal with this until she was older, like Bobbie, was baffling to her, but she felt special about becoming a woman. Her mama was a woman, her aunts, Trish, and Aunt Bobbie, so she was proud. She hoped she would be just as good as them.

"You know what I think?"

"What's that?" Amal felt strange wearing the weird piece of material between her legs. It felt like she was wearing a diaper. She was constantly trying to adjust it so it would feel a little more comfortable.

"I think we should have a period party. Just you, me, and that huge carton of chocolate chunk ice cream. What do you say?"

"Yes!"

"Let's go downstairs!"

When they were in the kitchen, Trish dug out the ice cream and Amal grabbed the spoons. There was no need for bowls. Between the pregnant woman and the newly minted woman, the ice cream didn't stand a chance. They sat next to each other on the couch with the ice cream in the middle. Amal was turned facing Trish with her legs folded under her.

"Word of advice: stay away from men. Far, far away from them until you find the right one," Trish said, waving her spoon in the air.

"I don't like men too much. They scare me," Amal said between spoonfuls.

"Sweetie, that's because you've been through some tough stuff, but believe me, when you find the right man, you won't be scared of him. Don't be like me. Choose wise-ly," Trish said with her spoon still in the air.

Amal thought it was funny how she punctuated every-thing she said with the spoon. "What do you mean?" Amal really didn't know. The only man she had loved was her father. Loving another man was perplexing. How could she love someone when she didn't trust them? The only thing men had brought her was pain and sadness. She didn't know if she could love one.

"When it's the right person, you'll just know. You won't be afraid."

Amal took in what she said, and they sat eating ice cream for several minutes before Amal thought of something to ask. "How was it when you started your period?"

"That's a funny story actually. I can laugh about it now, but then it wasn't funny. Me and Louis had been watching *Alien*. I don't know if you've seen it, but it's a movie about an alien that lays its eggs in people's stomachs and they burst out when they're fully formed. So we had been watching the movie before bed. After it had gone off we went to bed as usual, so I'm lying in bed and my stomach starts hurting, which wasn't unusual, as I had stomach problems growing up. But as the night went on, the worse it got. I have to say it was about an hour or so, and it was still hurting. I couldn't take it anymore, so I thought I had to go to the bathroom. I got up and went to the toilet and sat down, and I heard a weird splashing sound come from the toilet. I look down and see nothing but red. At this point, I'm panicking because I got it in my head that somehow the alien had laid an egg in

me and I had just given birth. I took off running and screaming with my butt hanging out. It took Mom twenty minutes
to catch me and calm me down. It was a mess—literally and
figuratively!" By now Trish was having a hard time telling the
story because she was laughing.

"Really?" Amal couldn't help but laugh too.

"Yes, and the whole time I'm screaming, 'I don't want an
alien baby!'"

Trish lay back on the couch laughing and coughing.
Amal tried to stifle her laughter, but the sound of Trish's
laugh made it funnier. Trish wiped the tears from her eyes
and looked at Amal.

"You know, I'm glad I met you, Lady Bug."

"I'm glad I met you too."

The lighting in the room began to change as the sun
started coming up. Amal began to cramp again, so Trish
gave her something and told her to go to bed. Amal remembered her sheets, and Trish followed her upstairs and made
quick work of them without waking Kenya, who was still
sound asleep when Amal slid back into bed. Trish winked at
her over her shoulder before closing the door. She savored
the taste of the chocolate flavor that was still in her mouth.
Hours before, she had been terrified, but Trish had made
things alright. She was a good friend and would be an even
better mother.

Bobbie

Present Day

After her shower, she dressed in her room and thought of what to cook for breakfast. It was only 6:00 a.m., but people would be waking up soon. Then she remembered the fish she had cleaned the day before. Fish and grits was what they would have. She ran a comb through her hair, making it wave and shine, and headed downstairs to the kitchen and was surprised to see Trish up and reading a book on the couch.

"Good morning, baby. How did you sleep?"

"I didn't get much sleep. I have something to tell you." Something in Trish's tone told her she would need to sit down for this, so she sat right next to her on the couch.

"What's the matter?" Bobbie asked, looking her over.

"I'm fine, but our Amal became a woman last night," she said, looking at her mother.

"You mean . . ."

"Yes," Trish said as she put down her book.

"Why didn't you wake me up?" Bobbie jumped up. "Oh Lord! My baby has become a woman, and I'm the last to know?"

"Mama, calm down!" Trish said calmly.

"How am I supposed to calm down? She needed me and you didn't wake me up!" Bobbie said as she paced back and forth in a small circle.

"The girl was so embarrassed she couldn't even say what was wrong. She had to write it down on paper. I took care of it, and she's upstairs sleeping," Trish reassured her.

Bobbie took a few calming deep breaths. She would never act like this in front of Amal, but she wasn't around so she could panic all she liked. "Did you give her something for pain? Or a heating pad?" Bobbie asked.

"Mama, she's fine. I took care of it."

"I'm going to go wake her. Maybe she needs something." Bobbie took quick steps toward the stairs. Trish stepped in front of her and grabbed her by the shoulders.

"She's fine. The only thing she needs is more chocolate ice cream. We ate it all. Sorry." Bobbie took an exasperated breath and put both hands on her hips. That was her signature look; whenever you saw that pose, you knew Bobbie meant business.

Trish smiled at her mom before yawning. "I think I'm going to bed myself. Mom, it's okay. She's fine, and please don't call too much attention to her when she does wake up. You know how you get."

"Little girl, you might be grown, but I'm still your mother. You don't tell me what to do. I'll do as I please."

Trish threw her hands up in surrender. "I apologize, Mom. You're right." Trish walked over to her mother and kissed her on the cheek. "Good night, Mom."

Chapter

Twenty-Eight

Amal

Present Day

She spent ten minutes looking at herself in the mirror. Trish had said she was a woman now, but she didn't look any different and certainly didn't feel much different. She was just in a lot of pain. Bringing up a hand, Amal traced the outline of her heart-shaped face slowly with her fingers until she was at her neck. *Nothing is different.* When she thought about women, she thought of her mama. Her mama had been a woman in every way she wished to be. Her mother was beyond beautiful; whereas Amal was just okay to look at. She wanted the beauty of her mother and grandmother, the kind that didn't age and only got better. She wanted her mother's smile, full bosom, and her flowery laugh. Standing in the mirror, she just felt plain; nothing close to her mother or her sister, even. She wondered when she would receive her share; when would God shower her with his favor and his blessings? Amal didn't know, but when he did, she would share it with anyone and everyone she could.

After her morning routine, she found herself in Kenya's doorway, watching Louis paint. He had a paper plate with dollops of every color in the rainbow on it. They looked pretty enough to eat. She had gotten used to having him around, so she was no longer terrified to be around him.

When he saw her there, he moved to the side so she could see his work.

"How long have you been painting?" He jerked his head up and looked at her as if he didn't think she would speak to him. It took him a minute to formulate a sentence, and when he looked at her, she smiled.

"I started painting when I was about your age."

"Oh, cool." Silence hung in the air for a few moments. "Well, it was nice talking to you," she said, turning to leave.

"I can teach you if you want." Louis said it so low she didn't hear him correctly.

"What?"

"I can teach you, if you want. To paint, only if you want to, though," he said, sounding a bit nervous. Amal could tell he wasn't much of a talker.

"Sure! I would like that."

"Cool, just meet me outback after lunch. I like to paint out there in the afternoon," he said before going back to his art. Last thing Amal saw was him dipping his paintbrush in a thick green glob of paint.

Downstairs, she could smell cooked fish. Bobbie and Trish were both sitting at the table talking when she walked in.

"Good morning, sleepy head. You slept in this morning," Bobbie said.

"Good morning. Yes, ma'am, I was just tired."

"Are you feeling okay?"

Amal had two choices: she could tell Bobbie about her period, or she could pretend it never happened and let Trish tell her. Amal chose the first option. She needed to get used to talking about it; plus Bobbie deserved to know. So she balled her hand into a fist and just said it: "I got my period last night."

"Oh my! You're a little lady now!" Bobbie smiled.

"I was scared at first, but Trish helped me."

"That's because she's my sweet girl, just like you," Bobbie said, giving Trish's hand a pat. "Now, if you need anything or if you start hurting, let us know."

Amal shook her head in agreement. "Where's Kenya?" Amal asked. She hadn't seen her all morning.

"She should be in the backyard. If you're going out there, be careful now. You don't want to have accidents." Bobbie said it in a way that Amal understood she meant her period. "Oh, and the yarn club is meeting in a few hours. You feel up to going?"

"Yes!" Of course she did. She wanted nothing more than to learn to crochet and visit with Aunt Bobbie's friends again. The thought of finally going to the group made her happy. She almost forgot about her cramps.

"Go ahead and take a shower if you need one. Henry will be here in a few," Bobbie said as she got up.

After taking a shower, she had the hard decision of picking out something to wear. Amal was so excited as she looked through her tiny closet, throwing out clothes that wouldn't do. After deciding on a blue shirt with jeans, she made sure she had pads in her pocket and grabbed her bag of yarn before running downstairs where Bobbie was waiting. She looked vibrant as usual in another one of her floral-printed dresses. It wasn't long before she heard Henry's car pull up in the driveway. She waited until she heard a knock to answer the door.

When they reached the church Amal saw a few cars parked out front. When Henry let them out, he told them he would be back to pick them up in an hour. Amal didn't like that she would only be there for an hour, but it was better than nothing. Holding her bag to her chest, she followed Bobbie inside. She was shocked to see how many women there were. Some were just chatting among themselves, and others were already working on their projects. When they saw Aunt Bobbie walk in they all flocked to her like they hadn't seen her in years. After being introduced to over twenty people, Aunt Hattie called everyone to attention.

"Hello, ladies!" she said brightly. Everyone said hello in unison. "Today we have a few announcements before getting started." She waited for the people who were standing to find seats. "We have a new member. Please give Amal a warm welcome." They all looked at her, smiling, some nodding their heads, making her feel self-conscious with everyone staring. She had to be the youngest person there, which added to her nervousness. Amal gave everyone a small smile back and looked down at the floor.

"Before we start our Healing Circle, I would like you all to know that we've got a big request from the hospital for preemie clothing and blankets. So when you all are ready, please move the chairs in the right formation so we can get started."

Amal didn't know what a Healing Circle was and was too shy to ask, but then Bobbie spoke. "We do what we call a Healing Circle. We put the chairs in a big circle and we crochet things for the community, and we also talk. In the Healing Circle you can say whatever you want and no one will judge you. We help other people, and we also help ourselves by talking about our problems. Some of these ladies have gone through some hard situations in life and just need someone to listen to them." Amal nodded, not completely understanding, but she was sure she would by the end of the meeting.

After the chairs were in the right position, they all sat down and got their supplies. Some started making hats, little socks, and the tiniest clothes she had ever seen, and when they finished an item they all added them to the same box. Amal liked that everyone worked together for a good cause.

Bobbie sat next to her and helped her start a granny square. "If you keep going, it will get big enough to be a baby blanket. Just do a few rounds, tie off, and drop it in the box."

At first Amal had a hard time doing it the way she was told. She dropped stitches or she didn't make enough, but Aunt Bobbie was patient with her.

"Don't worry. You'll get the hang of it."

She worked until she finally had something worth giving. "Look! I did it!" she said to Aunt Bobbie, who was working on a tiny hat.

"Good job! See? I knew you could! Is that going in the box?"

"Do you think someone would like it?" Amal asked, unsure.

"I sure do! Go ahead!"

And with that, Amal dropped her little blanket into the box. She sat back down feeling like she had conquered the world.

The room was full of chatter until it was time for the Healing Circle to begin. Aunt Hattie got everyone to quiet down. The rules were, anyone could talk and no one was allowed to laugh or make fun. Everyone waited from someone to speak, and soon an older woman started talking. She had a friendly face, but her eyes looked tired. Her son was addicted to drugs, and she had tried everything to make him better, but he just wouldn't stop. She said that she was afraid it would kill him and she couldn't stand the thought of losing him. As she spoke everyone listened quietly, respecting her feelings and words. You could tell she just needed someone to listen to her. She thanked everyone after she was done telling her story. A few of the ladies got up and hugged her tightly, telling her it would be okay and that they were praying for her and her son.

Amal loved the group for the creative outlet it gave her, but she developed a new appreciation for the women in the group. She fully understood why they called it a Healing Circle, by the time the hour was up. People spoke of their problems or their worries, and the rest of the group was reassuring and loving. Being a part of the group gave her a sense of peace, and when it was time to go, she left feeling like she wasn't alone. Amal decided that maybe she would speak next time, but she would have to figure out what she would say, as she didn't want to divulge too much information about herself. She still worried what people would think of her if they knew some of the things that had happened to her.

As they were riding back home, she looked out at the horizon past the fields of produce. Tiny puffs of white cotton stuck out among the green. The sky spread across the plains in a thin line of light.

"So how did you like it?" Bobbie asked.

"I liked it a lot," Amal said, still looking out the window. The dirt roads made the truck bounce.

"School's starting in a few months. You think you'll be ready?"

Amal thought about this for a second. She was frightened by the idea, but she would have to go. "I guess I'm ready," Amal said.

"You know there's nothing to worry about. You're a smart girl. I think you'll have friends before your first day is over," Aunt Bobbie said.

"I hope," Amal said, unsure.

"You will. I know it."

Once they made it back to the house, Amal was so tired. She didn't know why, but the idea of taking a shower and getting in bed was so tempting to her. "I'm going to go to bed," she said to Bobbie.

"Are you feeling alright? You need something for cramps?" Bobbie asked, looking concerned.

"No. I'm alright. I'm just really tired for some reason," Amal yawned.

"Oh, you're period will do that to you. You go ahead and go to sleep. You want me to save you some dinner?"

Amal just wanted to curl up in bed and go to sleep. She wasn't the slightest bit hungry. "No. I'm not hungry. If I need something later, I'll just make a sandwich," Amal said, yawning again.

"Okay. I hope you feel better."

She gave Aunt Bobbie a quick hug and made her way to her room. Kenya was sitting on the edge of her bed with a first aid kit. She had her pants rolled up, exposing her knee.

"What happened?" Amal asked.

"I fell out of the tree. It's fine. How was your day?" Kenya asked.

"I had fun. I'm tired though, so I was coming to shower and go to sleep." Amal went to her dresser and picked out some pajamas. They smelled clean and were buttery soft in her hands.

"I was going to ask if you wanted to sneak out and go hunting fireflies," Kenya said as she closed the first aid kit.

"And do what?" Amal asked.

"Fireflies! Lightning bugs! They glow in the dark, like they have little flashlights on their butts."

Amal laughed at this description. "Oh! Sure! That sounds fun!"

"Well, take your nap, and I'll wake you up when they come out," Kenya said, rolling her jeans over her bandaged knee.

Amal quickly showered, then fell into bed, so tired she couldn't keep her eyes open. Finally surrendering to her drowsiness, she slept peacefully until Kenya began poking her. It felt like she had only been asleep for a few minutes, but when she opened her eyes, everything was dark. She sat up, trying to wake herself up.

"What's wrong? Are you sick or something?" Kenya asked.

"No, I'm fine," Amal said through a yawn.

"But you slept for so long!"

Amal turned to look at the clock. It was 1:00 a.m. She wished she could lie back down, but she didn't want to go back on her promise to Kenya, so she got up.

"You don't have to get dressed. We're just going to the backyard," Kenya said, shoving a mason jar in her hands. "Follow me!"

Grabbing Amal's arm, she dragged her to the sliding door that led to the backyard. Amal could hear crickets and frogs chirping. It instantly put her in a better mood, but she wasn't ready for what she saw when Kenya opened the blinds. There were little holiday lights floating through the air. There had to be hundreds of them. Amal had thought the backyard was magical before, but now she was absolutely sure of it. She stood at the door gawking at the lights until Kenya pulled her outside. She was surrounding by these little insects. They swirled around her, buzzing with delight. She spun around slowly, trying to look at them all.

Her cotton nightgown swirled around her. She took in the backyard in all its glory: the garden, the hand-painted stone pathway, the fireflies, and the giant magnolia tree that was shedding its blossoms at will.

They spent about forty minutes outside. Amal took her seat under the tree and watched Kenya chase the little bugs. She tripped about eight times, and in the end she didn't catch anything. Kenya ended up convincing Amal to help her. Both of them clumsily ran around the yard with their jars in hand, but neither was fast enough to catch them. They ran until they were tired and ended up lying on the ground counting stars.

Kenya rolled over to look at Amal. "You know who's really good at catching fireflies?" Kenya asked.

"Who?" Amal asked, rolling over to look at Kenya.

"Louis. He can catch tons of them. Let's go wake him up!" Kenya jumped up to run inside. Amal caught her just in time.

"We can't go around waking people up in the middle of the night."

Kenya shrugged. "He isn't people. He's Louis! He'll be okay with it."

And she took off running toward the back door; Amal followed closely behind. When they got in the house Kenya started tiptoeing; Amal mimicked her—half because she didn't want to wake anyone up, but mostly for the sheer fun of it. Kenya pushed her door open until they saw Louis asleep on the floor.

Kenya whispered, "I'll do it. You keep watch."

Amal didn't know why she was keeping watch, but she did what she was told. She stood there until Kenya emerged with a shirtless Louis wearing a sleepy grin. Amal quickly looked away and covered her eyes. He noticed her embarrassment and decided to go back in and put a shirt on. When he came back out, he shut the door silently and led the way until they were outside again.

He twisted off the lid in one smooth motion. "Back up and let a pro teach you how to catch them." Kenya rolled her eyes as he rolled up his sleeves. "See, the trick is, you have to be very still and catch them when they least expect it."

Amal watched as he stood in the middle of the backyard holding the jar in position before he quickly pushed the lid on the top of the jar, catching about four of them. "See?" he said proudly.

Amal walked up to look in the jar. The little creatures inside flew around trying to find their way out. She couldn't help but think of how weird they were. God had given them their own little flashlights. It made her grin, looking in the jar.

"So I take it you've never seen them before?" Louis asked, taking in Amal's curiosity. "I've seen them. I've just never caught any. They're so pretty."

"I used to catch these all the time when I was your age."

"So what do we do with them?"

"Normally I just look at them for a while and then let them go. Mom doesn't like keeping things like that in the house."

Amal watched as he unscrewed the jar and let them go. She watched them fly away until she couldn't see their lights anymore. Remembering Kenya was outside with them, she looked around to find her friend gone. She and Louis went back inside, being careful not to wake anyone. "Good night, little lady," Louis said before he opened the door to the bedroom.

"Thank you for helping us," Amal said, truly thankful that he had given her a chance to experience something new.

"No problem. I'll be here whenever you need my services. All you have to do is knock."

Amal giggled as he did an exaggerated bow and flashed his pearly white teeth before going back into the room. Amal, still wondering where Kenya had gone, opened her door to find Kenya sitting on her bed. She didn't look at her when she came in, so she sat down beside her.

"Where did you go? I thought you wanted to catch the little bugs?"

"I did, until you got so fascinated with Louis. You like him or something?" Kenya looked at Amal strangely.

"Like him? No! I thought you wanted him to show me how to catch them. You went and got him."

"Well, you didn't have to start ignoring me," said Kenya, folding her arms on her chest and sticking out her bottom lip.

"Are you a baby?" Amal said jokingly, nudging her with her elbow. "Let me go get you some milk, baby." She messed with her until Kenya began to laugh.

"I'm not a baby!" she laughed.

"Well, don't act like one! I thought we were sisters? Sisters don't get jealous of other people. Friends get jealous. My sister never got jealous when I played with my friends, because she knew no one could take her place." Thinking about her sister made her heart ache, but she wasn't going to cry.

"You had a sister? I mean, before me?" Kenya asked. Her full attention was now on Amal.

"Yes, I did. She was older than me," Amal said as she got up to lie in her bed. The night's magic had worn off.

"Was she pretty, like you?" Kenya asked, clearly fascinated that Amal had a sister.

"No, she was prettier. Her hair was long and dark black," Amal said, picturing her sister in her head.

"Longer than yours?" Kenya asked.

"Way longer," Amal said with a sigh.

"She sounds pretty."

"She was and she was nice. She always played with me and took me to get candy."

"Do you miss her?"

"Every day I miss her and my parents, but I love my new life here as well."

"Hey, sorry about getting mad," Kenya said.

"It's okay. I was jealous of Louis too, at first, so I understand."

Amal waited for an answer, but hearing her breathing pattern change, she turned and found her friend fast asleep. That night her brain was crowded with thoughts of her family. She missed them and wondered how it would be if they were still alive. She loved nighttime, especially when everyone was asleep. It was quiet, but she also hated it for that same reason. She thought about things that she could ignore during the day. When she was with Kenya she didn't think about the things that made her sad. She closed her eyes and envisioned her mama and baba and how the days they spent together were her favorites. She was so happy then. Though she was happy now, it wasn't the same. At times she felt like she was intruding on someone else's life.

When she finally fell asleep, she dreamed of her sister in the prettiest dark-pink dress. She twirled like a ballerina from a distance until she got to Amal. They were face to face, and she was just as pretty as Amal remembered her.

"See? I'm okay," Jannah said before placing a warm kiss on Amal's forehead.

Amal watched as she twirled around and leaped through the air with grace until she was out of view. Amal frantically searched for her, wanting to spend more time watching her dance, but she was alone. Amal awoke feeling at peace with the dream. Hopefully, wherever her sister was, she was happy. She couldn't help but think that maybe, in some weird way, it was God letting her know she didn't have to worry about her anymore and that her sister was at peace.

Twenty-Nine

Bobbie

Present Day

When she rose from her place of sleeping, Bobbie immediately went to take a shower after turning on the sprinklers in the backyard. Everyone was still asleep, so she had more than enough time to start breakfast. After she showered and dressed, she was ready for her day. She had a list of things that needed to be done, but she noticed a pain developing in her back, so she decided to make a list and give it to her children. If each of them did something from the list, it would be done in no time. She sat down at the table with a pen in hand and wrote down exactly what she needed done until she was happy with it. Just as she finished Trish came bounding down the stairs. Her belly seemed more pronounced than it had the day before.

"Good morning, Mama!" she said cheerfully as she gave her a quick peck on the cheek. "What are you writing?" she asked as she went to the kitchen to get a glass of water.

"Just some chores I need done."

Trish came back, set her glass on the table, and plopped down in a chair beside her mom. She instinctively put one hand on her belly.

"Oh okay. We'll get those done for you. Are you feeling okay?" Trish asked.

"Girl, I'm fine," Bobbie said dismissively.

"Momma, come on. The only time you ask for help is when you're not feeling good." Trish looked at her sideward.

"I'm okay. My back is just bothering me," Bobbie said as she felt a sharp pain hit her lower back. She winced before she had a chance to catch herself.

"You need to go to the doctor. Something could be wrong." Trish held her hand.

"You know I don't like doctors. And something is wrong–my back hurts. It'll be fine. Tomorrow I'll be all better."

"Momma!"

Bobbie raised a hand to stop whatever Trish was going to say. "Don't 'momma' me! They'll charge me just to tell me what I already know. I'm not going. All I need is some prayer and a few aspirin. I had eight children without a doctor. I don't need one now."

"But Mom, its 2017! We do things different now. You have to give it a chance. A lot's changed in the medical field."

Bobbie didn't want to hear it. Like she said: she'd had eight children naturally. What could a doctor tell her that she didn't already know? She would take a few pain pills and relax on the couch with a book and her heating pad. She would let them do the rest.

"I'm fine and I'm not going anywhere. I'm going to make breakfast, and that's it." She struggled to get up, fighting with the sharp pain in her back. It was winning.

"I'll do it! You just stay still. After breakfast, I'll give you a good massage. Okay?"

Now, she would normally say no. Bobbie wasn't the type that liked to be touched, but if she could get rid of this pain to allow her to do some gardening, she would make an exception. Trish went into the kitchen, and before long the smells of breakfast wafted through the house. She came out with plates of French toast, eggs, and turkey bacon.

"Are the girls up yet?" Trish asked.

"I'm not sure. I haven't heard them get up."

"I'll go get them. I'll be right back."

"Girl, you need to be careful yourself. You don't want to stress yourself out with that baby in there."

Trish put a hand over her small bump and smiled. "I'm fine. I'm not stressed at all. I'll go get them."

"Well, at least take your time. Don't move so fast. You don't want to fall."

"Okay, Momma." And she went up the stairs one at a time for Bobbie's sake. When she came back down she was followed by some exhausted-looking children who needed a good hair-combing.

"Good morning!" Bobbie greeted them.

They croaked back a halfhearted good morning. About five minutes later, Louis came down the stairs, shirtless and beaming from ear to ear. He had always been a morning person. The girls, seeing him shirtless, made noises of disgust and covered their eyes. Bobbie couldn't help but laugh.

"Tell Louis to put a shirt on, Aunt Bobbie. He's walking around naked," Amal said.

"Boy, go put on a shirt before you blind the girls."

He left and came back quickly, wearing a wrinkled blue tee shirt. Still smiling, he apologized and told everyone to go on eating. The plates were empty within minutes. Bobbie loved to feed people. It was something she truly enjoyed. There was nothing like sitting back and watching someone enjoy food that was well prepared. Bobbie herself didn't eat much, but she urged others to eat their fill. Trish and the girls cleaned the table, then the kitchen, and Kenya went upstairs to shower, and Louis went out back to paint. Trish found some muscle pain ointment in the bathroom and gave her lower back a good rubdown. After she was finished, she didn't hurt as badly. She felt like she could go out and do some light tending to her garden.

"Now be careful, Momma! After you shower tonight I'll rub you down again so you can get some sleep."

Bobbie grinned to herself. Trish sometimes reminded Bobbie of her mother. As she changed into her gardening clothes she thought of Amal. Something seemed off about her that morning. She would ask after she finished getting dressed. She pulled her hair up and tucked it in her hat, and with her shoes in her hands, she left her room. She checked in Amal's room to find her lying down again.

"You okay, sweetie?"

Amal jumped a little as she sat up, and Bobbie felt bad for startling her. She walked into the room and sat on the edge of the bed.

"I didn't mean to scare you. I just saw you lying down and you made me worry. Are you alright?"

Amal gave her a pained smile, and she lay back down. "I'm okay. My stomach just hurts."

Bobbie had almost forgotten she was on her period. "I told you if you needed anything to tell me. I'll get you a pain pill and bring you the heating pad. You lie on it, and it helps relax your stomach." She rubbed her back soothingly and got up. "I'll be right back."

So Bobbie went to the linen closet in the hall and got the heating pad; then she went to her bathroom and got a couple of pain killers. After giving Amal the pills and positioning her on the heating pad, Bobbie sat on the side of the bed, rubbing Amal's back until she fell asleep. She got up slowly so as not to wake her up, and she closed her door behind her. She spotted Kenya coming up the stairs.

"Don't go up there and wake her up. She's not feeling good. Come outside with me."

Kenya loved gardening with Bobbie, so she didn't object. She skipped back down the stairs until she was at the bottom and held out her hand to Bobbie, who took Kenya's hand in her free hand, and they walked outside together.

On good days, she would leave the sliding glass door open to air the house out. The afternoon was warm, but there was a slight breeze that threatened to take her hat with it. The garden was alive with little creatures. She loved all God's creatures, but not when they ate her plants. She sprayed and dusted plants with pesticides, while Kenya poked at a tomato worm with a stick.

"Leave that thing alone before it stings you."

Kenya quickly dropped the stick. "Yes, Aunt Bobbie."

Louis was several feet away in the grass, painting his heart out. These were the times that she loved, when it was just her and her babies enjoying the day. She hated that Amal didn't feel well, but it would pass.

Bobbie stood as another breeze kicked up, and closed her eyes, letting the breeze blow across her face, drying the beads of sweat that clung to her. Her skin prickled under the fabric of her dress as the wind rippled like waves over her skin. She felt like she could stay out here for hours, but her body was telling her it was about time to go in and sit down. Maybe she would sit on the porch instead of going in, but until then her body would just have to be patient. The day was hers and she would enjoy it. She had been in the garden for an hour and her back was starting to bother her again, so she decided it was time to go inside.

Bobbie gathered her tools and rinsed them all as well as she could; then she and Kenya went inside, leaving Louis outside, still painting happily. The AC was on full blast; normally she didn't see the need for it, but today she would make an exception. She showered after checking on Amal, who was still sleeping peacefully. The warm water felt good on her joints, and she thought about standing in there for hours, just letting the water wash the pain away. The stream ran from the top of her head and down her back, landing in large puddles around her feet before running down the drain.

She stood comfortably under the water until she heard voices coming from downstairs. She turned off the water and dried off as quickly as her back would let her and dressed in minutes. She opened the door and could hear the voices of the ladies from the Healing Circle. As she got closer to the stairs she could distinctly hear Hattie chatting away. Aunt Bobbie had forgotten what day it was. It was their luncheon. Hattie was in pale pink with a pink-and-brown hat atop her head like a crown, and the rest of the ladies were in the exact same thing.

"Now, Bobbie, I know you didn't forget about us!" Hattie said with a flourish of her gloved hands.

Every Thursday, the women went to lunch and tea at either another member's house or a restaurant, but generally it was at a member's house. If she was correct, it was Cora's turn. She thought about Amal. Bobbie knew she would love to join, but she didn't want to disturb her rest.

"Nobody could forget about any of you," Bobbie said, rolling her eyes. "Just give me a minute to change. I'm not feeling the best today."

Hattie put a hand on her hip. "Well, why didn't you just say so? Are you alright?"

"Yes! Yes! I am fine."

Bobbie went back to her room and got dressed quickly after telling Kenya to get dressed. She checked on Amal before leaving and saw she was still asleep. She felt bad for leaving her, but she would be back before she woke up. They all filed off into two cars, with Kenya sitting in the back, right beside her. As she left, she saw Louis walking with his paint supplies and a big canvas bag.

She rolled down the window. "And where are you going?" Bobbie asked, but she knew the answer. Louis would often take a walk to find something new to paint.

"I'll be back before it gets dark. I'm just going to paint," Louis said.

"Okay! Be careful!" Bobbie said, and they drove away.

Trish
Present Day

She was standing behind the door in Kenya's room, looking at herself in the wall mirror that hung there. She looked a lot bigger than she had a week before. She would need to see a doctor soon. She didn't even know how far along she was, but she believed they would be able to tell her at the hospital. Trish took one last look in the mirror before going to pee. She felt like she lived in the bathroom now. Every five seconds she was running to the bathroom. She was getting better with smells. They just made her gag a little. *What shall I call you?* she thought, putting her hand on her belly. *I don't even know what you are. I feel like you're a girl, though. Are you a girl?* She swore she felt a light flutter, like an angry butterfly, on the inside behind her skin. *Was that you?* Trish asked, on the verge of tears. She couldn't help but laugh and cry at the same time when she felt it again. *So either I got it terribly wrong or you're saying yes.* She left the bathroom and lay down on Kenya's bed. She was so tired now and could only stay up for a few hours at a time. She fell asleep in no time.

Trish awoke to a note from Bobbie saying she would be back in a few hours and to check on Amal. It was written in her normal long, flowery letters that reminded her of a poet. She got up, feeling a little dizzy, and went down the hall and found Amal sleeping peacefully. She was so still that Trish wanted to go over and check to see if she was still breathing, but then Amal let out a light sigh. Trish smiled to herself, feeling her heart go soft. *Is this what it's like to be a mother?* she thought.

She went downstairs and called out for Louis, but got no answer. He was probably outside, she thought. She went to check and found the yard empty. *He is probably off painting.* So she was home alone—well, kind of. She didn't mind sharing her alone time with Amal. She had come to love the little girl dearly.

Beginning her cleaning routine, she started in the living room, wiping down all the surfaces until they shined; even the ceiling fan got a good dusting. She would wait to vacuum until the end to give Amal a chance to wake up before she started making loud noises. She felt another flutter in her lower stomach; apparently the little one was doing some work of her own in there. It made Trish's heart swell. She thought, *You're a little wiggle worm,* as she put a hand on her tummy before getting back to work. She moved to the kitchen, bleaching the counters and wiping down the fronts of the cabinets.

Halfway into it she felt like she needed a little music, so she retrieved her earbuds from the bedroom after checking on Amal again and found her list of soothing jazz music on her phone. She saw she had several missed calls and texts from the same unknown number. There had been at least thirty calls since the last time she'd checked. She shook it off and went back to cleaning the kitchen, humming to herself with the music. Because of the earbuds she didn't hear the noises coming from the back door. By the time she felt a presence, it was too late.

"You're finally up, Lady Bug?" But when she turned it wasn't Amal standing behind her, nor was it Louis or Bobbie. She jumped, ramming her back into the cabinets.

"Hey, love." It was Randy standing there, looking more menacing than he ever had. "You know, you had me worried. I've been looking for you for so long."

She could feel her heart hammering in her chest. She needed a way out. "Randy, I . . . ," she squeaked out.

"What? You left me," he said, taking a few steps toward her. His attitude was scary-calm, the way the weather gets right before a terrible storm. Looking into his eyes, she knew what he had come for, and he wasn't planning on leaving until he had her or he killed her. A part of her thought that maybe if she talked to him, it would calm him down, but she knew that when he got angry there was no talking.

"I didn't mean to . . . ," she said frantically.

"You didn't mean to pack all your things and leave?" His green eyes went cold, and on his face he wore a sly smirk. She had seen that face many times before. It was the way she knew when to brace for the hits or punches.

In the blink of an eye, he had reached out and was holding her by the shoulders. He lifted her up so he could look into her eyes. He was a good two feet taller than she was, even when she was wearing shoes. He glared at her like he was holding himself back from hitting her.

"Did you think I wouldn't find you? That's where you're wrong. I'll always find you."

He placed her feet back on the floor. The slap came without warning and was so hard she hit the floor and slid across it, bumping her head on the fridge. Her head throbbed and her ears rang loudly.

"Randy, please!" she begged, trying to shield her stomach.

Trish scrambled across the floor toward the entrance of the kitchen. His long legs made him way faster, and he lifted her up, standing between Trish and the rest of the house. She looked up at him, tears stinging her sore cheek. Suddenly she remembered Amal upstairs sleeping, and she didn't want to make noise and wake her up. She'd been through enough. Randy could beat her all he wanted, but she wouldn't allow him to hurt Amal. So Trish talked a bit lower, until her voice was a little louder than a whisper.

"So what did you think was going to happen? You would leave and you wouldn't have to pay? That's not how it works," Randy said through gritted teeth.

Another smack came, but she saw it and braced herself. Lights flashed like fireworks in her vision. This time she didn't fall, and stood her ground. She moved her mouth, making her jaw pop.

"I tried and tried, but nothing was ever good enough for you," she said, the words coming out of her mouth before she thought about it. "Who would want to live with someone like you?" Trish said, looking him straight in the face.

"What did you say to me?" he asked calmly, almost daring her to say it again.

Now she was the one that was smiling. "Are you having hearing problems now? I said, who would want to live with someone like you! I left because I can't stand you and I'm tired of being beaten!"

This time it was a fist into her head and her chest. Blood ran from her temple, and her mouth filled with it. But that didn't scare her; it angered her. She'd never felt like this. She walked up closer, waiting for him to hit her again and finish it, but he didn't. He just flashed a smile that made her sick to her stomach. Then in a flash came his fists raining a flurry of violence down upon her until she was lying on the floor in a bloody heap. She started losing track of the number of times he had hit her. She was only concerned with keeping Amal and the baby safe.

Amal

Present Day

Everything was a groggy blur as she woke up. She didn't just wake up on her own; something had awakened her. She strained her ears trying to decipher what was going on, as there was a lot of noise coming from downstairs. She thought of just going back to sleep, but something pulled her out of bed. That little voice inside her head that her mother had told her about was screaming for her to get up, until she found herself at the door and heard the strange sounds more clearly. There were thumps and yelling coming from downstairs. Not knowing why, Amal opened the door slowly, taking care not to make noise even though it was the middle of the day. In the hall the voices and noises were louder and sounded like an argument of some kind. *Who would be arguing here?* she thought. Something was telling her this wasn't right. The place just felt wrong. There hadn't been an argument in all the months she had been here. She needed to know what was going on.

Amal was almost afraid to go to the top of the stairs to look, but she went anyway, being careful not to make a sound. She had become good at that. What she saw from her position on the stairs sent panic through her whole body. Every inch of her ignited like electricity. There was a man in the house, a man she had never seen before, and he was standing over something. She had to strain to see what it was. He was yelling about something she couldn't under-stand, but she had to move in closer to see what it was. Then the realization of what the thing on the floor was hit her hard. Her brain was going a mile a minute. *What should I do? I have to do something!*

Trish

Present Day

She was going in and out of consciousness when he picked her up again, and they were eye to eye.

"Please don't!" she pleaded with him.

"It's until death, baby," he said with a laugh.

He was still holding her up when she saw movement from the stairs. She panicked when she realized it was Amal, looking so young in her nightgown. She turned her gaze to Randy's face so he wouldn't look around.

He would hurt Amal if he had to, so she looked him in the face and began laughing. "I think you should go take a nap. You look tired. Just go to bed," she said, hoping Amal would catch on and go back to her room. It did nothing to help the situation, though.

"You are crazy. Maybe I did beat you too much."

Trish gathered all the spit and blood she could in her mouth and spit in his face. He shook her before dropping her to the floor, kicking her once more.

"Dumb bitch! You're going to pay for that!" He grabbed her by the foot, dragging her outside and leaving a trail of blood behind her. "I was just going to beat you and bring you back home, but now I'm going to kill you," he said as he wiped his face with his shirt.

Trish saw the outline of a gun tucked into the belt of his pants. He was standing with his back to the sliding glass door, looking down at her like an angry giant. He smiled evilly as he retrieved the gun and took aim. So this is how she would die. She was okay with it as long as he didn't hurt anyone else. Her little worm wiggled a little, making her smile. *At least I got to experience what real love is like. I was almost a mother.* Hearing the gun cock, she closed her eyes and envisioned who her little worm would've looked like, what she would've sounded like when she started talking. *What would her first word have been?* Her brain was fixed on those thoughts when she heard a metallic thud and the sound of something heavy hitting the ground, but it wasn't a gunshot. When she opened her swollen eyes as much as she could, everything was blurry, but she focused on a figure in white a couple of paces in front of her, standing tall and holding something long and flat on the end. There was a big lump on the ground that she recognized was Randy. She was so happy that she began crying when the figure dropped what it was holding and ran over to her, putting a hand on the spot on her head where the blood was coming from.

"It's okay! I called 9-1-1! Please don't go to sleep. You have to stay up."

Trish gave her a sleepy smile, flashing blood-stained teeth.

"Hey, there's my Lady Bug," Trish said before drifting off to sleep. Someone kept shaking her, and she didn't know why. She just wanted to close her eyes for a minute.

Soon there where were loud noises and lots of people talking and touching her. She just wanted to be left alone. *Why won't they just let me sleep?* Their voices were so annoying, and her head hurt, and she didn't have the energy to make them stop talking and touching her. She felt them pick her up and felt something soft below her; then everything went bumpy until she could hear the sounds of an engine running, loud and low. She then felt a sting in her right arm, and the pain in her head and body washed away, lulling her into a deep sleep.

Chapter
Thirty
Bobbie
Present Day

Her heart almost jumped out of her throat when she saw the police and ambulance outside her home. Only a few minutes ago, she was sipping tea and socializing with the mothers and grandmothers of the church. She and Hattie jumped out of the car, racing to see what was going on. Her thoughts went to Amal and how she slept so hard after she gave her some pain medicine. *Did I poison her by accident?* Her four-inch heels didn't stop her from running at full speed through the lawn. A police officer met her halfway. She would plow through him if she had to.

"This is my home! What happened here?" She was so close to screaming her lungs out at him.

"You live here, ma'am?"

Is this boy deaf? she thought. Before she could say anything, Hattie took over. Bobbie felt like she couldn't breathe. Placing a hand on her chest, she tried to slow her heart so she could hear what was being said.

"This is her house. Is everything okay?" As Hattie asked, a man she recognized as Trish's husband came out on a stretcher, cursing at the EMTs. They paid him no mind as they loaded him into the back on the ambulance.

"Ma'am, there was an assault here. I can't let you past this point. All this is a crime scene."

Bobbie thought she hadn't heard the man correctly. "An assault? How? Who? Where are my daughters?"

"The girl? She's . . ."

Bobbie didn't wait for him to finish. She saw a police car door open and a female officer crouched on the ground, looking in and taking notes on a pad, and she made a beeline toward the car. Amal was sitting in the police car with a harsh gray blanket wrapped around her and dried blood smeared across her face.

"Amal!" she yelled, pushing past the officer to get to her girl. "What's happened? Did he hurt you? Where's Trish?"

"Ma'am, she's at the hospital being taken care of. This one here is a hero. You should be very proud of her," the officer said.

Bobbie looked at Amal, not knowing what to ask or where to start. She caught a glimpse of something in her eyes, though; something Bobbie hadn't seen until now. Ever since Amal had arrived, she'd had this look in her eyes, Bobbie had seen the look on the faces of terrified animals. It was as if Amal was waiting for something bad to happen, but looking at her now, she sat with her back straight and her head up. She was even looking the officer in the eye. Bobbie could tell she wasn't afraid anymore. Whatever had happened had helped her face something inside her that had been holding her inner strength captive.

The police officer moved away, giving Bobbie and Amal space. They just looked at each other for a while. Aunt Bobbie wasn't sure she could handle what Amal had to say, but she needed to know, so she asked, even though her heart probably couldn't take it.

"Tell me what happened," Bobbie said.

Amal shed her blanket, like a warrior dropping her shield, and told her everything she remembered.

Amal
Present Day

When she heard the cryptic way Trish told her to go to her room, she completely disregarded it. She must be crazy *if she thinks I'm going to sit up here and do nothing*, Amal thought. The first thing she needed to do was call 9-1-1, so she snuck into Bobbie's room where the phone was on her nightstand and got into the closet, and with shaking fingers she dialed.

"9-1-1. What's your emergency?"

"There's a man downstairs that's hurting my sister! Can you bring someone? Please hurry!" she pleaded and gasped.

"Okay, calm down and stay on the phone with me," the 9-1-1 responder said calmly.

"I can't! He's going to kill her! She's bleeding everywhere!" Amal cried.

She didn't wait for the responder to reply; she just hung up after hearing Trish scream again, and ran downstairs. The man was bigger than he had looked when she was upstairs. Everything in her said to run, but a part wouldn't let her do it. Not knowing what came over her, she walked out onto the porch and stood directly behind the scary man, and luckily he didn't hear her. He was too busy looking down at his wife, who lay in a crumpled heap on the ground. Her heart leaped, and she glanced to her right and saw a large metal shovel. In her mind she saw the faces of her friends and family and everyone she cared about that she had lost, and she was not going to let that happen again. Everything that she loved had been taken from her, and she'd had no say in it. Standing there with the sun beaming down upon her, making her white nightgown glow, she decided to take her life back. She would fight with everything she had in her to protect the ones she loved. She wasn't going to lose anyone else.

Amal grabbed and gripped the shovel tightly in her hands, like a baseball player going to bat, feeling the texture of the handle. She lifted it up as high as she could, then brought it down on his head with such force that she felt it connect with the bones in his skull. Bone crushed and sent shock waves through the handle to her hands and arms like electricity. His body hit the ground with a thump, and the man lay motionless on the ground. Not waiting for him to move again, something came over her, and she began striking him repeatedly, until her arms were tired and her nightgown was covered in blood. She breathed heavily as anger fueled her attack. Blood streaked her face and her hair went wild.

When Amal was sure he was down for good, she dropped the shovel and ran over to Trish. Badly hurt and lying in a crumpled heap of clothing, broken bones, and blood, she still managed to smile, calling her Lady Bug. Amal tried her best to keep her from falling asleep. When she heard the sirens in the background, getting closer, she breathed a sigh of relief before the sounds of people running into the backyard surrounded them. A strong arm gently pulled her away, and she didn't fight it. The gravity of the situation set in, and Amal began to shake. She didn't know why she was shivering so much. A female police officer saw her and assumed the girl was cold. She wrapped her tightly in an ugly gray blanket before sitting her in the back of a police car despite Amal's protests that she was fine. The woman had a comforting presence, so Amal didn't fight it for too long. She thanked the officer and sat in the back, watching the chaos from a safe distance.

The scene was surreal, but it wasn't the worst thing she had been through, by far. When she saw Trish lying there she couldn't help but remember her sister and the way she had looked when she found her lying there like a ragdoll torn to shreds. Amal had to shut her eyes and clear her thoughts. *Will everything be okay this time?* She didn't know if it would, but in that moment she shut her eyes and prayed. While the police and the EMTs swarmed the yard like honey bees, Amal had a long talk with God. She held the vision of Trish lying in the garden, looking so helpless, in her mind. Not knowing how long she had been praying, Amal opened her eyes and saw a kind face looking down at her. The same police officer squatted down so they were eye to eye and offered Amal a hand.

"My name is Officer Hunt." Amal took her hand and told the officer her name. The woman had big pretty eyes. "I know you've had a hard day, but I want you to tell me exactly when happened if you can."

Amal took a deep breath and told her everything she could.

Bobbie

Present Day

There was so much blood on Amal. Her nightgown was soaked through on the front, and the side of her face was covered in dried blood.

"Are you sure you're not hurt?" Bobbie asked her.

"No, ma'am," Amal said, shaking her head.

Bobbie was glad she was okay. What would've happened if she hadn't been there? Would she have come home to find her daughter dead in the backyard? She didn't know. What would she tell Kenya and Louis when they returned? She didn't want to think about that now. She just needed to figure out how her daughter was and where they had taken her.

"Will you be okay if I leave you here for a minute?"

Amal didn't say anything; she just shook her head.

"I'll be back."

She hated leaving her, but she needed to know where they had taken her daughter. Bobbie turned to make her way to the second police car that was parked a few feet from her. As she walked up a young policeman who was probably in his twenties got out. She could hear chatter coming from the radio in his car.

"Hey there, can I help you, ma'am?"

"I'm Barbara Bralev. This is my home. I just need to know where they've taken my daughter."

The officer rubbed the razor stubble on his cheek before speaking. "I'm not quite sure, but from the looks of her injuries, she's probably going to need a specialist. She sustained a number of serious injuries. I would ask the EMTs. They can let you know more."

She thanked the police officer and looked around for someone she could ask. She saw a young lady headed toward an ambulance, wearing gloves, and she walked toward her.

"Excuse me!" Barbara yelled at the fast-walking woman to get her attention.

The woman stopped and turned around, looking as exhausted as Bobbie felt on the inside. She walked quickly toward her until they were face to face.

"I was told I could ask you where they're taking my daughter. I'm her mother."

The seriousness of the woman's face fell away instantly. "Yes, ma'am. They're taking her to Saint Joseph's to evaluate her, but from the looks of her injuries, she may not stay there for long. If you head over now, you can probably catch them."

Bobbie thanked her and headed back to Amal. Another officer was standing next to her. When she got there an officer gave his sympathy and told Bobbie they were done questioning Amal and repeated what the other officers had told her. She was a hero. Bobbie knew this, but now wasn't the time. She politely excused them, grabbed Amal by the hand, and went inside. Before she could say anything, Amal looked up at her and said, "I'm going upstairs to get my things so we can leave."

Bobbie watched her run upstairs before heading upstairs herself to pack a bag. She didn't bother folding a thing before shoving it in a small travel bag and changing her own clothes. Her emotions tried their best to slow her down, but she couldn't cry, not now, not until she knew how her child was. When she was finished packing she came downstairs to find Amal cleaned up and packed, sitting with Hattie, who had an arm tightly around her. They both looked up when Bobbie appeared. She gave Amal's arm a rub before picking up her keys and announcing she would drive them to the hospital and come back to wait for Kenya and Louis.

Saint Joseph's Hospital wasn't a long ride from her house, but this time it felt like it was hours away. All she could think of was her daughter. *Is she okay? Is she scared? Is she lonely? Does she know that I am coming?* That was all she could think. Amal was in the backseat being as quiet as a church mouse. Bobbie wondered what was running around in that pretty head of hers. Again she wondered what the child had seen and gone through to do what she had done for Trish. This was all so messed up. Bobbie knew firsthand how cruel life could be, but it shouldn't be that way for children. Bobbie looked and watched Amal through the rearview mirror. The windows were cracked, so her shiny black hair blew in the wind, around her face.

Over time her features had sharpened, giving her a smooth jawline. She was becoming a woman right in front of Bobbie's eyes. The love she had felt when she first saw Amal had amplified. She couldn't imagine a life without her hero.

Amal

Present Day

The breeze from the window blew in her face, clearing her thoughts. Amal had finally stopped shaking, but she still felt a little odd. This couldn't be happening. She just wanted to get to the hospital to be with Trish. Her arms and hands were sore. She looked down at her hands as she closed and opened them. They were still dirty even though she had tried to wash them when she'd taken a quick bath. They looked weird, like they didn't belong to her. A gust of wind blew her hair in her face. She wrestled with her hair to get a few strands out of her eyes. *Why did this have to happen to her?* she thought. *Of all people, why did this have to happen to Trish?* Amal could never imagine her hurting anything or anyone, and she'd had to live with that man. How long had he been hurting her? And why didn't she leave? So many questions ran through her thoughts. She turned her eyes toward the bright, cloud-filled sky, and she could hear birds and other sounds of life going on around her like nothing had happened or like everything was fine, but it wasn't. Amal hoped it would be. She closed her eyes and sent her silent hopes to God that when they arrived at the hospital everything would be okay and they could all go home together. Wherever he was, only God could fix this.

Bobbie

Saint Joseph's Hospital

Present Day

When they arrived at the hospital, they exited the car, carrying bags and walking swiftly until they got to the front desk, where an older woman was sitting.

"We're here to see Trish Bralev."

The woman looked at them over her small, rectangular glasses, with her mouth pinched as if she'd just eaten a lemon.

She pushed back her chair and, with an annoyed sigh, said, "This way, please."

They followed her down the winding hallways until they came to a door that read, "Family Room." The older woman opened the door and ushered them in.

"A nurse will be in to talk to you in a moment," she said without looking at them, and left the room.

Bobbie and Amal found themselves alone in the cold white room. There were various chairs and a small couch along the walls. A tiny table held magazines. Aunt Bobbie looked at the smiling faces of the models looking back at her, and she wanted to slap them. *How dare you be smiling at a time like this!* she thought. They sat in the room, saying nothing, for what seemed like hours, until there was a knock at the door. A man wearing teal scrubs came in.

"Are you Mrs. Bralev?" he asked in a calm voice.

"Yes, I am," Bobbie answered.

He extended a hand and introduced himself as Nurse Jameson, then began speaking on Trish's condition.

"As I understand, she was beaten up by her . . . ?"

"Husband," Bobbie filled in.

"Her husband. Okay. Well, she has extensive damage in various places all over her body. Both legs are broken; she has cracked ribs, a broken collar bone, three fractures in her spine, and some injuries to her brain."

He paused as though to give them a chance to think. The room was silent as Bobbie and Amal both thought about what was just said.

"But is she okay? Is she talking?" Bobbie asked, wringing her dress in her hands.

"When she arrived she was unconscious, and she hasn't woken up. The swelling on her brain could be why, but we're not quite sure yet."

"The baby! Will the baby be okay?" Bobbie asked. The baby needed to be okay. She was so happy about the baby. If something happened, she knew it would make things worse for Trish.

"We are aware that she is pregnant, and the baby looks fine. If anything changes and it looks like she's not going to make it, you will have to make the decision to do a C-section to save the baby. Right now, we're cleaning your daughter up and getting her stable, and once we're finished you'll be able to go see her." He rose and straightened his outfit. "The doctor should be in to see you soon. Do you need anything?"

"No, thank you."

"Well, if you do, don't hesitate to ask. We're going to take care of her."

The nurse smiled before closing the door behind him. He seemed nice, but no amount of niceness could fix any of this. Bobbie watched Amal closely. She could tell her mind was going ninety miles a minute, just like hers. Amal reached over and held one of Bobbie's hands. Bobbie looked at her and smiled as much as she could. She wanted to reassure Amal that everything would be fine, but she didn't want to lie. Trish needed them, and they would be there for her. They would brave the storm until the very end. Amal reached over and wrapped Bobbie in her small arms the same way she had, and they spent their stay in the family room just like that. No one said a thing. They just existed for each other, and that meant more than words could say.

The doctor came in and brought them back to see Trish. She was tucked away in a special unit of the hospital. They passed people in beds with families standing over them. Some lay in beds alone in the dark, staring blankly at nothing or sleeping. Amal had to stop herself from looking; she had never been to a hospital in this role. She had always been the patient, and never the visitor. Her heart leaped every time she saw a sad face. They walked until they got to a room that was right at the end of the hall. Her heart pumped as the doctor opened the door and they walked in. He pushed back the curtain, and there lay Trish. Her face and eyes were swollen and blue. She was connected to a strange contraption that helped her breathe. It was taped crudely to her face and ran to a bulky white machine. Several tubes ran from her arm. Her thick black hair was loose and framed her head like a halo. Amal was aware of the fact that the doctor was speaking, but she didn't hear a word of it. This wasn't her Trish. They must have the wrong room, it felt so small. Amal stood looking at the person they said was Trish and had to fight back tears. She wished she were the one in the hospital bed. Amal could take the pain, but she couldn't take this.

She didn't hear the doctor leave, but when she saw Bobbie move in to where Trish was lying and put a hand on her head, she realized they were alone. Bobbie softly rubbed her daughter's head, and Amal, not knowing what to say, just stood there holding her things to her chest.

"Hey, sweetie. You're mama's here and so is Amal," she heard Bobbie say, so she stepped in closer. "I know you hear us. Come on and open those pretty eyes for me."

Bobbie was still rubbing her forehead. She and Amal waited for anything that would show them she was there, but she didn't move a muscle.

"Whenever you're ready to wake up, we'll be here."

Bobbie dropped her hand and walked out of the room, leaving Amal and Trish alone. Feeling so helpless, she moved quietly right next to the bed.

"Hi. It's Amal. I just wanted to say that I'm sorry that I didn't get there quick enough, and I love you. Please don't die. Everyone I've known and loved has left me. You can't leave me too. You got people here who really love you. You can take your time if you have to, but you can't give up. You have to fight. I'll be here with you, and don't you forget that. I'll stay here for the rest of my life if I have to."

Amal laid her hand on her bruised head and prayed for her, the way her parents had when she was sick. When she was done she kissed her on her forehead and took a seat next to the long window against the wall. She could see Bobbie at the nurses' desk, on the phone, as she settled into the chair with her yarn. The chair was uncomfortable, but it would do for the time being. If Bobbie was staying, so was she.

One of a parent's many fears is to lose a child. When she saw her daughter lying in the bed and looking very close to death, it ignited that fear in Bobbie. She wanted to cry, yell, scream even, but she couldn't. Her daughter needed her to be strong. She could cry later. After stepping out in the hall to gather herself, she called the house to make sure Louis and Kenya were home safe. No one picked up, so she called Hattie to see if they were with her. After speaking with her for a few moments, she was happy to hear that they were okay. Bobbie told her what was going on before hanging up the phone. She stood across from the nurses' desk for a while after that, trying to make sense of all that had happened. She didn't realize that she was getting dizzy before it was bad and she had to hold on to the desk for leverage.

One of the nurses came over and placed a hand on her back, steadying her swaying body. "Ma'am, are you okay?" She saw the words in her head but couldn't respond. "Sit here. Diana, can you bring me some water?" the nurse said over her shoulder to a woman sitting behind the long desk. "Here we are. Just take a few breaths."

Bobbie did as she said and breathed in and out as slowly as she could. By the time the nurse came with a cup of cool water, she was already feeling much better, but she took the water thankfully.

"I don't know what happened. Generally I'm levelheaded, but today has been rough." Bobbie adjusted to sit with her back straight.

"No worries. It happens, especially around here. Are you here to see anyone?" the nurse asked.

"Yes. My daughter." Bobbie pointed toward the door.

"I was here when she came in. I'm so sorry. We'll take good care of her."

"Thank you."

"No need to thank me. It's my job."

"Well, I need to head back to the room. I left my other little one in there."

"I'm working tonight, so I'll be making my rounds. If you need anything, just call the front desk."

Bobbie nodded and walked back to the room. She had to make herself push the door all the way open. When she did, she was met with the same scene. Her daughter was lying unconscious in a hospital bed with tubes everywhere. Amal was in a chair crocheting away, and when she heard Bobbie walk in she looked up from her work.

"Are you alright?" Amal asked attentively.

"I'm doing as good as I can right now. I'm just glad you are okay."

"Glad I'm okay? While Trish is like this? This is my fault!" Amal exclaimed, throwing her yarn and needle to the floor, her needle making a sharp, metallic pinging noise when it hit the ground.

"Why would you think this was your fault? You saved her. If it hadn't been for you, she'd be dead. You're a lot stronger than you think," Bobbie said. "I am so thankful for you."

Amal

Saint Joseph's Hospital
Present Day

The last time Amal had visited someone in the hospital, it had been her grandmother who was sick. It had started out with her forgetting to turn lights off or turn the oven off, but then she began forgetting things that time had etched in her memory. She would get lost on the way home, forgetting the faces of her friends; then, lastly, the worst: forgetting her family. A day Amal would never forget was the day her grandmother had forgotten who she was. Her aunts, uncles, and cousins had made a special trip on a Friday to see her.

There had been conversation, jokes, and laughter; then, out of nowhere, she had said, "I wonder why Amal hasn't come."

It didn't matter how many times the family tried to tell their grandmother that Amal was there; she didn't believe them.

"That's not my Amal," she repeated.

In the end, they had laughed it off and finished their visit. That night Amal had fallen asleep on a tear-soaked pillow.

As she stared at Trish, she hoped she would get better and wouldn't forget her. Amal thought about the night her period came and how Trish had turned that scary situation into something special. She wondered if she would ever get to spend a night eating ice cream and listening to funny stories again. Amal put down her crocheting, walked over to the bed, and rubbed Trish's forehead the same way Bobbie had. Amal talked to her like she would have if she were awake. She described the details of things going on outside and told her how much she was loved and missed.

The day quickly turned into night, and visiting hours were almost over. Only one person could stay in the room with the patient at night, so Amal had to leave. Bobbie hugged her good night since she wouldn't be able to do it at home. They waited on the ground floor for Mr. Henry. The front and the halls were quiet. Nothing but soft music could be heard, which Amal guessed was coming from the front desk. They sat in silence listening to the music, but Bobbie seemed to be buried by thoughts and stared off into nothingness until the familiar sound of Mr. Henry's truck could be heard. He pulled up in front of the automatic doors, and Bobbie walked her out. Before Amal got in the truck Bobbie looked down at her with tired eyes.

"Ms. Hattie will pick you up in the morning and bring you back. Just try to get some sleep, sweetie."

When Amal was secured in the truck Bobbie closed the door and Henry slowly pulled out of the driveway. Amal looked back to see Bobbie waving at the truck; she frantically waved back. What would haunt her that night was the way Bobbie's eyes had looked. She was normally so full of life, but staring at her through the window, she could see that the happiness was being sucked right out of her.

Amal

Present Day

When she arrived home, the yard, which had been over-run by police and EMTs, was completely empty and quiet. At the porch she was met by Louis, who had been sitting there waiting on her to come home. She didn't get a hello in before she was embraced in the biggest bear hug she'd had since her baba. She hadn't realized how upset she was until he hugged her. Every bit of emotion came pouring out, until the shoulder of his shirt was soaking wet. After a few moments, she pulled back.

"I'm messing up your shirt," she said between gulps of air.

"I couldn't care less about this damn shirt. How are you?"

"I'm okay."

"Bullshit!" Louis yelled, startling Amal. "There's no way in hell that after all that you're fine."

"I feel terrible. I should've helped sooner."

"No. You did what you could," Louis said through tears.

Kenya came barreling through the front door and wrapped her arms around Amal. She pulled back to look at her face and walked her inside. They climbed the stairs, and Kenya led her to her room. She had already picked out nightclothes for Amal.

"You should go shower. I'll get you some food."

Amal thanked her. She was really grateful for the small gestures. She grabbed the clothes that lay across the bed, then went to the bathroom. Normally she liked showers, but today she felt like taking a bath. She ran the water as hot as she could stand it. While the tub was filling up, she peeled off her clothes. She felt so vulnerable as she dipped a toe in the water and then slid in until everything but her head was submerged in water. She flexed her hands and feet, letting the hot water sting her skin, before bringing her knees to her chest. She was deep in thought when there was a knock at the door.

"You okay?" Kenya asked. Amal realized she had probably been in there for too long.

"Yes. I'm getting out now."

She pulled the stopper out of the tub after washing up quickly. After towel-drying she put on her nightclothes and left the bathroom, smelling like lavender and lemons. The house was so quiet, though there were three people occupying the small home. It still felt like something was missing.

Her laundry hamper was almost full when she put her day clothes in it. She would need to wash soon. For some reason, that semblance of normalcy made her feel a bit better. Amal looked at her bed and wasn't sure if she would be able to sleep tonight. Kenya appeared in the doorway in her own pajamas.

"The food's on the table. Ms. Hattie made lasagna. It's pretty good."

Amal wasn't hungry and knew if she tried to eat, it would probably just come back up, but she didn't say anything; she just thanked Kenya. They stood staring at each other for a while before Kenya broke down crying. Amal walked over, put an arm around her, and walked her to her bed, and they both sat side by side, the same way they had when Amal had just moved in.

"It's going to be okay. Everything is going to be alright. Please don't cry." Amal squeezed her before trying to wipe the tears from Kenya's eyes.

"I hope so," Kenya said.

"It will. She's in a good hospital. The nurses are taking good care of her, and Bobbie is going to stay there and make sure she's okay, so don't cry."

Amal held Kenya until she was all cried out and fell asleep on Amal's shoulder. She looked at her for a long time, feeling the warmth radiating off of her body. Amal saw then that she would have to be the strong one. She gently laid Kenya on her bed and covered her with a light blanket before going downstairs to put away the food. She searched the kitchen for plastic wrap, and when she found it, she wrapped the food and put her dinner in the fridge. Leaving the kitchen to go upstairs and get her clothes to wash, Amal saw Louis at the dining table. He had used a huge sheet covered in a variety of stains to protect the table. A small black easel sat on the table in front of him while he sorted through a box on his left side. She startled him a bit when she walked up to get a closer view of what he was doing. He looked up and waved at her to come closer.

"Have you ever painted before?" he asked, looking at her with those big brown eyes. They reminded her of chocolates.

"Ummm . . . no, I haven't," she said timidly.

"Would you like to learn?" he asked, raising his eyebrows.

"I don't know."

"I have more than enough supplies here, and I doubt you're going to be able to sleep."

He was right about that. Considering the only thing she was going to do was wash her clothes, she decided she would let him teach her.

"Let me start my clothes, and I'll come right back."

She ran upstairs and grabbed her laundry basket. Then she remembered she had no idea where the washer and dryer were. She came back downstairs with a handful of clothes.

"Louis, where's the washer and dryer?"

He got up, motioning her to follow him, and they went upstairs to the door she thought was just a closet. It was a small room that was just big enough for a few shelves and a washer and dryer that were stacked on top of each other. Once Louis turned the lights on and she could see better, she saw all the buttons on the appliances and got nervous. Her washer and dryer at home weren't this complicated. Louis must've seen the look on her face, as he started telling her how to use them without her having to ask. After her clothes were separated and in the wash, they headed back downstairs, where she found another easel on the table. This one was made of a light-colored wood, but had been splattered with a rainbow of colors. He had also laid out paintbrushes for her. The handles were bright green and shiny. She couldn't help but touch them. Louis came and sat down in the chair next to her and began dumping paint out on the table.

"If Momma was home, she'd have a fit. So let's just keep this between the two of us."

Amal could see Bobbie fussing the way she did, and it made the empty spot in her chest tingle. The house was an empty shell without her and her bright flowered-print dresses and garden hats.

"So what would you like to paint?" Louis asked, bringing her back to reality.

She thought about it for a few moments. In her mind she saw Bobbie in her garden collecting vegetables and watering her plants, humming happily to herself, and she decided that she would paint just that.

"Can you show me how to paint a garden like Bobbie's?"

Louis nodded and they got to work. First he gave her a paper plate, and before she could ask what it was for he began putting dollops of paint around the edge of the plate.

"This is your palette. You'll mix colors or use the colors as they are to paint on this canvas."

She looked at the white square that was sitting in front of her waiting to be transformed into whatever her mind could think up. Louis began talking about colors, different paints, and brushes. She listened intently to everything he said. She followed his every instruction when it came down to mixing colors and what brush to use. They began with sketching out the landscape, showing where the sky would be, the plants, the ground, the tree, and the fence.

"I would like to add Aunt Bobbie to it as well."

Louis smiled. "I knew you would. Okay, we'll put her right here," he said and then sketched the silhouette of a person in a hat, and Amal did the same.

When they were done sketching, they took one last look to make sure everything was in the right place. Amal thought Louis's sketch was better than hers, but he assured her it wasn't about the sketch; just the paint.

"They're just put there so we know where everything goes, that's all. And now for my favorite part of painting . . ." He began mixing colors for the sky. "It's the afternoon, so we're going to add yellow and a little white to the blue to make it look like the sun is bright and shining," Louis said.

Amal did exactly what he did. The paint went on the canvas as smoothly as warm butter on bread. She spread and moved the paint until the sky was complete, and then, although it was far from finished, they moved on to the ground. Shades of brown, green, and yellow were used to make the rich soil look almost lifelike. They formed the shapes of the garden vegetables and the green leaves on top. Once the landscape was done the tree was the last plant to add.

"Here is where you let the brush do all the work. Hold it in your hand like this and make slow upward strokes," Louis instructed her.

She did as she was told until she had a tree with little white blossoms. Once she was closer to being done, Louis encouraged Amal to take a step back and look at her work so far. Overall, she was proud of what she had made, but it was missing something. Besides Aunt Bobbie not being in the painting yet, she definitely felt like something wasn't right. The garden had this mysterious aura to it that she wanted to capture in the painting. She thought about this for a while before figuring it out.

"I feel like I want to add more color to the tree."

She looked up at her teacher to see if it was okay. He nodded, and she went back to her seat and dug through the box of paints, determined to find the right color. She stopped searching when she came across a tube of gold paint. She picked it up, moving it ever so slightly and watching the flecks of gold catch the light. She added some to her palette, trying to mimic the way Louis had arranged the paint on the paper plate. Dipping her brush in the paint, she carefully added gold to the base of the tree and a little to the tree limbs. The gold added exactly what she was looking for, but it wasn't quite there yet. She added a bunch of different colors until she was completely satisfied. She took a step back and looked at the whole piece.

"You're a natural artist. The tree was a nice touch," Louis said.

The tree looked the way it made her feel. It was strong, beautiful, very much alive, and full of wonder. The last thing they added was Aunt Bobbie. They painted her right in the middle of the lush plants, wearing a lavender flowered-print dress and her sunhat. The garden had looked empty without her, and now it was complete.

When they finally finished, Amal was surprised to see the yellow rays of the sun peering through the cracks in the curtains. She helped Louis clean up their mess. Neither one said anything as they returned the dining room table to the way it had been before they'd started their art project. She couldn't help but stare at her drying painting. She couldn't believe she had painted something. It wasn't as good as Louis's, but it was good enough for her.

When Louis came back to the table to gather the box of paint, Amal thought it would be a good opportunity to ask, "Can we do this again sometime? I really liked painting."

"Of course. Anytime you'd like, just let me know."

Louis abruptly stopped what he was doing and for the first time looked at Amal with seriousness in his face.

"Thanks," he said.

"For what?" Amal asked, honestly very curious as to why he was thanking her.

"For saving my sister. I appreciate it."

"Well, I just figured she'd do the same for me."

"But a lot of people wouldn't have done what you did. She could be dead right now if it wasn't for you."

Amal dropped her head, not sure what to say. She didn't feel like the hero everyone said she was, but she accepted the fact that people were thankful for her presence. Amal thought about the various times Trish had made her feel better. Then she thought about the man lying there on the ground and having beaten him the way she did. In a way, she felt bad about that also.

"You're a badass little chick. You know that?" Louis smiled at her, obviously joking around to distract from the serious situation.

Amal walked to the sliding glass doors and opened the curtain that blocked out the sun. As soon as she pulled back the thick fabric, the sun came flooding in. She let the warmth soak into the parts of her body that had gone cold. She touched the glass, looking through to the garden and imagining it was a normal day and Bobbie would be coming downstairs soon in her sun hat and floral-print dress to water and tend the garden in the early morning rays of the sun. She didn't know what came over her, but she went upstairs, finding Kenya still knocked out. She quietly put on some jeans and a shirt. She went to Bobbie's room and grabbed her sunhat. She hoped she wouldn't mind. She stood in the doorway looking around for a minute before closing the door and heading downstairs.

The sun hit her just right when she stepped outside. She greeted it with a smile while taking a deep breath. She put on the sun hat, which was far too big for her head, but that didn't bother her at all. She slid on a pair of Bobbie's garden boots and went around the corner of the house to grab the water hose. It was a lot heavier than she thought, but she handled it with no problem. She pulled it until she was standing in the middle of the garden and began watering the plants like she had seen Bobbie do so many times. It was therapeutic in a way. She watched how the water rained down on the plants, sending the leaves dancing this way and that. Tiny droplets clung to some parts of the plants, enhancing their signature shades of green. The smell of the damp soil filled her nose, and she had a sudden urge to take her shoes off, and that she did. She spread her toes in the mushy yet warm soil. It felt odd yet satisfying at the same time. She continued watering the garden until it looked the way it did when Bobbie was finished with it. Still barefoot in the soil, she turned around, slowly taking in the yard. When she thought of heaven this is what she would picture: being barefoot in a lush garden. But it was missing something, and she hoped that the people who were missing would be back soon. As soon as she thought this, a little bird, one that looked similar to the one that had landed on her shoulder weeks before, flew down and landed in a narrow space between the plants.

"Hello! You came back," Amal said.

It hopped in little bursts around her feet until it finally got bored and flew away.

Trish

Trapped in Her Head

Present Day

Trish didn't know how long she had been in this place of perpetual darkness. She walked with her hands out, searching for something to touch, like a wall or a piece of furniture. Beeping and the sound of her own breathing were evident, but she couldn't hear anything else. She recognized a voice, and she could see her face, but she couldn't say anything. *Why can't I speak? Where am I?* It didn't take long until she figured it out: she was trapped in her head. Trish wanted to scream and yell, but found she was mute; she often heard a familiar voice crying and wanted to tell her to stop. She wanted to be able to see, and searched and searched for a way out. *How long will I be stuck here?* It was cold, lonely, and she was so tired. Not knowing how much more of this she could take, she tried one last time to make a noise, but the sound seemed to be stuck in her throat. She finally gave in to exhaustion and allowed herself to fall deeper and deeper into the darkness.

Amal

Present Day

After she finished in the garden, Amal was in the shower, washing her feet, when she heard a male voice coming from downstairs. She finished her shower as fast as she could and came downstairs. There, sitting with Louis, was a police officer. They both acknowledged her when she came to the foot of the stairs. Amal was confused and thought the questions were over. What more did they need from her? She just wanted to be done with it.

"Hello, young lady," the officer said politely. He was huge and made the pencil in his hand look like a small twig. He had a gray mustache that curled at the ends.

"Hello," she said in return.

"Would you please come have a seat?" he asked, like she was a guest in his house, but she sat down nonetheless, directly across from him so she was looking right at him. "So since you are the only witness, I have to ask you a few more questions, just to be sure we got our information correct."

Amal wasn't stupid. She knew why he was here, and that was to make sure she wasn't lying. No one could understand how she had hit the man hard enough to knock him out, and she didn't understand either. Louis never left the room, and she was glad to have him keep her company. Talking about it the same way it had happened made the same emotions she'd had that day come back. At the end she was practically shivering, but she got through it. The officer seemed happy with what he heard.

"What's going to happen to him?" Louis asked. Amal could tell he was holding back his anger.

"He is being charged for battery, assault, and attempted murder. Since he came clean about everything, there probably won't be a trial."

He rose to his feet and thanked both of them for their time before leaving. They stood on the porch well after he drove off. Amal was stunned not to be in some kind of trouble, but she was glad it was over and Randy would be put in jail where he belonged. Now they could all focus on the most important things: Trish and the baby.

Bobbie
Saint Joseph's Hospital
Present Day

Bobbie stood at the bathroom mirror, looking at her bloodshot eyes. She had started developing bags under them, but she wasn't quite sure when it had happened. They must've snuck up on her overnight. After drying her hands on the brown paper towels that were automatically dispensed, she promptly threw them in the trash before leaving the sterile-looking room. The machines that were connected to her daughter beeped away. Periodically, the cuff on her arm would activate and squeeze her arm to take her blood pressure. The tubes in her mouth made funny hissing noises as she breathed. Bobbie stood next to the bed and laid a hand on Trish's forehead. As long as she kept breathing, it would be fine, she thought.

Sometime during the night, a nurse had come in and put a heart rate monitor on her belly to track the baby's heart rate. As the nurses came in periodically, she would ask how the baby was doing, and they said everything looked fine and that Trish was due for surgery any time now to fix her broken legs and pelvis. The doctors assured her they would monitor both of them closely, but it still made Bobbie nervous.

It was around 1:00 p.m. when there was a knock at the door, and in came Amal with Hattie.

"I just came to drop off the girl. I won't stay. How are you doing?"

She wanted to break down and cry, but she didn't. She held it together and answered honestly, "I am doing as good as I can right now."

Hattie put a hand on her shoulder, giving it a tight squeeze before moving toward Trish, who was lying absolutely still.

"Hey, girl! I know you can hear me. You need to get up now. Everybody's worried about you. We love you, sweetie."

After Hattie left, Bobbie turned to Amal before sitting down in one of the hospital's uncomfortable chairs, which was big enough for two, and patted the seat next to her, signaling Amal to come sit next to her. Amal had been standing in the corner of the room, looking at Trish but not saying a word.

"You brought your yarn with you." It was more a statement than a question. She knew Amal had brought along her yarn. She loved crocheting, and it delighted Bobbie to watch her work on little projects.

"Yes, ma'am. I brought clothes too, just in case you wanted me to stay."

When someone has a brain injury time slows down for the people they love. Bobbie waited for even the smallest sign that her daughter was there, a movement of a finger or toe, something, anything. They kept Trish on a breathing machine, and everything was the same. She left for surgeries and came back in the same condition. Bobbie prayed that she would finally wake up, but as the days went on, Trish never did. The only thing that gave her hope was the fact that Trish's heart rate would go up when she heard people talking, but that was it.

Amal

Seven Months Later

One double crochet and three singles, she repeated in her head, pretending to not be trying to hear what Aunt Bobbie and the doctor were talking about. Trish was still sleeping, but the baby was doing well. When the nurse would come in with her machine that helped them see the baby, they would always check and make sure everything was alright. It looked more and more like a person as the months went on. The monitor on Trish's belly sounded like galloping horses, and from what the doctor said, that was another good thing.

Bobbie and she would pray and pray over Trish, but she never seemed to get better. Amal was starting to think she would be stuck in that bed forever. *What kind of life would that be?* she thought. Suddenly wailing sounds could be heard from the hallway. Amal dropped her things to see Aunt Bobbie on her knees, crying. A few nurses had run over to help. Amal looked at the doctor, who was generally a seri-ous-looking man, but even he couldn't keep a straight face. His eyes pooled with water before he excused himself.

The nurses got Aunt Bobbie to a chair, and she sat in the middle of the hall, sobbing with a hand over her face. Amal kneeled down in front of her and put her hands in her lap.

"What's wrong?" she asked. Bobbie just shook her head and cried.

Bobbie

Present Day

"No brain activity" was the last thing she heard before her legs gave out. The doctor came back after she had calmed down and explained to her what would happen. They would do an emergency C-section, then take Trish off life support. If she breathed on her own, that would be good, but they didn't expect her to live for more than a few hours.

"I don't want my baby on that machine anymore. She deserves to die with respect," Bobbie said, tears dropping onto her dress.

"We understand this is a hard time for you . . ."

She didn't even wait for the rest; she just walked away. Bobbie didn't want to hear anyone saying another thing to her about how they knew what she was going through. At the nurses' desk she used the phone and called a few people. Her girl would need a coffin and an outfit to wear, so she made those calls as well, before placing the phone back on the hook. Part of her wanted to believe she was having a nightmare. She slowly walked back to the room where her daughter was lying, and stood and looked at her for a few moments before walking to the window. It was sunny, and she could see people going about their day. It seemed unfair that they could enjoy themselves when her daughter couldn't. Trish wasn't going to get better. She was going to die in this hospital, and Bobbie couldn't do anything to change that.

On the day of the C-section, Bobbie was peculiarly quiet. She was so full of emotion, she felt like she couldn't speak. This was happening. Today she was gaining a grandchild and losing a daughter. She dressed comfortably and spent her day standing at the head of her daughter's bed, lightly rubbing her forehead. She wanted to remember how she looked and felt. Everything on her was still swollen. The clock seemed to be going too fast today, and before she knew it Trish was being wheeled into the operating room, with Louis in tow. He would be the first to hold the baby. Forty-five minutes seemed like five, and soon Louis emerged in tears, cradling a bundled-up pink blanket.

"It's a girl, and she looks just like her," he said through sobs as he passed the bundle to Aunt Bobbie. She wasn't prepared for how much the baby would look like her mother. Bobbie had a hard time letting her go when the nurse came for her. They didn't keep her for long before bringing her to Trish's room in a little bassinette. The little girl was wide awake, looking around with big green eyes, and was the prettiest thing Bobbie had ever seen. It made her heart beat a little faster when she saw that tiny face staring up at her.

"Nosey, just like your mom," Bobbie said jokingly.

Not an hour later, the room began filling up with close friends and some relatives, all waiting to say goodbye. When they brought Trish back into the room everyone knew what was to come next. They each took turns telling Trish that they would miss her. Bobbie held the baby next to her so the baby could see who her mother was.

Aunt Hattie was the last to arrive, bringing her cello. She said one last goodbye, and when the nurse came in to turn the machines off, she closed her eyes and began playing, with the intent to serenade Trish into the next life. Bobbie was happy she had the company, because she didn't know if she could have done it without them. Once the machine was turned off people began filing out of the room until it was just Bobbie, the baby, and Trish. She held on to her daughter's hand for the last time. "Go to sleep, baby. Just go on to sleep," she said.

Amal

Three Months Later

Eight a.m. came without warning. It was good the bus stop was right around the corner. She and Kenya dressed in the same room, with their backs turned away from each other. Amal wore a bra now, though she still struggled to put it on by herself. She waved her hands around behind her back until she found the clasp and then pulled her shirt over her bare shoulders. She was wearing yellow, pink, and white. It was her first day of school, and she was nervous. Kenya laughed as Amal dropped and tripped over things all morning.

Once she got her skirt on, she went to the mirror and put on her hijab. She smiled at herself in the mirror after doing a deep-breathing exercise Amelia had taught her. *Everything will be fine,* she told herself before grabbing her bag and bounding down the stairs. Bobbie was sitting on the couch and smiled when she saw the two of them.

"You both look so cute! Are you ready?" Bobbie said, holding eight-month-old Marie. The baby had gotten so fat that it was hard to carry her.

"Yes, we're ready!" they said in unison.

"Louis! Are y'all ready?" Bobbie yelled while grabbing her house keys.

"Yes, ma'am!" Trish said with delight as she and Louis walked in together. Trish was wobbly on her feet, but she held on to Louis as they came downstairs. Louis helped her into her wheelchair with strong, steady arms.

"Well, don't you look lovely, Lady Bug!" Trish beamed with joy.

Amal said thank you before Kenya could cut her off.

"What about me?" Kenya asked.

"You look good too, Kenya." Trish had problems saying certain words, and it always took her a couple of tries to say the letters l and s.

"Let me get a picture of the two of you!" Bobbie said, grabbing her camera. Kenya and Amal both posed innocently. As they held their backpacks, they grinned from ear to ear as Aunt Bobbie snapped away.

"Come on, Ma. We gotta go! They're going to be late!"

"Okay! Last one!" Bobbie said as she took one last photo. Louis picked the baby up from her bassinette. She squealed with delight as he kissed her chubby cheeks before passing her to Trish. She held out her little arms to her mother, and Trish held her in her lap another placing a kiss on her forehead.

They walked out together to the bus stop and waited for the bus to come. Finally, after about twenty minutes, Amal could hear the engine of the bus roaring toward them until it slowed to a stop in front of them. The doors opened and Kenya got on first, waving at everyone. It took Amal a little longer, as she was terrified.

"You'll do fine!" Trish said.

"Love you both!" Bobbie yelled.

"Have a good day, you guys," Louis said with a wink.

Amal looked back to see Bobbie shaking her head in agreement, so she boarded the bus slowly and sat in the space next to Kenya. When the bus began moving, Amal looked back to see everyone waving. She waved back, making sure they could see her, and watched out of the back window until she couldn't see them anymore.

The bus picked up kids until it was almost full before stopping at the school. She couldn't believe she had never seen these people before. There were so many children her age; she lost count of all the bodies that packed on the bus.

All the kids filed out, and Kenya said she would see her after school, before getting in line to go to her own class. She followed the sea of children, with the map she had been given at orientation. She finally found her room after getting turned around a few times, but she wasn't late. She walked into the classroom, trying to avoid any eye contact, and sat in the back. She watched as other kids came in and sat down until all the seats were filled and the bell rang. A peppy-looking blonde who reminded Amal of Nurse Jackie came in the room and wrote her name on the board. "Mrs. Boyd," it read. She placed the marker down and took a look around and immediately noticed Amal sitting in the back. "So I see we have a new student. Can you stand up and tell us your name and a little about yourself?" she said in a chirpy way, like she was a bird.

Amal looked around and saw all eyes on her, but she stood anyway. What would she say about herself? That she was a refugee who had lost her family? That she had been beaten and used her first months here? Or maybe she could say something about the amazing family she had now.

Among all things, she was a survivor. Tons of other thoughts ran through her head, but she managed to find the words. She lifted her chin up high, as her baba had taught her. In her head she saw Aunt Bobbie's loving gaze, her parents, her sister, Trish, Louis, and the baby. She straightened her back and looked at the faces that gazed back at her.

"My name is Amal, but you can call me Little Bird, and I'm glad to be here today."